The One Who Brought Him Back

A. Elwood and C. Chapman

The 1st Cate Jenks, RN, Irish Cozy Mystery

ElwoodAndChapmanBooks.com

ISBN-979-8-9902452-0-4

This novel is entirely a work of fiction. The names, characters, and incidents portrayed in it are the work of the authors' imagination or are used fictitiously. Any resemblance to actual persons, living or dead, is entirely coincidental. The story has been set in a real-life small town because the authors mean to immerse themselves and their readers in the beautiful magic of Ireland.

Acknowledgements

It does indeed take a village to write a novel. We want to acknowledge the love and support of our entire family. We are especially grateful to our artist, Elizabeth, and our literary guardian angels, Suzanne and Jim, for their time, creativity, patience, and talent.

Chapter 1

Cate Jenks had never flown business class before. She stowed her small carry-on in the storage compartment after removing her medical kit. "Feeling okay?" she asked Brian who smiled and nodded, but his eyelids fluttered. He was sucking oxygen through the nasal cannula and blowing it out through pursed lips. Cate checked the settings of the oxygen concentrator in the seat beside him, with its carry strap still looped around his shoulder. She slipped a pulse oximeter on Brian's cool index finger. A few seconds later it registered 88%, then 90%, then 92%. "You're good," she said. Brian continued deliberate breaths that progressively came easier.

The flight attendant leaned in with a look of concern, but Cate smiled and nodded reassurance. Then she offered preflight beverage service. Her navy and green uniform contrasted sharply with her auburn hair secured in a sleek low bun, and her lilting accent made Cate feel like she'd stepped into an Irish travel commercial.

Brian ordered them gin and tonics, but Cate switched hers to club soda. "Can't drink when I'm on duty," she nudged his elbow with hers.

"Oh Lord, are you really going to be like that?" Brian sighed.

"I warned you," she arched an eyebrow and the corners of her mouth turned down.

"Well then you're fired," he muttered and took a deeper, slower breath.

"Not 'til we get there," she laughed. "Besides, I wouldn't know what to do with the free time."

But in reality that wasn't a joke. Cate reflected on the series of events in her life that resulted in her traveling internationally with her neighbor. Several years ago, she had been the youngest professional librarian at the regional archives when she became a late casualty of the economic downturn. She embraced the shakeup as a cosmic message that it was time to switch careers. Though she was a young librarian, she became the oldest student in her class of the registered nursing program at the local college. Cate landed the pivot to hospital nursing just in time to receive her husband's pancreatic cancer diagnosis. Four years of constant studying, then three years learning the new stressful job, plus non-stop double duty as wife and nurse at home kept her always on the move and maxed out with responsibilities.

Keith died on a Thursday night last April, one week after her 50th birthday. The years of disease and treatment had ravaged his body. Instead of ten years older than Cate, he seemed much older than their 70-something-year-old neighbor Brian.

After Keith died, it didn't even occur to Cate to cancel her upcoming shifts at the hospital. Her friend and fellow nurse Becky rubbed her shoulder and said, "I called the house supervisor and charge nurse to let them know what happened and that you'll be taking a few days off."

"Oh..." Cate answered, and became very still, puzzling what she would do with the days before her.

"Don't worry, sweetie, I'll stay with you if you want."

"No, that's okay, thanks. But there is still a lot to do. Maybe you can help me with some of the phone calls?" Cate automatically switched gears to her comfort zone and added a note to her to-do list. That was how she coped. And she hadn't stopped coping. It earned her a promotion to an informatics position at the hospital, which took her away from the bedside and into the administrative team where she was implementing plans, teaching her colleagues, and writing reports. Then, as the COVID-19 coronavirus threatened to spread across the world, elective medical procedures were abruptly canceled in many U.S. hospitals, including her own. "Non-essential" employees were shifted to telecommuting from home, and those with enough paid time off or money in the bank were encouraged to take a short sabbatical.

Cate interpreted it as another cosmic message: it was time to finally learn to relax. She volunteered to take the time off and after three days regretted it. On the fourth day she rose just as the sun was coming up, completed a yoga workout and showered. She blended up a healthful smoothie of kale, ginger, turmeric, apple, blueberries, and pomegranate juice. The residue in her empty glass initially rinsed purple, but then darkened as tiny green specks of kale swirled into the sink. "Now what?" she wondered. She had already overwatered the potted plants on the back porch and was pondering adopting a cat when her cell phone lit up with Brian's incoming call.

"Hello, Brian!" she answered a little too brightly. Brian Atley had lived across the street long before she and Keith moved in. He had retired early from some tech job in California and did well enough that the company had built the house for him in Florida as part of his golden parachute. She didn't know him well. Keith had had regular neighborly conversations with Brian when they both had dogs and would run into each other during walks. Brian's labradoodle lived to be thirteen; Keith's Brussels Griffon lived to a ripe age, too. After the dogs were gone the men rarely talked with each other at length, but Brian always checked on her after she called 911 for Keith's cancer emergencies.

Cate first summoned the ambulance the day before Keith was diagnosed with cancer. She had had a stomach flu the week before, and when he complained of nausea Cate assumed he had the bug too. But then he started running a fever, and after he threw up he couldn't stand up. His complexion had turned greenish-gray and he was panting with pain. The CT scan in the emergency room revealed "something" which turned out to be an inoperable plum-sized tumor whose growth was only temporarily stalled by immunotherapy, targeted therapy, and chemotherapy. The disease and brutal treatments stole Keith's strength, balance, and sense of humor. At increasingly frequent intervals, he was rushed to the hospital for falls, or fainting, or uncontrollable pain. Unlike their other neighbors on the street, Brian never came outside to gawk at the ambulances and fire trucks, but within a day or two he always called to ask how they were doing and offer help. Cate appreciated his concern but couldn't think of anything she would ask of the older man who seemed a bit fragile.

She was initially curious, though, how he got her cell phone number. She had no recollection of ever giving it to him. When she asked, he chuckled teasingly and answered, "Oh, I have my ways." Ultimately, she learned he had conned it from the exterminator who had her number listed on his work order for the quarterly outdoor treatment. She was more annoyed that the exterminator would give out her personal information, but Brian's acquisition of her number felt a little stalker-ish too. Ever since then, though, he'd been a perfectly appropriate neighbor and Cate appreciated his check-ins.

As the months passed, she settled into life without Keith and had not heard much from Brian. She had allowed herself to be consumed by her new job responsibilities so had not checked on him at all. As she answered Brian's call the morning of her sabbatical, she felt a twinge of guilt.

"How are you?" Cate asked.

"Well, I wondered if you might stop in sometime today," he replied, "I have a business proposition for you."

A short time later, Cate crossed the street and walked up the shallow circular driveway to the front door of Brian's Spanish Mission style house. The pale cream stucco walls contrasted with the terra cotta roof tiles. She pressed the doorbell button and it took Brian a full minute to open the door. His breathing was labored, but he greeted her warmly and invited her in.

"The coffee's still warm," he offered over his shoulder as he led her slowly inside. Cate had never been in his home before, but it was close to what she expected. The 20-year-old house was a time capsule of early 2000's design: non-descript, kept neat but never updated.

Cate followed Brian past a honey oak staircase, through the narrow foyer which opened into a carpeted living room separated from the kitchen by a single step up. Her nurse's eye assessed him from behind. He seemed weak, but his gait was careful and he steadied himself with a cane. His pale, hairless legs were skinny and his khaki shorts were sized to fit a distended abdomen so the fabric flapped loosely around his thighs. His ankles were slightly thickened with excess fluid despite the fact he was wearing beige compression socks with leather house slippers. An oxygen concentrator hung on his right side from a cross-body strap, and a clear nasal cannula was nestled into his nostrils. Brian's thinning hair was neatly shaped with visible comb tracks in it, and a faint high-end cologne wafted behind him.

"Pour yourself a cup, if you don't mind. Then we can sit outside on the lanai." Brian waved at the coffeemaker on the kitchen island and passed through the sliding glass doors to drop heavily into an all-weather swivel chair beside a glass topped patio table. She opened two different kitchen cabinets before she found ceramic mugs, poured half a cup, then joined Brian on the covered, screened-in porch. He raised his own coffee mug to her in a toast, but set it down again without drinking, "The dew hasn't quite evaporated yet, so we'll have enough morning cool out here for another hour at least. We only have two seasons, and pre-summer has run late this year."

"Yes, all the way into March!" Cate joked, "But I have to disagree with you: we have more than two seasons. This one is called The Pollening, and it's just getting started. If you don't have severe allergies, you haven't lived in Florida very long."

"I've got allergies, and more," Brian chuckled. "And I suppose you're wondering why I've asked you here. I've always wanted to say that."

"Well, yes, of course I'm curious. Especially with you sounding like an evil mastermind movie character. How long are you going to keep me in suspense?"

"No more suspense, Cate. I know it's been a rough time for you lately. Keith's been gone how long? A year? I was thinking you might consider a change of scenery about now. So I have a proposition for you." He held up a hand in response to her expression. "Don't answer right away. Please give it some time to cook in your head. I'm an old man. My health is not at all good. The doctor says I'm in a 'decline.' He told me I have six months to a year. And I'll tell you, nobody's gonna throw dirt on me before my time! Not even a doctor. But I do have a few things I need to do before that day comes. I need to go home to Ireland, to set something right, to make amends. So here's my offer: I'll pay your travel and a daily stipend to go as my health professional and travel agent. Just get me safely there and settled and then you're back to your home in less than a week."

Cate's throat made an involuntary cough of surprise.

Brian lifted both hands with fingers spread wide, "I beg you to think about it before you turn me down."

"Wow." Cate stared back, trying to take it all in and not sure what to say. "Ireland? You have a little bit of an accent I never could place, but I never would have guessed you're Irish."

"I left a long time ago. It's been more than fifty years. So what do you think? Will you help this old man get home before it's too late? Between my health and the way this virus is spreading across the world, if I wait any longer there won't be another chance."

It seemed daunting, but also an intriguing opportunity. A memory of her first semester of nursing school came to Cate's mind. Her instructor assigned each student to write on a slip of paper something that inspired them, and then submit it with their name written on the back. She was nervous about what kind of exercise in self-disclosure this would turn into, but she wrote out in block letters, "If it excites you a lot and scares you a little, you should probably do it." The next day the instructor returned the slips of paper to their owners, now laminated and hole-punched with a tassel threaded through, to use as a bookmark while they studied. After she finished school, Cate transferred the well-used bookmark to every novel she read for pleasure after those long, grueling years of study.

This surprise all-expenses-paid working travel gig to Ireland was both exciting and scary. It would be the perfect antidote to Cate's overabundance of free time. She felt her face flush with enthusiasm, "Let's start planning the details. Do you have paper and something I can write with?"

The full travel plan took almost a week to work out. Cate's passport was up to date. But there were flights and hotels to reserve, and a driver from the airport to the hotel, then from Dublin to Brian's hometown of Bunclody. Cate was excited to have a research project organizing the trip. She read up on Irish history and customs, in addition to creating a detailed spreadsheet of travel options and prices. When she brought the information to Brian for review, he was unconcerned. "Just book whatever we need," he said, placing a credit card from his wallet on top of the printouts Cate had laid out across the table. "I've been a saver all my life. No need to pinch pennies at this point. That's what the money is there for."

A few days later they boarded the overnight flight from Orlando to Ireland, and at altitude Brian became a little short of breath. Cate increased his oxygen by an extra liter and the remainder of the flight was uneventful. She watched two movies on her personal screen. One was an Academy Award winner that didn't pull her heart strings the way the critics promised, and the other was a slapstick romp of outrageous behavior that gave her a few chuckles before she nodded off. She awoke to gentle sounds of breakfast service and accepted coffee and an amazing scone, flavored with orange zest and a crunchy sugar crust on top. There was clotted cream to dab on, making it even richer. Brian looked tired but happy over his steaming cup of coffee.

They were met by airline staff with a wheelchair for deplaning, then transferred to a four-person shuttle that took them to customs then baggage claim, after which they met their driver.

"Welcome to Dublin." Cormac greeted. He was fit and friendly, mid-thirties, holding a tablet that displayed Brian's last name. He made sure Brian and Cate were nestled into the back seat of an idling black Mercedes sedan before loading their luggage into the trunk.

"To the Sasha, then?" he confirmed their hotel destination.

"Yes," Cate agreed.

"It's early yet," he said. "If you don't have an early check-in time you might end up waiting. I don't have another reservation until this afternoon. Care to stop for an Irish breakfast?"

Cate raised an eyebrow to Brian who shook his head, so she answered, "No, thank you. We just ate on the plane. But you can take the long way there, and can you give us a tour? This is my first time in Dublin and it will help to get my bearings."

The March morning was chilly and pearlescent gray. Spatters of rain flecked the windshield only enough that the intermittent wipers were needed. Cormac left the privacy barrier down between himself and the passenger cabin and narrated surprisingly helpful descriptions of the roads, buildings, and landmarks they passed. The landscape quickly became more urban. Cormac gave the history of the harp-inspired Samuel Beckett bridge that took them across the River Liffey and Cate was struck by the strange cadence of the naming convention. She tried it out on names of rivers in the U.S.: the River Mississippi, the River Colorado, the River St. Johns. The subtle oddity made her acutely aware she was now a foreigner.

"Does any of this look familiar?" she asked Brian. He seemed small, nestled in a new Gortex jacket with a flat cap pulled tight against his head. He'd kept his gloves on even though the car was pleasantly warm now.

"Very little," he sighed, "But she's a lovely city." Cate noticed a hint of Irish accent creeping into his expression.

Cormac drove them in a couple rough concentric circles to give them the lay of the land. They passed high-rises that housed financial and IT businesses. A glass wedge-shaped building sported only an iconic thumbs-up on its exterior which Cate recognized as Facebook headquarters. The stop-and-go traffic from block to block shifted the view to different types of businesses: shorter buildings with security bars on windows and doors, graffiti on the walls, bookmakers and curry takeaways. There were brick buildings that were clearly residential with regular windows, but varied and unique window treatments. Then there were more stately buildings and small manicured gardens.

"We're coming upon Trinity College," Cormac announced, his eyes crinkling a smile in the rearview mirror. "You'll know it as the safeguard of the *Book of Kells*, but more importantly it holds a copy of the Proclamation of the Irish Republic. Grafton Street is a short walk there to your right if you fancy the shops.

We'll soon arrive at your hotel, if there are no stops to make before?"

Brian shook his head and Cate directed, "Let's see if we can get checked in now." When they arrived, Cormac parked the car at the curb near the ramp to the front door. He took their luggage inside while Cate and Brian made their slow way to the entrance.

The Sasha Hotel was a dark stone building with modern, sleek furnishings, yet the lobby was cozy with evenly spaced pendant lights spilling pools of LED brightness that each ended several steps before the next. Rainy daylight glowed through the hotel's front wall of glass.

Cate and Brian were checked into separate corner rooms on opposite sides of the hall of the fourth floor. Each had a bedroom and sitting room with a view of the surrounding rooftops and streets below. Cormac was dismissed until the next day when he would drive them to Bunclody.

Cate assessed Brian in his hotel room and pronounced him stable. She administered a scheduled nebulizer treatment and unpacked his personal items so he could conserve energy. She strategically placed chairs in the room so he could easily sit if he grew winded while moving about, and then phoned room service and took delivery of soup and a sandwich. Brian dozed off sprawled on the sitting room sofa before his meal arrived. While she waited for it, Cate covered him with the duvet from the bed and texted his silenced cellphone to ensure they both had service. She placed his food and phone on the end table beside him, angled his cane within reach, then she pocketed his spare room key and let herself out. Brian's other key was lodged in a rectangular bracket by the door that activated electricity for the room.

Cate settled into her own room on the opposite side of the hall. Its windows were hinged at the top and opened only a few inches away from the sill. She levered one open and the most delicious cool breeze snaked through the toasty air. Cate's menopausal furnace kept her from ever getting too cold. She bent at the waist, stretching her back, and rested her elbows on the windowsill to watch the street below. There were rows and rows of kegs lining the side wall of a pub, leaving only half the sidewalk available for pedestrians. She thought either the kegs must be empty, or Dubliners are more honest than Americans. She wondered how much noise there would be at night. For now, the street was almost empty and produced only a few echoey vehicle sounds. Three pigeons were perched on the tiled rooftop directly before her. Their feathers were still fluffed for warmth, even though the sun had finally come out.

It was time for Cate to go out and explore. She had spent many hours researching and reading about Ireland in the days before their departure, and she was finally here for the first time. Now that there was no work to do, no duties to attend to with Brian, the idea of going out on her own was daunting. She had a list of sights that she had researched for her limited time in Dublin, and she had downloaded a taxi app. She was an experienced traveler and a methodical planner, but the adventure of it abruptly evaporated. Maybe she should rest instead?

The feeling of indecision overwhelmed her and she sat down at the room's small desk, smoothing the stapled itinerary she had prepared. "This doesn't feel like fun to do alone," she said aloud. Cate was an introvert. She did like people, but it took a lot of energy for her to be around strangers. When she was working, there was an agenda, tasks and goals, so she was comfortable with how she needed to interact with others. But it didn't come naturally to laugh and joke and just be casual with people she didn't know, and she had never actually traveled solo for pleasure. She felt the aching loss of Keith, and how his absence from sight-seeing transformed it from a delightful adventure to an awkward and anxious assignment. Did she even want to go out by herself? "No, I don't," she thought, "But I also don't want to be in an amazing new city and sit in my hotel room waiting to go home. That would be stupid." Her eyes watered with conflicting emotions and frustration. She sat unmoving for a while, feeling the inertia of stillness grow heavier. Imagining herself going to all the places she'd planned felt more and more impossible.

"That's enough!" she finally pushed back against the anxiety. "I'm going to go out and do at least three of the things on this list. If I have a lousy time I can come back after that." Cate felt a tingling energy at the base of her spine as nervousness mixed with the tiniest hint of excitement. She was going to just get out there and wander... "With my carefully planned itinerary," she sighed as she hauled herself out of her despairing sprawl. Then the six-hour time difference from home, the weird, muffled feeling in her head from flying, not sleeping properly, and getting upset all combined to produce a sudden giddy recklessness.

She geared up to go out. Her passport and most of her cash were in secure pockets of her clothes beneath her hooded, water-resistant jacket. She slung on a small shoulder bag with water bottle, rain poncho for downpours, ziploc bags to protect her phone, and a few Euros. Then she double-checked the taxi app she'd set up on her phone and reviewed the list.

Cate first started away from the hotel on foot, heading the short distance to Grafton Street. The shopping was "shite" she decided as she scanned the signage. Most of the stores were big name brands she already avoided at home. But there were fascinating buskers interspersed in the flowing crowds, and she paused to listen here and there. Then she walked to the National Museum where she saw the bog bodies, followed by a visit to the National Museum of Art where she browsed its world-class collection, then she ate a surprisingly good meal in the cafe. Cate loved museums and acknowledged she had been feeling comfortable wandering here alone, free to spend as much or as little time as she wanted without worrying about anyone else's interests. She was more comfortable eating here alone than in a restaurant or pub. "Baby steps," she congratulated herself as she took out her itinerary to decide what she would do next. Had she had enough personal growth for the day? Did she want to go back to the hotel or did she have the fortitude to do more?

She made a deal with herself as she used her taxi app to arrange a cab to take her to St. Michan's Church for a tour of the catacombs. If the app worked properly and the driver showed up, she would continue adventuring. If she couldn't get the app to work right, she would excuse herself back to the hotel. A notification popped up on her phone's screen informing her that her driver would arrive in seven minutes, and a map displayed where she should meet him. "Damnit," she sighed, anxious again, but glad she was now obligated to keep pushing herself because she was having a pretty good time.

There was only a handful of other tourists in the tour group at St. Michan's Church, and the guide was as entertaining and informative as she had read he would be.

When offered the opportunity, Cate touched the finger of the mummified crusader entombed there, and laughingly both added and crossed off the event in her mental bucket list. After the tour, she wandered inside the church to see the grand organ on which Handel had practiced his famous *Messiah*.

Outside, the sky remained overcast but not rainy, so Cate decided to walk the mile back to the Sasha. For her, the best way to handle jet lag was to just stay awake in her new location and go to bed at the normal local time. But after peeking in on Brian who had eaten his meal and was now snoozing in his bed, Cate's own bed was too appealing. She was glad she had pushed herself, but she was exhausted by the stress of her emotions. She stretched out for what was to be a short nap and woke up hungry at almost ten o'clock at night. The hotel restaurant was already closed and Cate was ravenous.

"So much for getting on schedule," she growled, debating what to do. Though Dublin was known to be a very safe city, she didn't want to go far, alone in the dark, and her phone told her most of the nearby restaurants were already closed. But she was feeling encouraged by her successful solo adventure earlier. "Guess I'm going to the pub," she decided. A glance out the window confirmed it was open. At street level she learned it was called Sullivan's and she was relieved to be seated at a tiny table instead of having to find a place at the crowded bar. There was no stage, and musicians were seated together within the crowd, playing loudly just a couple tables away. She ordered fish and chips and asked the server for a lager recommendation, since she knew from past experience she didn't care for the dark bitter Guinness.

"You'd like a Galway Hooker then," the young woman suggested and laughed patiently when Cate's eyebrows flew up. "Americans! Around here a hooker is just a boat."

"Okay, I'll try it."

Cate was soon glad she'd agreed. The pale ale was cold, clear, and citrusy. By the time her food arrived, the alcohol had helped her relax and its flavor paired perfectly with the fried food she craved and knew she would regret. She finished the beer but ate only enough of her meal to put a bottom under it, with plans to pop an antacid and sleep propped on pillows to combat acid reflux. She suddenly realized she was having a few moments of just being, without self-consciousness about eating alone, and that she felt okay for now. Then the musicians started playing a song she recognized but hadn't heard in a long time. She didn't even know the name of it, but she remembered the words. And since everyone else was belting them out, on the second chorus she joined in, too.

She continued singing in her head as she peeked in on a peacefully sleeping Brian before finally falling asleep in her own hotel room.

Chapter 2

Cate's 7:00 a.m. phone alarm was a violent intrusion because her body thought it was only 1:00 a.m. She dragged herself out of bed, showered and dressed, and packed her things then went across the hall to check on Brian. His long rest had done him good, and he had much more energy than the day before. She offered to order room service, but he wanted to eat in the hotel restaurant. "Now that I'm home, I'd like to actually see it."

Cate served Brian's plate from the buffet while he walked with his cane and pointed out what he wanted. Together they amassed a traditional Irish breakfast – beans, brown bread, grilled tomatoes, mushrooms, black and white puddings, and a small scone. It was more food than Cate had ever seen Brian eat, and he finished most of it while she worked on an almost identical plate. It wasn't what she considered breakfast food but it was all delicious, except the puddings which she tried only because she'd never tasted them before. Their flavor wasn't bad, but she just couldn't get past the idea of what she was eating: blood mixed with fat and grain.

They lingered a while after breakfast, sipping coffee and chatting. Brian asked how she'd spent the previous day and she recounted her explorations.

"You did so much in one afternoon!" He shook his head, "I'm so slow. Don't let me hold you back while you're here. Make sure you get out for all the sight-seeing you can."

"Thank you, I will. But you're my first priority on this trip. What do you feel up to today? Cormac will be picking us up at one o'clock. Do you want to do anything in particular?"

"I'm afraid I don't have many steps in me. Especially after this huge feast."

"Would you like to reconsider the wheelchair? I could work on getting one today."

"Absolutely not!" Brian scowled. "I'll come home on my own feet or not at all."

"It made a big difference at the airports," Cate encouraged. "There's no shame in it. And then you could conserve your energy for other things. If you'll use a wheelchair, you can come sight-seeing with me. I'd appreciate you reading signage; I can't even guess what the street signs say. Do you speak Irish?"

"Oh, it's been so many years, I'd be embarrassed to open my mouth, but I still can make out the written stuff pretty well."

"How does Irish work?" Cate asked, "I mean, like in Spanish, even though I only had a year of it in high school, I can guess what a lot of the words are because of similarities to English. And I can tell when a word is a noun because of the article in front of it. I can spot plurals, and pronouns, and verbs, and a lot of other parts of speech. With Irish, I can't even guess what I'm looking at. And the letter combinations don't make the sounds I think they would."

"It is a very different language," Brian conceded. "My parents mostly spoke English, but my grandparents, they only spoke Gaeilge." His pronunciation of the word sounded like 'gayl-guh' to Cate. "I learned it at home and in school, but once my granny died I never had reason to speak it much. The verbs come first in the sentence, and the adjectives follow the nouns that they modify. The sounds of the letters are different from English. And there are no words for yes or no, you just confirm the verb or state its negative. Like, if you ask if I slept, I would answer either 'I slept' or 'I didn't sleep.' 'Chas mé' or 'Níor chodail mé.'" Brian's pale cheeks actually blushed as he glanced around suspiciously and hissed, "Oh, God, I hope no one heard me butcher that!"

Cate leaned back against her chair and made a gesture of surrender with her palms turned up. "I'll try not to make you interpret for me in public, then."

"It's a deal," Brian chuckled. "Now let's see if my old legs can make it to the street. I'd like to have a look around if I can manage it." Brian waved off Cate's assistance and worked himself up from his chair by leaning against the table edge and his cane. Cate held onto the table to keep it steady.

They made their slow way out of the hotel restaurant into the lobby and out onto the sidewalk. Less than a block later, Brian paused, braced himself, and looked forward and backward along the street. He peered intently at the side street that crossed their path at the end of the block, then he scanned upward, surveying the sky. The motion played with his equilibrium and Cate slipped her hand between his body and arm, curving her palm into the crook of his elbow to steady him.

"This is my home," Brian's voice was quiet with emotion, still staring at the luminous sky.

"Welcome back," she answered softly.

They stood silently on the street for a few minutes longer, and then it was clear Brian was done in by the short walk. They returned to his room and he rested on the sofa while Cate organized his luggage. He had already packed most of his personal items before breakfast, so it only took her a couple minutes to place everything by the door and make sure nothing was left behind. Then Cate excused herself to her own room where she made ready for their next leg of travel.

Cormac arrived on time and ensured their luggage was stowed as they settled into the Mercedes. The town of Bunclody wasn't far. In their pre-planning, they had already established their route south of Dublin on the major road that paralleled the coast, even though it wasn't the most direct path. Brian had said he preferred to go that way.

Once they were on their way, Cormac closed the privacy barrier and Cate and Brian were alone. They rode in silence for a while, watching the passing scenery. On the outskirts of Dublin, the roads were slick again and the silvery sky was spitting rain. A masonry embankment on the roadside was graffitied with a single script word "feckers." Cate giggled and nudged Brian, pointing at its elegant derision. And then they were in the countryside. The vista was filled with the most extraordinary shades of green Cate had ever seen. Cows rested in pastures, many of them lying on the ground with their legs tucked under them, calmly chewing their cud. Again, Cate had the acute awareness that she was a foreigner. In Florida, the heat baked so much moisture into the air that the grass in pastureland was usually as much yellow and brown as green, and she rarely noticed cows lying down. The hot climate and sparser grass turned them into nonstop lawnmowers, constantly grazing.

"When we get to Bunclody," Cate asked, "who will you see first?"

Brian had avoided planning the particulars beyond his arrival to his hometown. He'd said he wanted to see who was still around once he got there.

"My sister," he stated plainly, without taking his eyes off the passing scenery.

"Will you need help looking her up?"

"No, I don't suppose so. It's still a small town."

"Is she the one you want to make amends to?" Cate probed.

"Yes." He continued to avoid her eyes. "And everyone else I knew back then. I left without telling anyone. No goodbyes. And I never went back. I think Mags will forgive me. At least, I hope she will. We're about to find out, aren't we?" He smiled weakly, only briefly glancing her way.

Cate was surprised. She realized when Brian said he wanted to make amends, she'd assumed he'd merely quarreled with someone and wanted to apologize. She hadn't given it much more thought once she got excited about the travel opportunity. Now she realized there were likely to be some emotional landmines and complicated family dynamics. She saw it regularly in hospital nursing. Emotions run high in times of illness, and it brings out the worst in many. She'd seen real-life dramas play out at the bedside that were too ridiculous to convert into salacious TV plots.

"I guess we are going to find out," she said tightly, rolling her eyes and raising her eyebrows. "You wanna tell me what happened, so I know what I'm walking into?"

"No," he answered quietly.

"Great," she breathed. Brian voiced a tiny ironic catch of laughter that she saw in the twitch of his shoulders more than she heard.

Cormac drove them into the town of Bunclody. The Turlough Hotel was located on Main Street and was more than two hundred years old. It boasted forty guest rooms that had been not-too-recently renovated, a small restaurant, and a bar. The building's facade abutted the narrow sidewalk, and Cormac's black Mercedes and suit garnered some attention at the curb. Cormac saw that his passengers and their luggage were deposited inside and would remain on call for the rest of the day. Starting tomorrow, they would use local taxis until it was time for Cate to return to Dublin.

Cate and Brian were checked into the only adjoining room option available in the hotel's offerings, which was a suite with access to a regular hotel room. Brian had wanted Cate to take the suite, but she insisted that he occupy it because she could better care for him in the extra space. She got Brian settled into his room then left the adjoining door on his side open and closed hers without locking it.

After refreshing herself in her own room, Cate knocked softly on the door to announce her entry but avoid waking Brian if he was sleeping. She entered and spotted him in a wingback chair using the hotel's curly-corded room phone. He signaled her to come closer and she waited quietly while he spoke into the receiver.

"Is this Margaret O'Connor? Who used to be called Mags Atley?... This is Brian... Your brother Brian.... It's me, really it is. Believe me.... I'm here in Bunclody. I've come back to see you. Can we arrange it?... Please, I know it's been a long time and I left without telling anyone, but time has passed and I need to see you... To tell you... er, well, to see you. Will you see me, please?... I'm staying at the Turlough Hotel. I can come to you.... Yes... Where shall I tell the driver, Mags O'Connor?... Did you marry Liam or Derry? Ah, Liam, then. He always was a good lad. See you soon, Maggie." Brian hung up the phone and slumped into the chair, closing his eyes. A few deep breaths later, he stated with his eyes still shut, "She'll see us."

"Us?" Cate echoed, but Brian didn't answer.

"Brian, tell me how you left Bunclody. I mean, you went without telling anyone? Can you remember exactly what happened?"

"Of course I can," he muttered, pinching the bridge of his nose with his fingers while blinking his eyes open and rolling them around before finally focusing on her. "Like it was yesterday. When I decided I needed to go, I just slipped into the house, went to my room, grabbed a few things, put them in a pillow sack and lit out toward Dublin."

"How old were you?"

"Nineteen."

"Why did you leave like that?"

"I had my reasons," Brian grumbled, "and they're private." He punctuated the statement by tightening his hand on the armrest of the chair.

"Did you go straight to Dublin?" Cate asked, changing tactics.

"No, first I walked to Gorey. But I knew somebody would soon recognize me and report to my family. So I hoofed my way to Dublin to seek my fortune."

"How long did that take?"

"A good week or so, since I didn't have an appointment," Brian cleared his throat ironically. "I had no need to hurry. I had few skills but I'm not without a brain and some practical sense."

"Tell me how you fed yourself. Where did you sleep?" Cate prompted.

"Oh, you know, I might've snagged some bread or maybe took a few things from the market. But I did a few odd jobs for people too. Really, the Irish are a kind, friendly bunch. Most people were good to me. I did alright. When men are on their own, they tend to use nature for their needs, if you get my meaning."

"Oh, I think I get it. And what about sleeping?"

"Well, there are lots of places to tuck into. I'd keep an eye out for opportunities. A shop closes and maybe there's a spot at the back doorway or a covered area to slip into for the night. I was young and kind of took to the adventure of it. I did okay."

"What did you do when you got to Dublin?"

"I met an American who took me on as a helper in his furniture business. That's how I got to the States. Mostly I moved furniture for a couple years, but it turned out I had a sense for business. He taught me, and I moved up in the company. I worked the tradeshows and such. And when everyone started using computers I got excited about them and he paid for my schooling. I wrote some inventory management software and then that got even bigger than the furniture business. We were one of the startups in Silicon Valley back in the early 90's. Didn't Keith tell you any of this?"

Cate shook her head, silently mouthing "Nooooo."

"Well, I must admit we usually talked about the neighborhood and mundane things like weather and gas prices. Your man was pure class though." Brian smiled, then sighed, "Let's call Cormac. You'll go with me to see Mags, of course?"

"Of course, but maybe you should rest a while first?" It was no surprise to Cate that he seemed more frail than usual. Though they traveled comfortably, she knew the journey was a big demand on his limited physical resources. She was concerned he might become overwhelmed by an emotionally charged reunion.

"No, I'll be alright. Now that I've finally come here, I don't want any more delays. It's time to make my amends."

Chapter 3

Cormac opened the Mercedes door and assisted Brian out of the car. With Cate at his elbow, Brian made his slow way up a flagstone path to the front door of an unassuming cottage, stopping at the bottom of three steps to catch his breath. He concentrated on recovering from the effort of the walk. Then one step, two steps, finally at the front door he knocked. The door opened and a small woman dressed in a gray sweater and dark slacks stood before them. Her face was tight with emotion, her blue eyes watering behind stylish rectangular glasses. Her wavy hair was plausibly auburn and her posture straight and strong, so it was hard to guess her age. The fingers of her left hand were pinched hard together and shaking as she dabbed her eyes with the facial tissue trapped between them. She drew a sighing breath between quivering lips as she took in Brian's cane and the oxygen tubing. Brian searched her face, saying nothing. Then they walked into each other's arms quietly, tearfully, clinging to each other.

Finally, Brian dramatically gasped, "Aw, Mags, I can't breathe!"

"Eejit," she snorted, stepping back, slicing a wide arc with her arm to acknowledge Cate. "We'd best stop gawping. Who's your woman?"

"Mags, this is Cate Jenks. She's my health professional and travel agent. You can blame her for transporting me here in my state of decrepitude. I couldn't have done it without her."

"Come in before you fall down." Mags sniffed at Brian, then, "Hello, Cate."

Mags pulled the cottage door open wide and Brian stepped through the doorway with Cate at his elbow. Mags led them through a cozy living room with broad windows that gave a lovely view of a vegetable garden. Cate spotted organized beds and rows of vegetables. Bright flower blossoms also spotted the landscape and Cate wanted a closer look but followed Mags and Brian to a warm kitchen with a well-worn wooden table and chairs.

"The kettle's just about ready," Mags said as she gestured for them to sit. Her face remained tense while she arranged tea things.

Brian attempted small talk. "You look well, Mags."

"And you look quite ill," she kept her attention on the cups and saucers.

"I am done for," he sighed. "I'll cark it soon anyway, if the coronavirus doesn't drop my body first. You know, I haven't had a real cuppa since I left. Yours was always best."

Mags didn't answer, but she sniffed and shrugged a shoulder to catch an escaping tear with the sleeve on her upper arm, keeping her hands clean while she worked. Cate felt compelled to ease the tension. "Your home is lovely, Mags. I noticed the garden out back. What are you growing?"

"I've got the usuals started already," Mags answered, waving a hand vaguely. "Broad beans, potatoes, cabbage, onions, leeks, turnips, peas, radishes, and some early lettuce."

"Do you mind if I go look at them?" Cate was hoping to remove herself and give them privacy, but Mags wasn't having it. "Tea's ready now," she replied tersely and began pouring. They all busied themselves with sugar and cream, and no one seemed to find words that flowed. Conversation bumped along unnaturally with polite meaningless statements. Finally, Mags cradled her cup in her hands and stared painfully at her brother. "Brian, what are you doing coming back?"

"Oh, I wanted to see you and whoever is left. I haven't a long life left. I just wanted to make amends before it's too late."

"Make amends!?" Mags cried as her eyebrows pinched together in disbelief.

"Yeah, you know yourself I left without the family's blessings – or knowledge, for that matter."

Mags choked and sputtered incredulously. "Blessing! You want the family's blessing?"

"Maybe that's not the best way to put it. But basically, yes. I want to apologize and reacquaint myself."

Bright pink flushed in two circles on Mags's cheeks and Cate's eyes darted back and forth between Brian and his sister, wondering if he realized she was on the verge of going ballistic, "Jaysus, Mary and Joseph! What are you talking about? 'Reacquaint yourself?!'"

Brian's shoulders hunched and he tucked his chin meekly. "I guess I'm putting my foot in it. I just mean I regret the way I left and regret that I didn't come back sooner."

Mags shook her head decisively. "Yeh shouldn't a come back at all. No good'll come of it. Time passes but a small town doesn't forget... or forgive."

Cate sat quietly watching the two siblings in their odd conversation. She looked from one to the other like a tennis match, comparing their expressions and postures. Would Brian have come so far knowing this would be his reception?

"Ah, Maggie, Maggie, times have changed. And I've grown old. I am who I am. Course, if you can't accept me, I'll just pack up and go back to the States. But I'd hoped for a better ending."

"Oh, that would certainly be for the best. People in the town are already talking about you and what you... what happened. Even though it was a long time ago. But no, it's too late now you're here." She spoke quietly, setting her cup on the tabletop and avoiding Brian's eyes, staring out the window sadly.

"But time has passed, Mags, even in Ireland," Brian sighed, "though you're making me feel like I've traveled right back to 1969. Maybe this place is just too small."

"Well, you don't understand at all! P'r'aps you've suffered a stroke or maybe dementia's setting in. For your own sake, you should leave Bunclody straight away. Go! Now!"

Mags stood abruptly, and Brian slowly rose from his own chair, levering himself up with hands spread flat on the tabletop. Cate hooked a hand under his arm to assist, but he waved her off in frustration. He straightened himself as best he could and balanced against his cane. She noticed his hands shaking but he remained surprisingly steady as he made his way to the door. He turned to Mags with tears in his eyes, opened his mouth as if to speak, then changed his mind and stepped outside. In the cool silver daylight, Cate turned to close the door behind them and witnessed Mags collapsing back into her chair with her hands over her eyes, her shoulders shaking with sobs.

Brian hurried to the car faster than Cate had ever seen him move, but Cormac was attentive and holding the door open. Brian collapsed into the seat, sucking in desperate gasps of air.

"Howya?" Cormac asked nonchalantly, but his eyes showed concern.

"Not sure yet," Cate answered, twisting the meter up on Brian's oxygen concentrator as she slid into her own seat. "Take us back to town, please. On the way I'll let you know if we're going to the hotel or the hospital."

Cormac drove quickly on the narrow roads and Cate was glad she needed to keep her eye on Brian because the speed the driver maintained was unnerving. By the time Brian inhaled a dose from his rescue inhaler, they were nearly back on Main Street. Then his color started to look a little better and he was stabilizing, so she directed, "Take us to the hotel, please, Cormac."

Chapter 4

They sat in the car for a few minutes to give Brian time to recuperate for the walk back to his hotel room. The formal-looking Mercedes attracted the attention of every passerby, and Cate felt exposed despite the tinted windows that prevented people from making eye contact. Though Brian's breathing eventually returned to normal, Cate left his oxygen rate turned up to support his exertion during the walk back to his room. She would turn it back down to his normal rate when he was safely recovered. Brian allowed Cormac to help him out of the car, then waved him away saying, "Thanks, lad. We'll see ourselves in."

She stayed close to Brian in case he became unsteady. As they passed through the lobby door side-by-side with Cate's hand under Brian's elbow, they were nearly run over by a woman who was hurrying to exit. All three stopped just short of a collision.

The woman gasped, "Jaysus!" Her hands flew up to her face, covering her mouth momentarily, and her dark eyes were wide beneath bobbing curls of charcoal hair, once-black but now shot through with gray, "It is you!"

she cried. Her hands lowered to her sides and tightened into fists. "Oh my God! They said you'd come back! Why are you here?! After all these years! Oh, God, oh God!" she wailed, then she flew past them and out the door.

Cate and Brian stared after her, shocked. "Jaysus, Mary, and Joseph!" Brian muttered with more Irish accent creeping into his expression. "Is there no end to the madness here?"

Two women, one young and the other middle-aged, were working the desk and observed the commotion. The older one, Moira, had checked them into the hotel earlier. She nudged the younger woman, Rose, to stop staring and both quickly arranged their expressions into professional neutrality. Cate made sure Brian was steady where he stood, then she took a few steps out the door to see which way the woman had gone, but couldn't spot her. When she returned, she asked Brian softly, "Who was that?"

"No idea," he barked back, shaking his head.

"Well, she seems to know you," Cate said. As they passed the front desk, she asked Moira and Rose, "Who was that?"

"That's Anna Dooley, of course," Moira replied.

"Of course," Cate echoed in confusion, then she looked at Brian with a shrug, checking if he recognized the name. He shook his head gruffly and continued making his slow way to the elevator.

They didn't speak again until they were in Brian's room where he dropped himself heavily into the blue wingback chair. He closed his eyes and breathed through pursed lips. Cate gave him a minute to rest while she gathered her thoughts. Something bizarre was going on here. She didn't know any of the pieces of the puzzle, and it wasn't clear what Brian knew. He was holding back details of something that had happened long ago, but he seemed a bit clueless too.

"Brian, do you know that woman? Anna Dooley?"

"No. I remember the name, but no, I never really knew her."

"Well, she seems to know you," Cate probed. Brian didn't answer. "Has Bunclody always been this... odd? I mean, not just the way people are acting so strangely. I've got a weird feeling. What happened that made you leave so abruptly all those years ago?"

"It's old history," Brian muttered. "I had my reasons. And they're my business and nobody else's!" His voice rose with all the breath he could muster, "If this is the reception I'm going to get, we'll just pack up and go back to Dublin tomorrow. To hell with 'em!"

"But can you think why people would be treating you like this? Even Mags. Why was she so upset to see you?"

"To hell with 'em!" Brian wheezed, shaking his head as his eyes watered.

"Okay, to hell with 'em," Cate echoed.

She left Brian in his chair and prepared a nebulizer treatment and his medications. After he settled down and took them, she tidied the room and exited into her own quarters where she sent a couple texts and photos to her daughter and friends. Her efforts to switch to local time were a losing battle. It was only 5:00 p.m., but her body was confused and wanted a nap. Instead, she ordered room service for herself and Brian and flipped through the Irish TV channels while she pondered his bizarre homecoming.

Men, she thought, were so often indifferent to the dynamics of their families of origin. They seemed to jettison easily without attachment or concern, and then wonder why those they abandoned were hurt. She saw it play out like that in the families of her patients frequently. Keith had been disinterested in his own family connections too. As soon as they'd married, it suddenly became Cate's job to remember all the birthdays, make social invitations, and send thank you notes. She was grateful she liked his family. And since most of them were located in south Florida, they were sweet and supportive from a distance, and not too big of a job for Cate to take on.

Keith was a nice guy. He was a joy to Cate: fun, sexy, thoughtful, and adventurous. His friends considered him dependable, and he had a stellar professional reputation. He just didn't do family relationship maintenance. And neither did any other man Cate knew. It appeared Brian lacked the nurturing gene too. Maybe he wasn't so unusual, just a regular guy who had dumped everyone years ago. Just up and left without saying why, leaving everyone who cared about him to wonder whether he was alive or dead. Was that reason enough for a whole town to be so angry when he turned up again? Yes, Cate thought, she'd be that mad if her brother had done the same to her and her parents. And was Brian clueless enough to expect a warm welcome? Maybe.

A while later Cate answered a knock at her door, took the room service delivery, and placed Brian's meal on the small table in his room. He was asleep in the chair. She softly closed the door between their rooms and enjoyed her solitary dinner immensely, plugged into some of her favorite music. Brian woke after a couple hours. He grumpily ate some brown bread and soup she warmed in the room's microwave, while avoiding her attempts at conversation by answering only in monosyllables. Finally, he said, "I'm tired, Cate. I just want to go to bed."

She observed him carefully, looking for signs of physical decompensation that might be hidden by his emotional upset. The travel itself was a tremendous stressor for a person in his condition, and Cate had expected him to have some increased difficulty upon arrival. Today's conflict and his outburst and exertion only added to it. She decided he was currently stable and helped him get settled. Then she went to bed early too, sleeping in stretchy athleisure clothes just in case Brian needed her in the night. She got a full course of uninterrupted sleep and awoke easily when her alarm went off at eight. She peeked in on Brian and found him already bathed and dressed, sipping coffee, with an Irish morning news show on the TV.

"Good morning," she greeted, finger-combing her messy sleep hair.

"Morning," he raised his cup to her.

"Shall I call for the car to take us back to Dublin?"

"Nah, not yet," Brian harumphed and smiled slightly into his mug. His temper seemed to have cooled.

"Want some breakfast?"

"No. It seems I'm off my feed again. It happens. This coffee's enough to fill me up. You take some time to yourself this morning while I have a long think about things. Enjoy yourself. Go see the sights. I don't want to slow you down."

"Okay," she was relieved he'd changed his mind about leaving, and he looked better than he had last night. This might turn into a little vacation for her after all.

It didn't take her long to shower and get dressed, then she checked Brian's vital signs and gave him his treatments. She made sure he had everything he needed, then she geared herself up for some exploring. She wandered up and down Main Street and found Market

Square. Cate ordered breakfast in a little cafe, then strolled up Irish Street to the bridge over the River Slaney. She had read that the river's name came from the Irish word for health, so she stood on the midpoint of the bridge watching the water flow and reflected on the meaning of health and what it was in her life. She came from a family of fairly healthy people, and had taken her own health for granted. Then she studied health and made it her career, spending her days with people whose health was poor or in crisis. Then Keith's health disappeared practically overnight and became not a full-time job, but a constant consideration like a monotonous drone in the background. Now Brian's health had brought them across the ocean and through the decades to a wound that had never been resolved. "Physician, heal thyself!" she muttered, then added, "And, Nurse, you get the dirty work!" The river was indifferent and continued to flow. "Sláinte!" she called out to the water the Irish word for health that was also a traditional toast.

She walked further along the road away from town and took a right at every fork. That way she could find her way back easily by always going left. Eventually she came upon stacked street signs for Carlew and Gorey. She remembered them from yesterday, and realized she was now on the road to Mags's house. She couldn't remember exactly how far they'd driven, but it had only taken a few minutes by car. Should she continue on to Mags's house? Cate wasn't one to drop in on people uninvited, but at least she now knew where she was, and walking the distance would be a nice way to spend the rest of the morning. If she didn't come to Mags's house soon, she would just turn around when she felt halfway tired.

It wasn't her business to go to Mags without Brian, and yet, Cate had questions. If she just happened to run into Brian's sister out for a walk or driving by, maybe they would have a chance for a conversation. She wasn't even sure what she would say, but Brian had come all this way and Cate had put a lot of energy into getting him here. It was a shame to have their reunion fall apart without really happening, especially with Brian's health so fragile. Maybe she could help get them talking again. And if she was honest with herself, Cate was very curious about why Mags reacted the way she did. She was conflicted about nosing into Brian's business, so she kept giving herself little ultimatums about turning back, then revising them: if the driveway wasn't around the next bend, she would stop and go back. Then, she would walk just ten more minutes and if she didn't see the driveway by then she would go back. Eventually, she came upon it. "Well, now that I'm here, I might as well..." she rationalized. And she also really needed to pee.

She knocked softly on Mags's door. "She's probably not even home," she thought. "And that's a sign I should just stay out of this." As she turned to go, the door opened. "Uh, hi, Mags, it's Cate."

Mags peered beyond her, "Where's your car?"

"I can't imagine driving in Ireland. There is no car. I walked."

"You walked all the way? Come in." Mags motioned her toward her prior seat at the kitchen table and put on the electric kettle. "Tea?"

"Yes, please. I'm sorry to drop in without calling but I went out walking and then recognized the way to your house. I'm so sorry to ask, but could I use your bathroom?"

Mags directed her to it, and when Cate returned, she found the older woman in the kitchen. "Your home is lovely."

Mags nodded, quietly assembling cups, spoons, milk, and sugar, "Biscuit?" she asked.

"Thank you, just tea will be fine," Cate replied, remembering that a biscuit was what she would call a cookie.

"Never say no to a biscuit," Mags instructed, tipping four wafers onto a plate from a red and blue packet labeled Digestives. She placed the plate between them and continued organizing the tea things on the table.

Cate was full of questions but trying to ease into the subject to keep Mags from shutting down or getting revved up like before. And the peace of the cottage felt like a haven she was reluctant to disturb. She wished she could curl up on the tufted sofa with her tea, and sip and read until overtaken by a nap. Quiet reigned until she tasted her tea and sighed, "It's perfect."

Mags answered, "Mmhm, it's Bewleys Irish Tea."

Cate decided not to make a case for Brian, not to speak of him at all yet. "Mags, can you tell me about Bunclody? It's so charming."

"It's pretty much just your typical small Irish town."

"You know everyone here, don't you?"

"Course I do. I'm older than most of them. I've seen them born, schooled, married, and make their own families."

"In the U.S. we have a very mobile society. People seldom stay where they're born. I've never lived in a place where everyone knows each other."

Mags chuckled softly, "Well now, there would be some who would call that an advantage. I'm one that prefers the closeness. It feels comforting knowing a neighbor will lend a hand or let you know when something's awry."

Cate nodded without comment.

Mags continued, "I suppose a disadvantage would be that the people have long memories. Forget and forgive are not Irish characteristics. We hold onto things, the old ways, the old language. It's a way of protecting our Irishness."

"I can see that," Cate replied with a gentle smile, "and I've read up a little on Irish history."

"T'is true we all carry the long suffering of our country's history, but the town's history is a little different. That's about each other, don't you see? What your family did to mine and t'other way around. Then of course a bit of taking sides, and that's not even touching on who is related to whom and how they can't side with anyone outside of family. I think it must be that we're an ancient people," she harumphed softly, "and that's not just meself I'm refrerrin' to."

Cate chuckled and stirred her tea nonchalantly. "Ancient people, ancient history... Do you think many people remember Brian?"

Mags paused mid-sip and nodded deliberately. "He's part of Bunclody's history. Sure they all know about him."

A knock sounded at the front door followed by whispering hinges, light, and a current of cool air as the door opened without waiting for an answer. "Mags? Ye home?" a man's voice rumbled.

Mags called back, "In the kitchen, John, with a visitor. Come in, come in. Liam's not here now, ye know."

A tall, burly man with a lantern jaw and hawk nose strode into the room. He was about Brian's age, but in much better health, moving easily with purposeful steps. He startled when he spied Cate. "Sorry, I didn't know."

"John, this is Cate Jenks," Mags offered. "She's come all the way from the States with me brother Brian. Cate, this is John Kelley, our local publican."

John touched his cap, nodding at Cate, "Howya?" then he turned quickly to Mags, "Didn't mean to intrude. I didn't see a car. No way of knowing you had company."

"Not a bother," Mags soothed, "Cate didn't drive. She's American, but she walked all the way here."

"What, from the hotel?"

"Well, it's not all that far," Cate tried to curtail her defensiveness. "I like to walk. It's good for the body and soul. It's nice to meet you, John."

"Yes, yes, nice to meet you too," he barely glanced at her before turning away. "Well, I'll just go seek out Liam. Where'd you say he was, Mags?"

"Liam went over to help out at Murphy's farm to sort out something with the sheep." She turned to Cate, "Liam's the authority. He retired some years back, but they still call him if there's a problem. Though I've come to think 'sheep problem' is what they call an afternoon pint."

"Alright then, I'll see him later," John said as he turned to go.

"If you're going back to town, why don't you give Cate a lift to the hotel?" Mags suggested. "It's beginning to rain and the walk back might not be so pleasant."

John stared Mags down for a couple seconds. Cate noted he was uncomfortable, but she had more questions. If Mags was getting rid of her, John might give her some answers. Maybe he would warm up during the short drive.

"O'course, o'course I'll take ye back," he relented.

"Thank you so much for the tea, Mags. I hope I can see you again before I go home," Cate said.

"That would be lovely, dear," Mags answered. Cate was sure she didn't mean it at all, but she felt drawn to Brian's sister and her cottage life. She was curious about Mags and wanted to spend more time at her kitchen table.

John's car was a classic Volkswagen bug, brown, with a chrome gear rack on top. It was clearly long-used but well kept. John stepped heavily toward it and Cate darted through the rain after him. Surprisingly, it seemed he was leading the way to open the door for her when she remembered the driver's side was on the right in Ireland. She changed direction and let herself into the passenger door feeling utterly disoriented. The car's interior consisted of simple painted metal surfaces and coarse basket-weave cloth upholstery. She had to exert extra effort to pull the door closed. It swung heavily on its hinges and latched loudly in the small echoing space, then John opened his door and slid behind the steering wheel to her right. As he turned the key in the ignition, the engine fired up like a lawnmower behind them. She had to suppress giggling with amazement because John was already so clearly uneasy.

She tried to initiate small talk. "Do you live nearby, John?"

"Down the road a bit."

Silence.

"Thank you for driving me back. I guess I didn't think about the rain when I started out."

"Not a bother."

More silence. Cate kept her eyes on the countryside through the rhythmic blurring and clearing view caused by the slower-than-normal windshield wipers. Was the local publican actually incredibly shy? They rolled to a brief stop where the narrow lane joined the wider road at the edge of town. Only a few people were visible here and there on the streets.

Finally, she tried, "John, have you lived in Bunclody all your life?"

"Not yet, no."

Surprised, Cate barked a laugh, and John smiled just a little. "Yes, I see," she tried again, "Well, have you lived here until now?"

"I left for a bit when I was young. Spent some time in the Army."

The rain was letting up. As they slowed before the hotel entrance Cate gave up trying. "Well, thanks again. I appreciate the... lift." She'd almost said ride but vaguely remembered something about the word being slang for something she didn't mean.

"Not a bother," John repeated, and Cate was rankled by the blatant fallacy of it.

"I most certainly am a bother," she thought to herself as John's car rolled away even before the door was fully closed. "The question is, why?"

Chapter 5

Rather than go straight back to her room, Cate decided to first buy some mineral water from the Eurospar just a couple doors down, at the end of the block. She followed the sidewalk toward the market, passing a health store and a salon before coming to the Eurospar's adjoining car lot. There was a great deal of activity in the back corner of the lot, including a cluster of police cars and an ambulance. Several uniformed officers were busy managing the scene, and people were gathered to observe the goings-on, abuzz with talk. Her path didn't take her close enough to hear details, so Cate minded her business and went into the store where she wandered the aisles thinking through anything she might need in her hotel room. She noticed the products that were unfamiliar, even if some of the brands were recognizable. Canned mushy peas. Potato waffles. She considered buying several of these things to take back for friends as souvenirs from her trip, but that would be a decision for a later time. Instead, she selected two liter-bottles of mineral water and headed to the register.

The clerk was at the door talking with another woman who had been watching the police as Cate came in. She didn't seem pleased to be interrupted by a sale, but she perked up when Cate asked, "What's going on in the parking lot?"

"Man's been found dead."

"Oh! Do they know what happened?"

"Nora found him when she came round to open her shop this morning. Poor dear's in a state, and she was going to do my roots today." She pointed to her hair significantly.

Cate wasn't sure which the cashier found most distressing – the dead body, the upset beautician, or the delay of her own hair appointment. "Oh, sorry to hear that," she said as she swiped her credit card to pay the bill. The clerk handed her a receipt but did not bag her purchase, nor did she offer a bag. Cate wasn't sure what was going on, then remembered reading it's common practice to furnish one's own bags. Cate was glad she didn't buy more items, and was able to fit one bottle into a large exterior pocket of her jacket. She held the other in her hand as she exited the store and made her way back to the hotel. She went to her room and unloaded her purchases then knocked softly on the door to Brian's suite. He didn't answer, so she pushed the door open to find him asleep in his bed.

She quietly returned to her own room. What to do now? She wished Brian was awake to provide a diversion. She wasn't tired but she had pushed her introverted self outside her comfort zone and needed to recharge. She didn't want to just sit in her room, but right now facing the unfamiliar felt overwhelming. She sat dejectedly in the chair, staring at the walls around her, sipping a glass of water. When she felt like this at home she would simply clean or organize something, distract herself with busyness, but there was nothing to rearrange here. She was alone with her thoughts. She sat until the quiet was too much.

"Put on your big girl panties," she told herself out loud, then she gathered her things to continue exploring. She returned to Main Street with no destination in mind and was rewarded with a bit of sunshine that seemed rare. She headed in the opposite direction of the police investigation at the Eurospar, thinking how in Florida, this type of blazing light would send the recently fallen rain rising up in humid clouds, making her clothes stick to her skin and her hair frizz out. Ireland's sunshine merely subtracted the chill from the air. Cate removed her jacket and tied it around her waist, then pushed the sleeves of her sweater up to her elbows. She strolled Main Street heading toward Irish Street. First, she only gazed into shop windows, but eventually she stumbled upon a charity shop with funky displays that featured old-timey housewares, eyeglasses, and shoes. This was her kind of shop. She pawed through several racks of clothing with an eye out for anything she might suddenly "need" on this trip. She didn't find anything that called to her strongly enough to bother with buying and washing. Then she looked at the tchotchkes and glassware. In recent years, she'd become a huge fan of Mid-Century Modern design, and its influence was growing in her home as she added thrifted pieces whenever she came across them. She already had more than enough drinking glasses for a full dinner party, but she couldn't resist whimsical Atomic Age patterns. And here she found one lone little Blue Heaven patterned juice glass amid a cluster of much more recent glassware. Cate had a set of three mixing bowls in the same pattern in her kitchen cabinet at home. Their milky white curves nested perfectly into each other, and their rounded top edges tapered into two flattened handles. Their printed designs were quite worn but still utterly charmed Cate. She had paid $65 for the set in a little antique store close to her home.

This juice glass was sparkling clear and the design was pristine. And it was priced at only one Euro. Cate took the little treasure to the register. The shopkeeper was a stout woman about Cate's age. She was squatting behind the counter, organizing a display of costume jewelry. Her dark hair was caught up in a loose bun and she peered up over reading glasses perched low on her nose. "Howya?" she smiled. "Found something pretty now, haven't ye?"

"I certainly have!" Cate beamed.

The woman stopped her work and placed both hands on the countertop, levering herself up. "Are ye going to want that wrapped? I've got a bit of paper to cushion it."

"Oh... Yes, please," Cate nodded gratefully. "I already have a set of mixing bowls in this pattern. I guess this one officially turns me into a collector. I want to get it home safely."

"Well now, I'm just doing the wrapping, the rest is up to you," the woman chirped as she rolled and taped the protective paper around the glass and tucked it into a paper bag. "It'll be well-traveled by then. You're American," she stated.

"Yes."

"Then you're the one brought Brian Atley back to Bunclody," she added knowingly.

"Uh... Yes?" Cate was taken off-guard. "I mean, no. I didn't bring him back. I came with him. I didn't know he was so famous."

"Hmmmm," the woman tucked her chin to stare over her reading glasses.

Cate was uncomfortable, and not sure how to proceed. Obviously, Brian had quite a reputation. But for what? And why wouldn't he talk about what had happened? This lady was acting like Cate should know better.

"Well, thanks." Cate took the small package in hand and pushed the shop's heavy door open. She crossed the street into the median space filled with trees and a series of rectangular canal channels constructed from brick and stone and walked purposefully for a full block before she slowed and took a seat on a park bench. She never imagined she'd be so recognizable under any circumstances. It was a strange feeling of celebrity that didn't seem to come with any perks, just lots of uncomfortable attention and a bizarre puzzle she couldn't figure out.

She inventoried all she knew about Brian and his strange return to his long-abandoned home, as she watched the street before her. Parked cars buffered some of the sounds of vehicles rolling smoothly on the streets. Traffic was one-way on each side of the canal park, so she felt she was perched on a small island with movement flowing before and behind her. A green Toyota Corolla eased along the street headed who-knows-where. She realized she wasn't sure exactly what lay in that direction beyond this little town's border. Was Brian the talk of all of County Wexford? How far did his infamy spread?

From less than a block down the street she heard a bang and crunching metal. She stood to find what caused it and spotted the Toyota angled into one of the parked cars. "Oh, shit," she sighed. No one else on the quiet street was closer than her, so Cate gathered her belongings and trotted toward the accident.

A wiry middle-aged man sat behind the wheel of the car; its driver's side quarter panel was plowed into the back fender of an empty car. A few bits of broken plastic and fiberglass lay on the ground from what was obviously a slow speed crash. Cate observed the man's behavior. He was dazedly looking around. She moved a little more in front of him, waving and knocking on the glass to catch his attention, and in a couple seconds he met her eyes.

"Are you alright?" she called. "I'm going to open your door!"

The unlocked door swung wide without resistance and Cate leaned down to get a good look at him. The heat was running full blast and she detected no fuel odor, nor alcohol on his breath. He was not bleeding from anywhere she could see.

"My name's Cate. I'm going to help you. Can you tell me your name?"

"Huhhhh...." He blinked at her and she noticed he was moist with sweat. Heart attack? Stroke? She pressed her fingers into his wrist and detected a racing but regular pulse. His facial expression was symmetrical, without noticeable drooping, and she could see no signs of paralysis to any of his limbs.

"Let's turn off the car," she encouraged loudly. He didn't follow her command, so she reached through the steering wheel to turn the key herself.

"Are you hurt?" No answer. "Are you diabetic?" she asked.

"Mmmmuhhhhhhh..." He was becoming more agitated. By then several people had joined the scene, including a uniformed police officer.

"Does anyone know this man?" she called out to the group in general. "Is he diabetic?"

"That's Fergal Doyle," the young officer answered and shouldered in to share the space looking in on the driver. "What happened?"

"He ran his car up into this one just a minute ago. He's confused, diaphoretic, looks hypoglycemic – low blood sugar. Let's get some sugar in him fast and see if that helps. Can you get some juice or soda?" Cate was glad to have someone else to start handing this over to. The officer sent a man into a cafe just a couple doors down the street then made a call on his radio.

"Does anyone happen to have any candy on them?" Cate asked. No one did. "Does he have a blood sugar meter in his car?"

She directed the other two people to look in Fergal's car while she continued to monitor her unexpected patient. No equipment was found, and Cate found no medic alert jewelry to explain his crisis. A few seconds later the man who had gone to the cafe loped back across the street, breathless, with a bottle of apple juice in hand which he opened and passed to Cate.

"Fergal! Fergal! Listen, you need to drink this juice. Be careful. Take a sip!" Cate put the bottle to his lips and he sloshed messily but swallowed without choking. "Good! Drink some more." She kept the bottle to his mouth for a longer drink before pausing again.

An ambulance arrived on the scene within a couple more minutes and Fergal was beginning to perk up. He'd stopped shaking and was able to speak. Cate stepped back and gave a brief report as the paramedics took over. Then the police officer turned his attention to her. "Nicely done," he said.

"Thanks for getting more help," Cate replied.

"I'll need to get a bit of info before you go." The tall, lanky, young man fished a notebook from his jacket pocket. "Your name, please?"

"Cate Jenks."

He nodded but had already started writing before she answered. "Tell me again, exactly what you saw."

Cate described the accident again.

"And how did you know what to do?"

"I'm a registered nurse in the U.S. 'Cold and clammy, needs some candy' as they say. I just started with the basics."

"And what's brought you to Ireland?"

Cate paused, suddenly careful about her answer. To say she was working wasn't an official statement she wanted to make to a police officer. Her informal arrangement with Brian might have some visa implications she hadn't considered. "I'm traveling with a friend."

"Would that be Brian Atley?"

"Yes." Clearly the officer was in the gossip loop too. "Word gets around fast in this town, I notice. Why is he so famous?"

The officer glanced up from his notepad with a sharp look straight into her eyes, measuring his words before replying with a shrug, "It's a small town. People don't often disappear under unusual circumstances. And now he's reappeared, there are questions."

"What kind of unusual circumstances?" Cate probed.

"I'm not familiar with the details," he replied. "How long have you known Brian Atley?"

"We've been neighbors in Florida for more than ten years. His health is failing, so I've come along just to keep a nurse's eye on him and help get him settled back in Bunclody."

"Did he tell you why he's finally come back?"

"You'd have to ask him that," Cate sidestepped his question just as the officer had done with her moments before.

The young man stopped writing, nodded, and closed his notebook. "Thanks, then." He flashed a smile.

"My pleasure," Cate returned. "Can I have your name?"

"It's Rowan Ryan."

"Thanks... Officer?... Ryan." Cate wasn't sure what a police officer was called here.

"Garda Ryan," he corrected.

Chapter 6

Cate returned to the hotel. After checking on a still-sleeping Brian, she took the opportunity to catch a nap too. She woke disoriented, not sure of the day or time. The jet lag was still playing with her senses. She checked her phone and confirmed she'd slept less than an hour. When she knocked on Brian's door his voice was strained and a little wheezy. "Come in."

"How are you feeling?" Cate looked him over carefully.

"Oh, I've been better. I guess the travel is catching up to me," he said, not meeting her eyes.

Cate slipped the pulse oximeter on his finger. "You probably should stay resting for now." She increased his oxygen, checked his blood pressure, and was satisfied with the result. "Are you hungry?"

"Not especially. Maybe a nice Jameson sip would do me good."

"If you like," Cate replied. "But I wouldn't advise you to walk anywhere for it. Your oxygen's a little low and we don't want you keeling over before your mission is accomplished."

Brian sighed, then said, "Considering the way things are going, we may be aborting the mission altogether. I don't know why I thought Mags would be happy to see me, but I knew I'd be so happy to see her. I just thought it would have gone differently. Never occurred to me that she'd throw me out. I know I hurt her, but... I just never expected her to act like that." Tears welled in his eyes again.

"Oh, Brian, I don't think she..." Cate began, but wasn't exactly sure what she meant to say. Something wasn't adding up, even if Mags hated Brian. "Well, just the way she... She seemed almost afraid for you."

"Hmmm... That's clearly a woman's take. I felt unwelcome," Brian sniffed, converting his sadness to resentment. "Anyway, what have you been doing while I've been shut up here?"

"I went for a walk."

"In the rain?"

"It wasn't raining when I left." Cate sat in a chair at the little table. "Brian, do you know John Kelley?"

Brian looked up sharply. "Why do you ask?"

"I met him today. He seems about your age. I thought you might remember him."

"Yes, I knew him. We were mates when we were young."

"Tell me about him," Cate encouraged. "You know, he drives an old VW Bug," she offered nonchalantly.

"Ah, Cate, it was so many years ago! But he was a good fella, and we were pretty close back then. His family owned The Green Man pub just down from here."

"Maybe we can try it out at some point. But we need to make sure you get enough rest first. And we need to get you set up with a doctor, too."

"Not today, Cate. You can care for me. I'm just too done in to see anyone." He rubbed his eyes hard.

"Have you eaten anything since this morning?"

"Don't think I could get anything past my Adam's apple. I'm even choking on words today. How'd you meet John Kelley?"

Cate busied herself with setting up the nebulizer. "He gave me a ride in the rain."

"He gave you a ride?"

"I mean a lift," she amended. "Well, it was raining and I had gone for a walk, and he took pity on me and brought me back to the hotel. Now, why don't I order you some soup so it will be here after your breathing treatment? We need to keep your strength up."

Brian placed his palms on the table and squinted at her. "We don't know each other well, but I get the feeling you're holding out on me. If you're trying to get me to relax, you'll tell me what's going on."

Cate waded in, not sure where her words would take her, "No, we don't know each other well at all. But you trusted me with your health, didn't you?" Brian nodded. "Well, my intuition tells me something wasn't right about your visit with your sister. She seemed worried and sad, not so much angry. So I went back to see her."

Brian's mouth opened to speak, then he bit it into a frog mouth frown.

"Well, that's where I went."

"And what came of it?" Brian sputtered.

"We didn't really talk about you."

"What was your point in going, then?"

"I just wanted to know her a bit. Get some insight into why she reacted the way she did. I wasn't going to ask her directly... I guess it was a little presumptuous."

"A little?!"

"Okay, yes, but I did learn some things about Irish small-town life, and it was a pleasant visit. Your sister really is a lovely woman. And your friend John might be nice too, but they both wanted to get rid of me fast. There's something weird about it all. Oh, and there's plenty of other drama in this place too. I've had quite a day."

Brian said nothing, continuing to frown at her, so she added, "They found a body down by the Eurospar. The lady from the salon found him and it messed up her schedule so the checkout lady at the Eurospar missed her appointment to get her hair dyed. Police, I mean gardaí, were all over the place. And Fergal Doyle had a low blood sugar and a fender bender!"

"Fergal Doyle? Ah, he was a wee one when I last saw him. And now he's a bad driver like his da," Brian finally replied with a note of reminiscence.

"Diabetes is the most likely inheritance here, but maybe he got the bad driving gene too," Cate shrugged and sighed. "Now why don't I get you something to eat? A sandwich? Do you want tea with it?"

"Nah, I don't want anything," Brian grumped.

"You need to eat at least a snack," Cate encouraged, "You won't be able to keep your strength up if you don't put fuel in. How about cashews?"

She served them each mineral water and a single-serving packet of cashews she'd packed in her luggage. Brian reluctantly ate a few nuts while she sat with him, but he seemed distracted. He waited long enough to be polite then dismissed her. "I'm tired, Cate. You go enjoy yourself."

He looked stable enough, so she gave him his space, "I'll be back to check on you again later."

Cate wanted more than cashews. And she didn't want to sit cooped up in her hotel room watching TV, so she left the hotel with a destination in mind: The Green Man. Her cellphone GPS showed the pub was a couple blocks up and over, just a few minutes' walk.

The pub name was painted in simple lettering high across the building facade. Cate took two steps up to a narrow entryway with a tall green door. Its knob was in the center and she pushed in slowly. The pub was dimly lit. Only two other patrons were present, seated at a small table by the fireplace. She took a seat at the bar. John entered from a doorway behind it, hesitated briefly upon spying her, then his expression resolved. "What'll ye have then?"

Cate considered another Galway Hooker but couldn't bring herself to ask for it without feeling awkward, so she said, "I'll have a mineral water." It was still an adjustment to call it that. She wasn't sure of the difference between seltzer water, club soda, and mineral water – and it didn't matter to her which one she drank, as long as it had fizz.

John nodded and placed a bubbling glass of water before her without comment, then busied himself at the other end of the bar. A woman in her late thirties emerged from the room behind the bar, calling to John while she hefted a plastic crate full of glassware through the doorway, "They can't shut down deliveries, and we qualify as essential, John. Or there'll be an uprising. Oh..." She trailed off when she noticed Cate. She set down her supplies, washed her hands, and came straight over.

"Howya?" she offered as she dried her hands, stopping directly in front of Cate. "I'm Addy. So, you're the one brought Brian Atley back, are ye?"

"I wouldn't put it that way, but yes, I am the one who came with Brian. I'm Cate Jenks."

"Nice to meet you, Cate Jenks. Now I don't have to keep calling you 'the one.'" She laughed infectiously and Cate smiled with relief.

"We seem to be the talk of the town," Cate offered.

"Oh, more than that, yeh yeh."

Addy leaned her elbows on the bar and John abruptly called, "Addy, we'll be needing set up for tonight."

"Yes, John, I always get it done, don't I? I'm just taking a break." Then she continued, "So, Cate Jenks, how long are you here for?"

"Just a couple more days, until Brian's settled."

"You think it'll be just a couple days?" Addy looked surprised, and then John barked from the doorway behind the bar, "Addy, you're needed in the back, NOW!"

"Aright, aright. Talk to you later, Cate Jenks." Addy shrugged her shoulders, spun away, and John frowned at her angrily.

"Okay, bye." Cate took a sip as Addy and John disappeared. "How odd," she thought. What did Addy mean when she asked if it would only take a couple days to settle Brian? What would Addy even know about it? She must have been born more than ten years after Brian left.

Cate watched the bubbles rise in the water before her. Why did everyone seem to have an opinion of Brian? Cate had lived in multiple cities throughout her life, in the same place for years at a time. It was rare for her to know many of the people next door to her immediate neighbors, much less have knowledge of their personal lives. After all these years, why did people remember or care about Brian's departure?

Cate sighed, took out her cellphone and checked her emails, then browsed the news. The COVID-19 virus was spreading, and things were looking grim. China was in lockdown and some other countries were following suit. Cate needed to get Brian set up with a home health service tomorrow so she could make sure to be on her return flight Friday. Already she expected she might be quarantined upon landing. Each article she read led to another with more harrowing details of the virus's devastating effects. The pub grew busier and noisier as Cate read on. Two men took seats at the bar on Cate's left.

"Oi, Addy!" A thick older man with florid features roared jovially as he leaned against the bar next to Cate, holding up his thumb, forefinger, and middle finger indicating three drinks, "This round's on me!"

"That's a fret, Jack!" Addy called from behind the taps, "Did your pension check come early?"

"That'll never happen, but we're celebrating all the same!" He draped his arm across the other man's shoulders and gave a rough clap on his back, seeming a bit drunk. Cate glanced sideways, observing his grizzled hair and toothy yellow grin.

Addy arrived moments later with three foam-topped pints that she placed on the bar as she nodded to another patron who came through the pub door calling "Oi, Addy!" Cate watched her move on, multitasking fluidly, barely looking at her own hands as she joked with the new arrival.

"One for the lady." The man called Jack said as he slid one of the glasses sideways in front of Cate.

She was caught off guard. It had been decades since a stranger bought her a drink. She felt awkward and a little flustered, "Oh, thanks, that's very nice of you, but no."

He extracted his arm from his friend, then turned to her and said, "At least have a toast with us."

"What are you celebrating?"

"We are celebrating Brian Atley's long overdue return to Bunclody!" he inhaled sharply then sighed as if deeply satisfied.

"Oh! I'm sure he'll be happy to see an old friend," Cate looked more closely at the two men. The younger one probably wasn't old enough to remember Brian, but Jack was most certainly the right age.

Still grinning, Jack replied, "Oh, he's no friend of mine."

Cate was puzzled. "Then why are you celebrating his return?"

"Because the right-bollix will finally pay his dues."

"What?" Cate startled.

"Jack Dooley!" Addy admonished, reappearing in front of them.

Jack barked a laugh and raised his glass, "Then I'll drink to the lady who brought him back." He gulped sloppily while Addy scowled.

"That's enough!" she warned. "Sean, get him away from my bar."

Sean draped his arm across Jack's shoulders and turned him away from Cate, "C'mon, Jack."

"Bollix!" the older man cackled and allowed himself to be led away.

Addy rolled her eyes, "Jack's some tool."

"What did he mean by 'pay his dues'?"

"Oi, Addy!" another patron called as he entered the pub.

Addy moved away from Cate toward the new arrivals saying, "No time to talk now, love. Ask John."

But John was nowhere in sight. "What is going on here?" Cate wondered. She glanced around, trying not to look as rattled as she felt, then she focused on the pint of beer in front of her and watched its foamy head diminish while she inventoried what she knew, which wasn't much. The old man Jack said Brian would finally pay his dues. Obviously, Brian had made quite a few people angry before he left Bunclody. Why hadn't he told Cate what had happened? Of course, if she had known about the situation beforehand, she might not have agreed to come here with him, but now that the trip was completed why hadn't Brian just told her?

A young man took the seat on Cate's right. "Howya," he muttered.

"Hello," Cate returned warily while trying to concentrate on the problem with Brian.

Moments passed and she could feel the man's continued attention angled toward her, eyeing her beer. "Not a drinker then, heh?"

"Not beer so much, no."

"I'm Padraig O'Connor," he continued.

"Cate," she replied carefully, wondering where this was going.

"You were at my house today. Mags O'Connor is me mam."

"Ah, O'Connor! I'd forgotten her last name. Nice to meet you, Padraig. I had a lovely visit with your mother. She gave me tea." Cate relaxed a little.

"Yeah, she would do that. She thinks tea can fix more than even cloth tape can."

Maybe Padraig could fill her in on the mystery. She asked, "Does she ever talk about your uncle Brian?"

Padraig's eyes darted about as if to find who'd heard her, and he murmured, "This is not the place to talk of my uncle." He lowered his voice even further, "But she never believed he did it. She's beside herself he's come back!"

"Did what?" Cate asked, her eyes widening as she struggled to keep her voice low.

"I told you, this is no place for such talk. Mam's right though, Brian needs to leave Ireland now. Take him back where you came from while you still can."

He slipped off the bar stool to leave, but she pivoted toward him and continued softly, "Brian's not going to do that. He's come home to make amends."

Padraig kept his voice low enough that she strained to hear him, and his expression was grim as he said, "He won't fix anything. Just the opposite." Then he walked away without saying more.

Cate felt she'd entered a world of riddles. Were all Irish so cryptic? What could Brian have done? She decided it wouldn't help to ponder it more on an empty stomach while hoping to get a chance to ask John her questions. She moved to a small table for two for an early dinner, positioning herself by the window so she could watch the comings and goings. She was a people watcher by nature, and the last two days had become a bizarre social experience. As she waited for John to reappear, more people drifted into the pub. She felt their attention as they noticed her.

Addy stopped at her table, "Howya, Cate Jenks?"

"I thought I'd order some dinner. What do you recommend? Do you have any specials?"

"No specials. Nothing's special. But the fish and chips and the cottage pie are always fair good."

"What's cottage pie?

"Like shepherd's pie, but the meat is beef instead of lamb."

"That sounds good. I'll have that." Cate suddenly realized how hungry she was. A short time later, Addy delivered a steaming dish of classic comfort food. The top layer of mashed potatoes was burnished golden brown with darker crispy points. The stewed meat and vegetables beneath were a savory delight seasoned with onions and sage. As she tasted her food she felt eyes upon her. Though the crowd was abuzz with conversation, almost every time she looked up from her meal, one patron or another was staring at her and would quickly look away. "Is this about Brian?" she thought. "Or maybe they just don't get many tourists here. But Ireland is flooded with tourists half the year," she rebutted her own explanation. "I can't be such a curiosity just because I'm a stranger."

Though uncomfortable, she continued to wait for John to reappear. She decided to enjoy her food in the meantime and when every last morsel was gone, she sighed with satisfaction. Three musicians had been arranging themselves with guitar, fiddle, and the traditional Irish drum, and they began to play a rousing tune that livened the pub. She sat back and enjoyed as one song seemed to wind into the next without pause, except for punctuation by the listeners' applause and cheers. It was a strange mix of traditional tunes and kind of an 80s punk rock vibe. Eventually the musicians paused and the crowd quieted as the guitar player spoke into his microphone, "It's a sad day as we've lost one of our own. We'll send Billy off now with 'The Parting

Glass.'" He raised his glass in a toast, and all the patrons followed suit, so Cate lifted hers too. "Here's to beefsteak when you're hungry, whiskey when you're dry, all the women you'll ever want, and heaven when you die. God's speed, boy-o." Then the trio played a slow, sweet song Cate had never heard before, but everyone else sang along. The unity of their voices, and their togetherness in loss brought a tear to Cate's eye. As the tune ended the pub was silent, and then it erupted in clinking glasses and murmuring voices.

Cate smiled at the warm sadness of the moment this community was sharing. Everything may be everyone' business in a small town, but that might not always be a bad thing. She thought back to the days after Keith died, and how strange it was to do normal activities like grocery shopping. She remembered swiping her card at the register and as she waited for the transaction to be approved she thought, "This lady has no idea that my husband is dead." It was weeks before Cate stopped feeling so constantly aware of the significant event. She must have looked normal on the outside, though she felt anything but normal. The strangers she brushed past on her errands were oblivious to her life turned surrealistically upside down.

Cate sent up a prayer of peace and comfort for Billy's family on this night of their loss. The musicians had resumed their upbeat tunes and she thought about the walk ahead of her in the chilly evening. She would drink just a half-cup of coffee to finish dinner off and if she didn't get a chance to talk with John by then, she would return to the hotel. As she scanned the room to catch Addy's attention, her gaze locked with a youngish man staring from a seat at the corner of the bar. His bright blue eyes were filled with emotion. Cate blinked in astonishment at his intensity, then frowned disapprovingly to rebuke his intrusion. Instead of looking away, he rose from his seat to approach. Cate watched carefully.

"So you're the one, I hear," he accused.

Cate had had enough. "The one, what?" She squared her shoulders and stared him down but the man neither answered nor moved. Instead, he continued to loom over her, his blue eyes sparking. Cate stood so he was forced to step back. "Why did you say that?" she demanded.

He blinked as if surprised, then sputtered, "Are ye jokin'?"

"No. Why did you say I'm the one?"

"Cause you're the one brought him back!"

"Him? Brian? Brought Brian back?"

"Yes, Brian!"

"I didn't bring him back! I came with him. Who are you, anyway?"

"My name's Aiden Atley. And that lazy hole can rot in Hell."

Cate's mouth opened but she didn't know what to say as Aiden turned angrily and stalked out the door. The pub wasn't silent but its ambient noise level was definitely lower than normal, with many eyes on her. Cate's cheeks flushed as she suffered their attention. She sat back in her seat and conversation picked up immediately, but she was ready to go. When Addy appeared she quickly settled her bill and returned to the hotel, going straight to Brian's room. She knocked softly on his door.

"Come!"

Brian was sitting in the wingback chair with his cane propped against the arm rest. The room was darkened even with the curtains open, as only a little light came in through the windows. Cate switched on the lamp that sat atop the dresser, but the room was still too dim for her to properly assess him. "It's getting dark out. I ate at the pub." She switched on a torchiere lamp beside the bed. "What can I order for you? Or would you like to go to the dining room?" She assembled her tools to check his vital signs and listened to his lungs. The familiar crackles sounded a bit wetter, and she heard an expiratory wheeze with each breath. She wanted to ask him questions and get to the bottom of things, but he seemed more fragile than usual. "I think we'd better order in. What'll you have?"

"I don't care," Brian grumbled.

"Well, I had the cottage pie at the pub. It was delicious. Want me to see if room service has it?"

"Yeah, that sounds good." His flat tone contradicted his words, but Cate called in the order anyway and started a breathing treatment. As Brian rinsed his mouth afterwards, Cate weighed whether or not he needed to see a doctor, "You haven't been out at all today, have you?"

"I'm a little winded," he sighed, not meeting her eyes.

"And maybe depressed?" she offered. "I know the meeting with Mags wasn't what you'd hoped."

"Bullshit!" he barked. "Everyone's depressed. That's life! I'm just wondering what to do next, that's all. Just sorting things out." He coughed and wheezed.

"It would be normal to have hurt feelings," Cate offered.

Brian grunted, "Enough talk about feelings. How was the pub? Delicious, you say?"

"It was!" Cate dug in deeper. "But I felt like I was on display. People are talking about you... and me." Brian didn't reply so she continued, "I met Addy. She's the server. Seemed friendly but I didn't get to talk with her much. John called her away to the back and she kind of cooled when she took my order and brought my food. Maybe I imagined it, but I felt like John told her not to talk with me, you know, like to back off. She had been chatty earlier."

"Aw, he probably just wanted her to do her job. Nothing personal."

"She said a strange thing earlier."

"What was that?"

"She said, 'So you're the one brought Brian back.' It was weird, almost like an accusation. And she's not the only one who has said it."

"Well, it's a small town. I'm sure there's been gossip. My leaving without goodbyes was disrespectful, and I left them all in the lurch."

"I wonder if it's more than that. I met a man named Jack who was about your age. He sounded like he knew you, but not in a friendly way. There was a younger man too. He said the same thing about me bringing you back."

"Probably just an Irish turn of phrase that sounds funny to you."

"He told me his name is Aiden Atley. Same last name as yours. Is he a relative?

"Hell if I know! Probably!" Brian choked. "I abandoned them. I don't know anyone anymore! Are you trying to make me feel worse about it?" His voice cracked with emotion then broke into coughing spasms.

"No, Brian," Cate soothed, "Relax, put your hands on your knees, lean forward and breathe out slow."

He followed her direction and stopped struggling to speak, but glared at her with watery eyes. He stabilized with a couple minutes' quiet breathing and Cate decided to not to stir the pot again tonight or she'd have to get him to a hospital. When Brian's dinner arrived he agreed it looked delicious but took only a couple disinterested bites. He then declined help getting ready for bed, so Cate made sure everything was in close reach before excusing herself. "If you don't need anything, I'll say goodnight."

"That's fine," he sighed. "See you in the morning. Maybe I'll have the trip behind me and get some of my energy back."

"We'll count on that," Cate offered. "Then you can show me more of Bunclody and teach me some Irish lore and customs. Good night, Brian."

She closed the door between their rooms and tried to settle down. She turned on the TV but nothing caught her interest. The unfamiliar channels seemed like too much effort, so she opened a book that she brought with her but couldn't get caught up in it. She found herself pacing and feeling restless with so many questions circling in her head. "I just keep bouncing around," she thought. "I can't settle down and relax but I don't know what to do with myself."

Cate concluded that she needed to tire out her body to try to quiet her mind. There were enough people still moving in the well-lighted street below that a walk in the fresh air seemed safe. She set off in the evening chill, passing The Green Man. Through the window she observed that the crowd had thinned, but a few people still sat at the bar. A couple blocks down she crossed the street to peer into a jewelry shop window with a display by a local jeweler. A gleaming Brigit's Cross caught her eye – so lovely! She would certainly come back to try it on. After zigzagging a few more blocks she felt she could relax so she turned back toward the hotel, but when she entered the lobby she went toward the bar instead of her room.

* Brigid's cross

There were no other patrons, which was no surprise. There seemed to be only a few other people staying in the hotel. A tall, slender bartender looked up at her from where he worked cleaning the taps. His nametag read Arek. He smiled and asked in an Eastern European accent, "What will you have?"

"Do you have Jameson?"

"I do, indeed. How would you like it?"

"With water."

"I'll serve, and you spill in the water to suit yourself."

"Thank you." He placed two glasses in front of her. She swirled the amber whiskey in the glass, watching its legs form as it clung to the sides. Then she dribbled in just enough water to take the stab out of the alcohol. "You don't have an Irish accent. Where are you from?"

"Originally from Poland."

"How long have you been in Ireland?"

"About ten years," he continued to tidy up behind the bar.

"Did you come here directly to Bunclody?"

"No." He paused his work to stand in front of her. "There's quite a few Polish in Limerick. I stayed there for a while."

"How did you come to settle here?"

"Mmmmm I'm not sure I'm settled yet." He smiled and tucked his chin down, "But in Limerick I met a fellow student from here. We became friends, so I came to check it out and have not left."

"So you really like it here?"

"It's a little town. It's okay. Not that far from Dublin if I want more excitement."

"Do you drive there?"

"No, I go public trans. That way I can return ossified and no damage to anyone but myself," he laughed softly, and she did too.

"Oh, I'm not much of a drinker myself. These days one glass of wine gives me a headache and no fun. But this Jameson is just what I needed tonight. Is it always so quiet in the hotel?"

"No. This time of year is usually a little slow, but with the current health concerns it's practically dead."

"Well, I hope we will see quick resolution of this virus, but I think it's probably going to get more complicated before it gets better," Cate sighed. "How often do you go back to Poland?"

"Now that I have kids, I try to go at least twice a year. But travel is expensive. Kids are expensive," he chuckled at his own joke. "My mother, she comes here sometimes."

Cate was relieved that this younger man seemed to have no interest in her story at all and wasn't asking about Brian. She wanted the normal conversation to continue, "How many children do you have?"

"Two daughters."

"How old are they?"

"Eight and six."

"Such sweet ages. They must keep you busy."

"See these gray hairs?" he pointed to his temple, laughing, and Cate joined in. Then two men came into the bar loudly laughing at some joke between them, and one called out, "Oi, Arek, draw us the black stuff!"

Cate turned to find garda Rowan Ryan in civilian clothes and Aiden Atley, both looking as surprised as she felt. All lightheartedness in the room had evaporated.

"Aye, lads." Arek moved to the taps with two pint glasses wrapped in his long fingers.

Aiden looked sullen as he leaned against the bar, not making eye contact with Cate. Rowan hovered halfway between them and spoke politely, "Evening, Ms. Jenks."

"Hello, Garda," Cate greeted them, "Aiden." Aiden only nodded unhappily, so she turned her attention to Rowan. "How is the man from the car accident?"

"He's quite recovered, thanks to you."

"Good."

An uncomfortable silence followed, so Cate excused herself, "Good night, all. Thank you, Arek, this was perfect."

As she returned to her room, the long, strange day caught up with her and the Jameson felt gritty against her eyelids. She blinked uncomfortably as she puzzled through all the unanswered questions. What had Brian done to upset everyone? How was Aiden Atley related to him, and why was he so angry with Brian if Brian had no idea who he was? What had Brian done to him? He was born decades after Brian left. He was an Atley, so not one of Mags' children. Did Brian have a brother? What happened to Brian's parents after he left? Wouldn't they have been devastated by his disappearance? Maybe they didn't fare well in his absence. Was Aiden angry because of that? But Brian didn't seem to know. Maybe Mags would shed some light on it all, if Cate had an opportunity to see her again. Cate made ready for bed. Her mind was running in circles, but it let go of all the questions as she burrowed under the duvet and she was asleep moments later.

Chapter 7

The next morning Cate rose before her alarm clock went off. She washed and dressed then knocked on Brian's door thinking they might share breakfast. He was dressed and looking better than he had since they arrived in Ireland.

"Top of the morning to you!" she greeted him in an attempted Irish brogue.

"And the rest of the day to you!" he answered laughing, "That Lucky Charms crap won't win you any friends here, Cate. Don't do it outside this room."

"I'm terrible with accents," she conceded. "Does my real voice sound like an American hillbilly to these people?"

Brian's eyes crinkled and his shoulders rose in an exaggerated shrugging apology, as if delivering bad news. "Well, not too much..."

So she laid on a thick Southern accent and sighed, "I knew it! Hey, I'm actually pretty good at this one." Then she returned to her natural speech which was General American neutral with soft Southern influence, "You look good this morning. Let's get a real meal into you. Want to eat here or in the dining room?"

"Let's venture down to the dining room. I could do with another Irish breakfast!" Brian rubbed his hands together. Cate slipped the blood pressure cuff on his arm and the pulse oximeter on his finger, and began preparing his nebulizer when a knock sounded at the door. She opened it to find a sturdy looking middle-aged man. Rowan Ryan was behind him.

"May I help you?" she asked.

The older man said, "I'm here to see Brian Atley."

Brian called from where he was seated, "Who is it, Cate?"

Cate looked questioningly at the man and waited for him to introduce himself.

"I'm Detective Sergeant Michael Rooney of An Garda Síochána. And you are Cate Jenks?"

"I am," she replied.

"I understand you are already acquainted with Garda Ryan," he nodded over his shoulder toward Rowan.

"Yes, we met yesterday. Good morning, Garda Ryan." She stepped aside allowing them into the room and turned to Brian who was rising stiffly from the chair where he had been sitting.

"What's the story?" he wheezed, looking a little shaky.

The detective sergeant re-introduced himself and commanded, "Sit, please, Mr. Atley. I need your account of your time yesterday."

Brian remained standing, with his hand on the chairback. His eyebrows pinched together and his chin jutted aggressively. "I'll need to know why you care," he countered.

"Well, now, I can't divulge that until you give your account. But I can make note that you are uncooperative."

"Hmmph," Brian snorted, "You'll have to do better than that."

Rooney smiled without warmth while watching Brian carefully. "Alright then, an acquaintance of yours has met with an unfortunate circumstance and your name came up. How's that?"

"Well, that's better, but it doesn't make sense. Who is this acquaintance?"

"The same man who phoned you yesterday. Billy Collins."

"Ah," Brian seemed surprised and uneasy. "Alright, I was in my room most of the day. In the morning I got a call to meet yer man. But you're wrong about him being my acquaintance. I didn't meet with him, and I didn't know his name until you said it now."

"You didn't know him?" Rooney drilled. "Then why'd ye agree to meet him?"

"Well, he sounded quite urgent, upset like. Said he had information I needed to know. Said it wasn't right what happened. He wouldn't say more, but he was quite insistent we meet. Then he never showed. As you can tell," Brian motioned to the oxygen pack, "I'm on a short leash. I waited a bit for him then I came back to my room. Felt I'd been a fool. Maybe he'd meant to rob my room while I was out, but nothing was amiss."

Cate realized she was staring open-mouthed at Brian's revelation and had to deliberately put on her "nurse face," an expression that conveys no disgust with the foulest bodily odor, nor distress over mortal trauma, nor surprise by outrageous human behavior. That face. She'd told Brian yesterday that a body had been found.

She had told him all the details of her day. Why hadn't he shared what he'd done? Why had he not mentioned the phone call and his trip to meet Billy Collins? Why would Brian omit those details if he had nothing to hide? Billy was dead, and he'd called Brian that same morning?

Rooney probed for more detail, "Will you start with the day's beginning, please. And leave nothing out."

"Aw, I had some breakfast delivered to my room after Cate left. Then I read for a bit, checked my emails. And then I got a phone call. By the way, how do you know I got a call?"

"A witness put the call through the hotel switchboard," Rooney answered tersely, but refused to be taken off track, prompting, "Go on."

"Ah, well, the fella said to meet him in an hour, so I went out."

"Where were you to meet?"

"Funny that," Brian replied. "He first said to meet in the church yard and I said 'Hell no.' I'd never make it that far on foot, but I didn't tell him that. And he said he didn't want to be seen with me. I said, 'Then why did you bother calling?' See what I mean? Funny. But I felt I needed to hear what he had to say. So he finally said he would meet me at the back of the hotel. But he never showed, so I came back up and that alone about did me in."

"You were seen walking from the direction of the Eurospar," Rooney stated flatly.

"The Eurospar?" Brian seemed confused, "Oh, well, I did walk a little ways down the lane. Just a few steps, thinking if he didn't want to be seen with me that he might not come right up to the hotel. It's foolish, I know, but things aren't going at all the way I expected. I came all this way, and my own sister has received me terribly. I know I'm no hometown hero, but I came to make things right. This town may not have changed as much as the rest of the world, but I'm not going to give up yet. So I wanted to hear yer man out. When he didn't show, I waited a bit then came back to my room. I was completely knackered and slept most of the day after that."

Rooney turned to Cate, "Can you confirm this?"

Cate took a breath to gather her thoughts and before she could begin to answer, Brian interrupted, "No, Cate was unaware of this adventure. She came to check on me later. I didn't need her to know what an eejit I am. And I didn't go out again – too winded."

Rooney let silence hang until it became uncomfortable, but neither Brian nor Cate was compelled to break it. Finally, he said, "That is all for now. Garda Ryan will type your statement and we'll return later for you to sign it. Ms. Jenks, what is your relationship to Mr. Atley?"

Cate replied, "I am his friend and neighbor, and also a nurse. Because of his medical condition Brian is unable to travel alone. I'm traveling with him to provide assistance, administer his prescribed medications, assess him periodically, and escalate his care if necessary."

"Right, then. Thank you for your time." Rooney signaled Rowan toward the door, then turned back to Brian, "I will need to speak with you again, Mr. Atley, and until further notice you are not to leave Bunclody. Understood?"

Brian gasped, and Cate quickly intervened, "Is he under arrest?"

"Should he be?" Rooney shot back.

"Of course not!"

"Then he is not... yet."

Rooney stalked out of the room with Garda Ryan behind him. As the door clicked shut, Brian sagged against the back of the chair, but Cate didn't move to help him. She was seeing him in a new light. He certainly wasn't sharing all he knew. Was he doing things he shouldn't do? Was he a bad guy? Rooney didn't actually say that Billy had been killed, but his investigation and implication of arrest sounded like a crime had occurred. However, he never actually said the word arrest. Cate was the one who'd said it. Rooney used the situation to plant doubt, to throw them off balance, so he could get to the bottom of things. It was a successful tactic. Why was Brian keeping secrets? Cate felt anger rising in her. Why had he dragged her into this mess without disclosing it beforehand? Cate answered her own question: because she never would have made the trip with him. But what exactly had Brian done?

Brian was glaring indignantly at the door where Rooney last stood, "Gobshite. Why would he be asking me all those questions?"

"The detective said your acquaintance met with misfortune. And Billy had called you to meet, but never showed. I'm pretty sure his was the body that was found yesterday, and that means he died unexpectedly sometime after his call to you. They even played a song for him in the pub last night. The police have to investigate. As for your adventure, anything that affects your health also affects me, so you should inform me when you plan to go out," she demanded.

Brian looked angry and not at all contrite. "I didn't plan the adventure, it just happened!"

"Brian," she stood firm. "We are not joined at the hip and you are free to do what you want to do. But until we get you settled in with another caregiver..."

"Alright, alright!" he cut her off. "I'll give you a ring if I decide to go anywhere."

"Thank you." Cate paused, taking a breath to settle herself, then redirected him to another topic, "I'm sorry to revisit a painful subject, but you didn't receive the welcoming you were hoping for."

"That's an understatement," Brian said as he moved from where he was leaning against the chair back to seat himself again.

"What are you going to do next?"

"No idea," he frowned deeper, shaking his head.

"Well, what were you going to do if you'd been received differently? What did you have in mind before you were unwelcomed?"

Moments passed while Brian considered his answer. Cate watched anguish and regret and longing shape his expression. Finally, he said quietly, "I dreamed of buying a cottage here in Bunclody and enjoying my last days with Mags and her family. Getting to know them." His fingertips traced absentminded patterns on the chair arm.

Cate shook her head empathetically. "If that's what you wanted after all these years, you must be deeply disappointed."

"I'm sure I'll figure out something, given time. Perhaps I could convince you to stay on a few more days? Maybe get me a little more stable?" Brian sighed dramatically and made himself look as pitiful as possible.

Cate smiled at his request but reasoned gently against it. "I'm going to need to stick to the original plan. Flights are already being canceled. If I don't catch my plane on Friday it might be hard to find another one. At this point there's no quarantine required when I land, but that could change anytime. I read there are some cruise ships that have been turned away from ports. We need to make calls today to get you set up with a doctor and find a home health service to look in on you. I assume they'll come to the hotel if you haven't settled somewhere else by then."

"I'll be flying back with you Friday if the people here are going to keep treating me like a pariah." Brian's tone was gruff again.

"Unless Detective Rooney says you have to stay put," Cate reminded him.

"Rooney can kiss my arse!" He rolled his eyes and broke into a coughing fit.

"So..." Cate changed the subject when he quieted, "Do you want to stroll down to the dining room and give the locals something to talk about? Or would you like your breakfast brought up to you?"

"Let 'em talk!" Brian was defiant.

They went to the hotel restaurant where Brian ordered another traditional Irish breakfast, and Cate ordered porridge oats with milk and maple syrup. Afterwards, they took a short, slow walk in the canal park. They sat on a park bench before turning back, and the morning chill cut through Cate's jacket where the bench planks pressed into her backside.

"Where was it they found Billy Collins?" Brian asked.

"Just down there," Cate pointed to the Eurospar. "See the parking lot right before it? He was in the back corner, the one closest to the hotel."

"He must have been on his way to meet me," Brian mused.

"Brian, do you have any idea what he wanted to tell you? I mean, it's a strange coincidence that he dropped dead just before you were to meet."

"No idea."

"You said he didn't want to be seen with you."

"Aye."

"Why not?"

Brian's expression was stiff, "He didn't say."

"But you must have some idea why," Cate pushed.

"I may. But that's my business."

An uncomfortable silence hung between them and Cate finally sighed, "Fine. So, I guess we need to go make some calls to get you set up with nurse visits and you can start looking for a place to stay."

It was a slow journey back to Brian's suite because, despite increasing his oxygen flow for his exertion, he had to make several stops to rest on park benches and then again inside the hotel lobby. In his room, he dropped himself heavily into the blue wingback chair. Cate reminded him to tripod, and helped him reposition on the edge of the seat. She brought the side table in front of him, placed a pillow on top of it and had him lean there on his elbows.

"You'll need to set up this arrangement wherever you stay so you can use these breathing techniques," she urged him, not for the first time. "Make sure you put chairs around your place so you have somewhere to sit in each room." She knew patients needed to hear information about seven times before they would reliably retain it. They also learned by doing, so Cate was preparing to leave Brian in Ireland by beginning to back off handling arrangements and instead coaching him through them.

Cate started the electric kettle and excused herself to her own room for a few minutes to let Brian recover. When she returned, she noticed he had reduced his oxygen flow back to his normal setting and was breathing comfortably while still leaning forward with the TV remote caged loosely in his right hand, watching a program in Gaeilge. She listened while she made tea.

When the program broke for commercial she placed a cup in front of him, asking, "Do you understand what they're saying?"

He shrugged, "Ehhhhh, some."

"Let's start making calls to get you set up with a local nursing service. Where's your insurance card?"

Brian dug out his wallet and produced the card from the international private insurance he had purchased for both of them before leaving the U.S. Because of the rapidly spreading coronavirus, the premiums had been outrageous and the deductible was also astronomical, but Brian had waved his hand unconcernedly when they'd received the quote. As an Irish citizen he would be eligible for national healthcare, but Cate had worried he might need intervention before all his long-dormant paperwork was resurrected. He placed the card on the edge of the table then sunk back in the chair with his eyes closed.

"So... Have you looked up any phone numbers for nursing services?" Cate asked.

"No," he kept his eyes closed.

She took a deep, quiet breath, "Well then, let's get started with it."

"If you insist." Brian didn't move.

"Brian, your behavior is called passive-aggressive." Exasperated, Cate took the card and his wallet to start the research. She used her cellphone to find numbers for the health center and a couple doctors in County Wexford. She got no answers to her calls, so left messages with Brian's phone number for callback.

As she was finishing, Brian excused himself to the toilet. When he was returning to his chair a knock sounded at the door. He detoured to open it. "G'way! The sight of you!" Brian gasped.

Cate had a clear view of John Kelley in the doorway as he replied dryly, "Word is Brian Atley's ghost is haunting this hotel, so I came to see for m'self." Then the two men laughingly embraced. John's long arms slow-clapped against Brian's back.

"I'll live a while yet," Brian finally wheezed, "If you let go before you smother me. I'm so happy to see a friendly face, even if it is old as dirt. Cate, this is me old mate, John Kelley." He motioned John to a chair and returned to the blue wingback.

"We've met," Cate said. "Hello, John, it's good to see you again."

"Hello, Cate," John nodded, seeming more at ease than yesterday, but still guarded.

"What's the story?" Brian leaned forward eagerly.

"Aw, Brian, it's a twisted one. I've come to fill you in," he coughed and shifted in his chair.

Cate noticed his pause. "I'm going to go next door and make a few more phone calls," she said, "So you two can talk."

She stood, but Brian waved her back. "Stay, Cate. We're going to sort things out here and now."

"Um, okay." It seemed to Cate that John really preferred to talk with Brian alone, but she was also dying of curiosity and relieved that Brian wanted her there. She tried to set John at ease. "Let me get you a cup of tea."

He shook his head, "I don't want to put you out."

"I just poured some for us and the water's still hot," she said. "Please join us."

She placed a cup on the table beside him and Brian urged, "Tell me what's happened."

"Tell you what's happened in Bunclody in the last fifty years? Then I'll want to hear what you've been up to all these decades." He shook his head regretfully, "But let me begin with Aiden Atley. He thinks you are his grandfather and you are responsible for his granny having such a hard life. He thinks you abandoned her."

"What? Who was his granny?"

"Claire Fitzpatrick."

Brian's face contorted with shock and confusion. "But John... I never! You know that! Why would he think that? Why?"

"Ye knew that Claire had fallen pregnant when ye left."

Brian put up a hand in protest, "And I never breathed a word of it. I held her secret."

"Yeh, but she couldn't. When you took a runner she named you as the father. Sorry, lad. I wasn't in a position to contradict her, ye know. And I think the lie ate at her. She did live a hard life. You can see then, growing up with that tale, why Aiden is angry."

"Oh, dear God! Why would she do that? My family must have gone mad."

"It did cause a stir. She begged me to keep her secret," John sighed and his shoulders sagged a little.

"All these years," Brian shook his head, "Wait! What became of Claire and the baby? Was it a son or a daughter?"

Cate blinked, opened her mouth and then closed it without saying anything.

"It was a daughter," John confirmed. "The Fitzpatricks were harsh to them. And really browned off at you, by the way. But your da and mam did right by them both, as much as they could. Claire fell into poor health and passed years ago. She looked twice her age, poor soul. Her daughter Mary Margaret took care of her. She took care of Aiden too, as best she could. He was another fatherless baby, so he got your name. Mary

Margaret has had her share of troubles, you see. She's in Dublin now for work and Aiden's been on his own from a young age. He's built up a head of steam all over again now that you've returned, and he's... unpredictable."

Brian seemed locked in intense thought, but his breathing was growing ragged.

"I met Aiden in the pub last night," Cate said softly. "He seemed very angry."

"Aye," John replied.

"Brian, are you alright?" Cate asked. He was even paler than usual and his eyes were downcast, His head shook almost as with a tremor. Finally he whispered, "No... No, how could I be alright?"

"I'm afraid there's more," John stated.

"More?" Brian moaned and broke into a coughing fit that escalated until he couldn't catch his breath. His eyes watered and his face blazed red.

Cate reached for his rescue inhaler and shook it hard as she removed the cap. Brian used both hands to scoop it from her. He closed his lips around the mouthpiece and inhaled shakily. Cate increased his oxygen. She placed the pulse oximeter on his finger and moved the side table back in front of him, urging him into the tripod position again.

"Shall I call 999?" John asked.

"No!" Brian wheezed.

"Hang on. Let's give it a minute," Cate answered as she watched Brian's breathing pattern, his coloring, and the oximteter. She was on the verge of calling for help. His oxygen saturation had dipped dangerously, but as his breathing became less desperate the readings increased. They all waited as minutes passed. The only sound in the room came from Brian's laboring lungs.

"Do you want an ambulance, Brian?" Cate finally asked.

He shook his head no.

"Your oxygen has improved a little now. If we can keep you there I think you'll be alright."

Braced on his elbows, Brian's head hung exhaustedly and his eyes were closed as he nodded. Then he opened them to look at John and croaked, "Tell me."

Cate intervened, "No, not now. It's too much. If you get worse I've got no way to help you."

John looked shaken and his expression was grim as he nodded. "She's right. It'll keep until you're better, Brian. I'll pop by again tomorrow. You can find me at the pub if you need me," he said as he opened the door to leave.

"Thank ye, John, for telling me," Brian coughed and wheezed, then took another breath and his eyes watered, "It's a mighty shock, but at least now I can deal with the young man."

"Ta' bron orm," John spoke softly.

"Slán," Brian sputtered, and waved him on. The door clicked as John closed it.

Cate quietly maintained her position beside Brian, monitoring his recovery. As minutes passed, his breathing continued to improve. After some time, Brian sighed, "What a Godawful mess!"

"It is," she agreed.

They sat silently. Brian stared at the floor, occasionally shifting his gaze and sighing, deep in thought. Cate would have given him privacy but she needed to make sure he remained stable, so she turned on the TV and set the volume low. Throughout the hour she periodically rechecked his vital signs and decided he had safely returned to his baseline. "It seems like you're okay for now, but, you know, too much stress is dangerous for you."

"That's the least of my worries. How am I to make this right?" He coughed, then continued, "If I deny it, I make my friend Claire a liar to her family and the whole town. If I don't, the lie continues and Aiden will suffer more, and I'll still be despised. I wish I'd never come home. Not just for myself. Oh, what a mess. What a mess!" He covered his eyes with his hand and squeezed his head at the temples.

"It is a terrible situation, Brian. I'm so sorry you're going through this," Cate patted and squeezed his shoulder. "And I'm sorry that Aiden is going through it, too. He has reason to be angry, but that's no excuse for bad behavior. He was very aggressive when he talked to me in the pub last night. He actually made me pretty nervous, the way he came right up and got in my face. John said he's unpredictable. You'll just need to keep that in mind if you plan to see him."

Brian slid his hand down to cover his mouth while raising his eyes to meet Cate's. He shook his head slowly in despair.

"What will help at this point?" Cate asked. "Is there anything I can do?"

"I've no idea," Brian sighed. "Why don't you go exploring? I've no energy for anything else right now. And no one's taking your calls, I noticed." He gave a small smile.

"You don't have to be smug about it," Cate huffed, "Seriously, though, you've had quite a shock. Do you want to talk about it?"

Tears glistened in Brian's eyes and he looked away from her as he drew a tremulous breath. "No, I really don't want to talk about it. Thank you, but I would rather be alone right now."

"If you're sure." He seemed to have stabilized, and Cate felt he was safe to be on his own.

"I am. Please go. I just need some time to think."

He waved her away and she patted his shoulder as she headed to her room. "Call me if you need anything."

Cate closed the door to give him privacy. What could she do to help him? She was worried about the stress heaped on by the allegations of fatherhood and abandonment. Was this why everyone was so angry with Brian? In his absence, things must have gone terribly wrong for his friend Claire, her daughter, and grandson Aiden. And since Brian had never known that Claire named him as the father, he had never defended himself. But if he wasn't the father, he had left Bunclody for some other desperate reason, and he still hadn't said why. What could the reason be?

Cate was pacing, trying to puzzle it all out, and she could barely keep herself from going back to Brian with her questions. She sat in the chair and stared at the door between their rooms, willing him to call for her. But he didn't, and the silence irritated her.

She thought, "I'm going to go crazy just sitting in here. I'll double-check to make sure he's okay and go take a walk." She geared up for any weather she might encounter – jacket, boots, and a rain poncho in her bag in case of another soaking rain. She knocked softly before entering his room.

"Hey, Brian, I'm just checking to make sure you're still doing alright."

"I'm fine, Cate." He sounded a little annoyed by her intrusion.

"I'm going out for some fresh air, like you suggested, unless you feel like you need me to stay close by?"

"Nah, go on. I'm fine."

"Is there anything I can bring back for you?"

"No."

She made sure he had his cellphone and the room phone within reach and headed out of the hotel without a destination. She wandered back to the bridge over the River Slaney. Shortly past it, she found a well-trod but unpaved path split off to the left of the pavement. Cate paused to consider, should she take it? "Why not?" she dared herself... "Because this is the way horror movies start," she answered, and then she felt reflexively defiant. It was terrible that women in particular, but people in general had to be so careful. It wasn't wild animals she was concerned about, rather it was the danger of other humans. She stepped off the pavement to follow her curiosity. After passing through the hedgerow she was immediately rewarded with a most beautiful view. A short stroll across pastureland led to a copse of trees then followed beside a stream. Then the path angled upward on a hill. She continued, and as she descended the second hill a circle of brush lay ahead, and she decided it would be her turnaround point.

She came within a few feet of the circle's edge and decided not to go in, even though it seemed like exactly where she should go. It was like going to the beach and not putting her feet in the water. Years ago, Cate had taken karate lessons and there was a ritual of respect for entering the dojang, bowing to the flags and to the instructor. And if class was underway, students waited for permission to step onto the floor. This place felt significant, like a ritual of respect might be appropriate. Maybe it was one of the faery circles she had read about, and Cate didn't want to break any rules she didn't know. She didn't believe, but she also didn't disbelieve. Who was she to question another culture's mythology? Irish faeries weren't beautiful, winged girls that danced on mushroom caps. They were capricious.

Instead of going in, Cate tracked the outside of the circle and found it was not-quite-complete. She was able to get a clear view of the whole space and there was nothing inside but grass. Still, she didn't venture in. She completed her walk around the outside, back to where she had started on the path, put her hands on her hips and stood to take in the sight once more before turning back. A movement in the corner of her eye caught her attention. It was a little animal she'd never seen in the wild before. A spiky hedgehog scurried about, rooting and snuffling in – of all places – the hedge. Adorable! She laughed out loud and startled the creature. It stopped dead still and so did Cate. After a long pause measuring for danger, the hedgehog continued its industrious business and Cate was completely mesmerized. When it finally ambled off out of view, she took a deep breath. She felt as if she'd been meditating, refreshed but a little tired from the intensity of her attention. A twig snapped behind her and she turned fast to find a small, thin old woman on the path. She wore her socks over the cuffs of her pants, and her red waterproofed shoes were well-muddied. Her smile pushed the wrinkles around her face. A braid interwoven with feathers and bits of colored yarn hung over her shoulder, and flyaway strands of long silver-white hair brushed her face. Her eyes were like buttons, bright and shiny and her gnarled hand clutched a basket of herbs. "She's a cute one," the old woman remarked.

"The hedgehog?"

The woman nodded in reply.

"I've never seen one before. It's so sweet!"

"Sweet?"

"I mean dear, precious."

"Ah, dear indeed," the woman turned to go.

"Do you live nearby?" Cate asked.

The woman turned back to her, "I do."

"I'm just visiting Bunclody for the first time. I'm from the U.S."

"I know who ye are, Cate Jenks. Yer the one brought Brian Atley back to face his past."

"Well, I am the person who came with Brian. I'm his nurse." Cate sighed. "I don't know anything about his past except that this is his home."

"So you say."

Somehow the old woman's words were not combative or accusatory, just statements. Maybe she could fill in some of the missing pieces of the puzzle. "What's your name?" Cate asked her.

"I'm called Cailleach."

"I'm happy to meet you, Cailleach." Cate tried to repeat the name as she'd heard it, but she knew she was mispronouncing it. It came out sounding like Ka-lock.

"Mm."

"What is it about Brian's past? What is he facing?"

"Sometimes one day changes everything; sometimes years change nothing."

Cate squinted. "I still don't understand. What does that mean?"

"You're the one who will help him understand," the old woman said evenly, as if the answer made perfect sense.

Cate shook her head, "This is confusing. I don't know what you mean, and I certainly don't understand what's going on. Can you please just explain why everyone here is so upset with Brian?"

"There's more than one tale to be told. You're the one to bring truth to light."

"Everyone keeps saying I'm 'the one.' I'm the one who brought him back. Now you say I'm the one to 'bring truth to light.'"

"Truly ye are, dearie."

"I'm just Brian's neighbor and I don't really know him very well at all. I came along to help him with the travel so he could get home safely. I don't know anything about his past and I'm leaving on Friday, so I can't help if I don't know what's going on. Can't you just tell me?"

"No, you must be getting back to the hotel now. Don't be late. Continue on the boreen, it's the quickest way back."

"The boreen?"

"This path," Cailleach pointed to the well-trod track that had brought Cate to the faery circle and indicated she should continue past it rather than retrace her steps. Then Cailleach turned away and ambled off in the opposite direction.

Exasperated, Cate watched her go and complained loudly, "That doesn't clear up anything!"

Cailleach chuckled and called over her shoulder, "Leg it, Cate Jenks."

Chapter 8

It took Cate only about half the time to return to the hotel. The boreen, as she now thought of it, merged with a narrow, paved road that crossed the River Slaney with a single-lane bridge, then led straight to Main Street. All was quiet in the town, and in the hotel. Cate went upstairs to her room, then knocked softly on Brian's door. When there was no answer, she looked in on him and he was asleep in his bed, breathing evenly.

"Looks like I got back just in time," she thought sarcastically. "I guess I can take Cailleach's recommendations with a grain of salt. What to do now?"

It was too late for lunch and too early for dinner, and Cate wasn't hungry even after the walk. She wandered through the hotel and when she looked into the bar the long, tall bartender was on duty and alone. After the rollercoaster ride of the day, she decided she deserved a drink.

"How are you, Arek?"

"Very good, and yourself?"

"I'm trying to decide what to do for the rest of the day. What's the best drink you make?"

Arek's brow arched over his deep-set eye, "The Prince has complimented my martini."

"You've served Prince Charles?" she was looking forward to this story.

"Nyah, not exactly. My friend Aiden's dog Prince once got to a spilled one and wagged a compliment."

Cate laughed along with him. "Well, that's a good review. I'll have one of your Prince-approved martinis." She watched him mix, then he placed a perfectly chilled glass in front of her and waited for her to taste it. She sipped and sighed, "Oh, Prince was right! That is good. Thank you."

Deadpan, Arek said, "Now we see that it is also fit for human consumption."

"Well, let's not jump to conclusions," she joked back. "Check back on me to make sure."

He pointed to his own eyes then arced two fingers at her, motioning that he was watching, while he assembled a small plate of salted peanuts that he placed in front of her.

"If I eat these, how will we know if it's the drink or the food that's the poison?"

"Exactly," he chuckled, as Cate popped a couple peanuts into her mouth.

Arek made himself busy behind the bar and Cate sat silently, reflecting that here she was in Ireland, with no one close to her to share this bizarre experience. She didn't feel lonely, but she did feel alone. She weighed the difference. Right now, she was content and curious on this adventure, but when she returned to her everyday life there would be no one to share the story and laugh about how strange it all was. Her memories would be hers alone, and most people weren't interested in stories that didn't include them. This is what made her miss Keith most. For a year, there had been no savoring of memories together.

Sharing memories was a big part of their marriage, and Cate had only realized its full importance when it stopped. Through the years they had traveled regularly, and from time to time they would relive their trips. It was usually the disasters and ironies that became the favorite stories they laughingly re-described to each other again and again. For their twentieth wedding anniversary Keith planned a trip to Arkansas to "hunt a sparkler" for her in the Crater of Diamonds State Park. They packed inappropriately for the April weather, which was blazing hot in Florida. When they landed in Little Rock it was unexpectedly dreary and cold, so they stopped at a WalMart to buy jackets and rubber boots for slogging in the mud. But at that time of year the store was stocked with summer clothes and not a long sleeve was to be found in the men's or women's departments. They ended up buying overpriced windbreakers from the camping section then drove a couple hours to Murfreesboro, and by then the sky had cleared and the temperature had climbed into the eighties. They spent the afternoon sweating, and finished the day sunburned and diamond-less. But the jackets were much appreciated the next day when they took a Duck Tour on an amphibious vehicle in Hot Springs. They rode around town on the repurposed military vehicle and learned about the history of the place, then splashed into lakes where the whipping wind and chilly spray left them both bedraggled. For years, they called the windbreakers their "Arkansas jackets," and retold the story with each wearing.

When Cate returned home from Ireland, who would care about this strange adventure she was on now? No one would want to hear the story more than once, and certainly not in all its detail. Would she be able to securely hold onto her memories without a dear partner to cherish a shared past? She suspected that was one of the health benefits of a good relationship, and a reason why married people tend to live longer. But she had no desire to find another partner now. The idea of dating, trying on new people to see if they fit, learning about their lives and interests and needs, held no interest.

She thought, "Maybe I can be enough good company for myself instead, and intentionally practice enjoying my memories on my own as a mental exercise. It might become a habit that eventually feels natural."

Cate was jolted from her reverie as she glimpsed Detective Sergeant Rooney and Garda Ryan pass through the hotel lobby toward the elevators. Rooney had said Ryan would type up Brian's statement. Was this a routine delivery or were they going to question Brian further? Were they even here to see Brian, or for some other reason?

Cate didn't want Brian left alone if any official business was underway. She sprinted after the two guards, trying to decide what she would say if they were waiting at the elevator. Thankfully, the doors closed just before she arrived and she waited a couple seconds before pressing the up button to call another car. By the time her elevator reached the third floor, which was called the second floor here, Rooney and Ryan were knocking at Brian's door.

"Come!" Brian called from inside.

Cate frowned at Brian's response and called to the two men, "I'm here, I have a key." She hurried toward them, feeling the half of the martini she had drunk. "Are you here to finalize his statement?"

"We are here to see Mr. Atley," Rooney replied tersely.

"He had an asthma attack earlier and was sleeping when I last checked on him. Let me make sure he's steady." Cate moved between the officers and the door, opened it slightly and announced, "Brian, it's the police here to see you again." She opened the door fully to step inside and found Brian awake and sitting in the wingback chair again.

Rooney didn't pause for pleasantries. He moved past Cate, directly in front of Brian. "Brian Atley, you are being arrested for the murder of Timothy Dooley."

"What?!" Brian and Cate cried simultaneously.

"I am arresting you for the murder of Timothy Dooley," he repeated.

Brian roared back, "I heard what you said, now what do you mean? What is this insanity? Has the whole town gone mental?"

"I'm taking you to the station to be formally charged," Rooney replied. "You are not obliged to say anything unless you wish to do so, but whatever you say will be taken down in writing and may be given in evidence."

"Whatever I say? Like, what would I say?" Brian gasped, "This is ridiculous! I've only been in Ireland a couple days. How could I murder anyone? Not that the bastard didn't deserve it."

Cate interrupted, "Brian! Stop talking! Detective Rooney, can you explain why he's being charged?"

Rooney replied, "He's being charged because we have evidence that he murdered Timothy Dooley."

"Who is Timothy Dooley?" Cate asked Rooney.

"He's a local bullying gobshite," Brian interrupted. "I can't say I'm surprised he finally got murdered. He mucked up so many people's lives. But I haven't been in Ireland in fifty years so I can't see that you would have evidence that I've done anything but walk a few steps in the town. What evidence do you have? I can hardly breathe, much less kill anyone." Brian's statement was punctuated with a high-pitched wheeze as he finally inhaled.

Cate turned to Rooney, "I am so confused, Detective Rooney. Will you explain, please?"

"No, I will not. Not here." He kept his eyes on Brian, "Now, get yourself together and we'll go to the station where you will be formally charged."

"Am I dreaming?" Brian moaned. "Is this a nightmare?"

"It is for you," Rooney replied stonily. "Now come along with ye."

"I'll get our things," Cate launched into motion.

"No, Miss," Rooney intervened, "We'll be taking only Mr. Atley."

"But wait! You can't!"

Rooney glared at her, "Can't what?"

Cate adjusted her tone. "I mean, doesn't he get an attorney or something? Someone to advise him?"

"He may request a solicitor," Rooney acknowledged.

"Alright! I request one." Brian's gaze was bouncing between the two nervously, "Cate, can you find a solicitor? I don't know anyone here anymore. In fact, it feels like the whole place is upside down."

"I'll figure it out, Brian," Cate reassured him, then turned to Rooney. "Will you let me give him a breathing treatment before you take him in? And I need to send his oxygen concentrator, battery packs, and medicines with him. You'll need to rotate charged batteries and keep on schedule with his doses or you'll end up having to call an ambulance."

"Fine," Rooney was unmoved.

She feared for Brian's safety in the uproar. Cate took a firm position directly in front of the detective. "I know you're doing your job. I have to do mine too. I need to make myself completely clear. Brian is oxygen-dependent, and his airway must be protected. He has already had an episode today when I nearly called for an ambulance. If you lock him up in a cell without medical supervision, he can get in trouble fast. We're talking minutes, not hours. He must have access to oxygen, his rescue inhaler, and breathing treatments at all times. Delaying any of those could result in his death. I'm asking each of you to acknowledge what I've just said." She looked to Rooney, "Detective?"

"Understood," his voice was hard, "and you should understand, Ms. Jenks, that you are in County Wexford, not L.A. This is not one of your American television dramas."

"You're absolutely right," Cate replied. "I have no idea how legal matters work in Ireland, so I can only go with what I know. Garda, do you also understand what I said about Brian's breathing?"

Rowan looked surprised when Cate turned to him. "Yes, understood."

As she then turned to Brian, from the corner of her eye she saw the younger garda steal a glance at his boss.

She continued, "Brian, you tell them if you need help. Do it the minute you notice anything changing. If you start wheezing or feeling tight, don't wait. Take your meds, and if you don't feel improved, ask for an ambulance."

Brian looked stunned and miserable, shaking his head in disbelief.

"Brian, do you hear me?" she prodded.

"Oh, yeh yeh. Ask for an ambulance."

"Right," and she looked pointedly to the two officers before setting up the nebulizer and getting Brian ready to go. Then, as they walked him out of the hotel room, Cate reminded Brian, "Don't talk until I get you an attorney... Solicitor... Whatever."

The gardaí took Brian toward the elevator. In the hallway, Cate cautioned them, "Go slow. He can't walk the whole distance to the car at one stretch. Let him sit and recover in the lobby."

Rooney nodded without looking back at her and answered, "We will do what's necessary."

When the doors closed, Cate returned to Brian's room in search of a phone number. He had used the room phone to call Mags so it wouldn't be in his cell phone which was plugged into the wall, charging. On the tabletop beside the room phone was a scrap of paper with a number in Brian's spidery handwriting. Cate dialed and was thoroughly relieved when Mags' voice answered on the third ring, "Hello?"

"Mags? This is Cate Jenks."

"Sure and how are ye keeping?"

"What? Listen, Brian's been arrested. They charged him with murder of someone named Timothy Dooley."

"No! But it was only a matter of time!" Mags wailed.

"Brian seemed totally surprised. Anyway, he needs a lawyer, a solicitor. I told him not to talk until the solicitor's with him but I don't know if he can control himself. I'm in over my head here. How do we go about getting him some help?"

"It's Declan O'Keefe that Brian will need. I'll ring him straight away."

"That's a solicitor?"

"Aye."

"Okay, can you see my cell phone number on your phone or do you need to write it down?"

"I've got it here."

"And is this your cell or a landline?" Brian's sister confirmed both her phone numbers. After writing them down, Cate continued, "Mags, I'm worried about Brian. He's fragile and with all this turmoil and activity... well, he could have trouble breathing. He already had one asthma attack today and I nearly called an ambulance. Will they keep a close eye on him while he's in custody? Or will they toss him in a cell with a bunch of other people?"

"What other people?" Mags huffed. "He's likely the only one being detained, but you're right, that lot won't care for him the way you do. Go to the station, dear. Mick Rooney does his job but he's class and may let you look after my brother even while he charges him."

Cate ended the call with a reminder for Mags to give the solicitor Cate's cell number, then she looked up the garda station in her GPS app. Fortunately, it was only a few minutes' walk away so she didn't have to call a taxi or figure out other transportation. She made herself stop and take a few deep breaths – inhale for a count of four, hold for eight, then exhale for eight. It was her way of tricking her body into calming down, even though she did not feel calm at all. Her mind was racing. She looked around the room for anything she had forgotten to pack for Brian. She mentally walked through his care routines. Was there anything she missed sending with him? Was he dressed warmly enough?

"I'm stalling," she thought to herself. "I don't really know what I'll be walking into at the garda station." When and how could Brian have murdered someone? And what made Rooney sure enough to charge him? Cate dug an additional backup battery for Brian's oxygen concentrator out of his luggage, slipped it in her bag, and ensured their rooms were locked before making her way downstairs.

The walk to the garda station went much quicker than Cate hoped. She still hadn't decided what she was going to say. Rooney had specifically stated that they were taking Brian alone. She didn't want to get on his bad side and make things worse for Brian. She also considered that it might be very foolish to insert herself into legal matters in a foreign country. She didn't recall Ireland ever being in the news for harsh treatment or locking up tourists for obscure infractions, but she really had no idea what the country's reputation was in handling criminal matters. She didn't want to get herself detained for the Irish version of obstruction of justice or somehow as an accessory to Brian's charges. Had she somehow facilitated a crime by bringing him here?

Why was she marching into a garda station to try to see a murder suspect? "It's about patient advocacy," she reminded herself. Cate had taken care of hundreds of patients with diverse backgrounds, and details of their lives often unfolded during care. She had tended convicted felons, gang members, victims of violence and trauma, and neglected and abused elderly. With their families and friends often at the bedside, the details emerged sometimes through observations and overheard conversations, and sometimes through deliberate disclosure. Humans, Cate had learned, are capable of just about any behavior. As a nurse, her patient was always her first priority, no matter who they were in their everyday life or what they had done. Patient advocacy was her compass in uncomfortable conversations. Making sure her patient was safe was her goal, even if it upset families or doctors. Without having eyes on him now, Cate didn't feel at all sure that Brian was safe.

And Brian was her patient. Was he also a murderer?

The garda station was a nondescript block building with only a blue insignia-marked lantern as signage. A communications tower rose impressively behind it. There were only four parking spaces and all but one were empty. Cate steeled herself and opened the door.

Inside she found a reception area with a couple seats and a countertop with a guard behind it. Glass partitions separated the space from the rest of the building.

"Can I help ye?" the guard asked.

"Yes." She still hadn't quite decided what she was going to say, so she was a little surprised that she sounded reasonably confident, "My name is Cate Jenks. I'm from the U.S. and I'm traveling with Brian Atley who has just been brought in by Detective Rooney. I don't want to get in the way of police business, but Mr. Atley has medical conditions that might require urgent intervention with equipment and medications. I'm a nurse and have been taking care of him. Honestly, I'm just worried about him and wanted to be close by in case I'm needed."

The guard looked at her skeptically but politely said, "Please have a seat, then. I'll let Detective Sergeant Rooney know you're here."

She sat in the chair closest to the door where she could see a little of the goings on through the glass panes into the next space. There were multiple desks in an open area, but only two of them were occupied by gardaí who were typing on keyboards with screens that were angled away from her. The reception officer also typed on a keyboard but did not use a phone or radio, so she wasn't sure if he'd actually informed anyone she was there. Most offices in the U.S. now had instant messaging utilities, so people could communicate from computer to computer without speaking aloud. Cate was hoping he had alerted the detective sergeant or Garda Ryan by instant message, and that he wasn't just leaving her to sit. Whatever the case, she'd done all she could do for now, so she sat as patiently as she could.

As an hour crawled by, Cate took out her cellphone and began to read about Irish criminal justice practices. According to an official website, when a victim reports a crime to An Garda Síochána, the gardaí take a witness statement from the victim, and the witness statement is the written record of the complaint. The gardaí then investigate the crime and, given appropriate evidence gathered during investigation, they arrest a suspect. The Director of Public Prosecutions then independently makes a decision about whether or not to prosecute. That was the stage they were at right now; Brian was arrested, so there must have been a witness or other evidence to indicate he had killed Timothy Dooley. Rooney would be taking Brian's statement and from that there would be a decision whether or not to prosecute. What would they do with Brian between those two events? Would he stay in jail? Would they keep him in Bunclody? She couldn't find more detailed descriptions of what to expect.

And, backing up a few steps, what witness could have accused Brian of murdering Timothy Dooley? Cate had been with Brian much of the time they'd been in Bunclody, but there were also many times that Cate was out or had the door shut between their rooms. Every time she'd checked on him, though, he'd been in his room.

However, he did go out yesterday morning without telling her and she never would have known except that he'd been questioned by Rooney about Billy Collins. And that happened because Billy Collins had turned up dead too, which didn't improve her confidence in Brian at all. Was he a cold-blooded murderer?

"Slow it down, Cate," she thought to herself. "Don't jump to conclusions. What you imagine is almost always worse than what actually happens."

She forced herself to stop thinking about Brian's mess by switching to reviewing emails and social media. Ten years ago she thought she'd been kind of trendy having a Facebook account. She hadn't moved on to Instagram or other media, so realized she had become more of a social media dinosaur. Many of the younger nurses at the hospital didn't even have Facebook accounts these days. But the app was mainly how Cate stayed up to date with family, friends, and old colleagues. Most of the people she was connected with had stopped posting photos of their breakfasts a long time ago, but they continued to share achievements, disappointments, quirky funny things, and political opinions. Today she found that the usual lighthearted content in her feed was nearly crowded out by posts about COVID-19. Her friends in health care were sharing about personal protective equipment supply shortages in medical facilities. People were starting to wear masks in the community, not just in health care settings, and there was intense debate about mask effectiveness and necessity. There was a prayer chain for the brother of a former colleague whose parents and wife had died of the viral infection while he was lying intubated in an intensive care unit. Cate's heart and mind were heavy with this news, and the current situation with Brian.

A woman approached the door of the garda station and stepped into the reception area. She looked formidable and a bit glamorous, though she was wearing a simple orange wrap dress with a soft gray cardigan. The handle of a stylish designer bag hung in the crook of her elbow. She eyed Cate then proceeded to the guard behind the counter. "Hello, Lorcan, I'm here for Brian Atley."

"Cheers, Clodagh, come on through." The guard stood and opened the door at the end of the counter that allowed her access to the next room.

"Wait!" Cate cried, and as they both turned to her, the guard Lorcan pulled the door shut again. "Sorry," she said, realizing he was securing the area because of her, and she wasn't sure what to say to dial things down. "I'm traveling with Brian Atley. He's requested a solicitor. We've called for one. If you're here to question him, or... or... move things forward, you'll need to wait until he has representation."

"Ah, and who are you?" the woman tilted her head slightly.

"I'm Cate Jenks. I'm a nurse, and I've been taking care of him."

"Hello, Cate, I'm Clodagh Walsh. I will be representing Mr. Atley."

"I believe Brian's sister was calling a solicitor named Declan. Sorry, I don't remember his last name. I'd like to check with Mags O'Connor to make sure of what's happening," Cate said.

"No need. I'm a colleague of Declan O'Keefe. As he's unavailable, he's asked me to come in his place."

"Oh, okay. Well. Then, thank you for coming to help Brian. I'll let you get to it," Cate remained standing.

Clodagh smiled without warmth, "Right." She turned and Lorcan re-opened the door and Cate was left alone in the reception area.

She wondered, "What am I even doing here, hanging around a police station waiting to get in? Brian has a lawyer now, so there's really nothing I can do. They're not going to let me see him. Maybe I should just go back to the hotel. If they're detaining him, what should I do with his other things? The driver is due to pick me up Thursday afternoon, and I've got to sort it out before then. I'll go back and give Mags a call. I'm sure she'll take possession of his belongings."

Lorcan returned to his place behind the counter. Cate couldn't quite bring herself to leave yet. She had started making a to-do list in her phone when he spoke, "They're askin' for ye now."

Cate raised her eyes from her phone, surprised, "Me?"

"Yeh."

She popped up out of her chair and tucked her phone into her pocket then pulled the hem of her sweater straight. Lorcan opened the door and allowed her through. He led her to a small room with a window where she could see Brian and Clodagh seated across from each other at a table. Brian looked bad. His color was off and he seemed smaller, slumped in his chair. Lorcan knocked twice quickly then opened the door without waiting. Their conversation ceased abruptly. Cate stepped into the room and the guard shut the door behind her. The three were alone.

"D.S. Rooney has allowed you to be here," Clodagh stated. "It's an unusual concession."

"Okay." Then Cate looked to Brian, "How are you?"

"Terrible," he croaked.

"That is why you are here," Clodagh explained. "You will provide medical supervision when Brian is formally charged."

Brian's eyes were heavy-lidded. "Formally charged, buncha bullshit," he grumbled, then he perked up a little to focus on Cate. "Where have you been?!"

"I scrambled around trying to get you some help, then I waited outside until they finally let me in. Mags got Ms. Walsh to represent you, so behave yourself, okay? You're going to need to help her to help you. Are you okay with me being here with you?"

"Of course," Brian patted her hand.

"Call me Clodagh," the solicitor's manner was warming a little.

Cate nodded gratefully. "Thanks. I'm glad you're here, Clodagh." Then she said to Brian, "Let me check you out." The pulse oximeter and blood pressure meter were laid out on the table and Cate put them to use. "His blood pressure is a little high but not imminently dangerous, and his oxygen is okay for now. Can you explain why he's being charged?"

Clodagh shook her head. "D.S. Rooney will come in to make the formal charge and we'll hear it together. Brian, you've done well not to speak before I arrived. Keep your head and we'll deal with things. Everything you say will be held against you, so let's hear Mick Rooney out and I will advise you what to answer." She moved around the table to sit on the same side as Brian and Cate.

"Jaysus! What can I say?" Brian huffed. "I know nothing about this! Nothing!"

"Brian, slow down a little," Cate urged quietly.

A quick knock sounded on the door and Rooney and Garda Ryan entered and seated themselves. Clodagh asked, "Detective Sergeant, will you please state the charges to Mr. Atley?"

"That's why we're here." He tapped the case folder he had placed on the tabletop, "Brian Atley, you are charged with the murder of Timothy Dooley. Do you wish to confess?"

"Oh, Jaysus! No, I do not!" Brian sputtered. "I know nothing of it. I haven't seen the man in some fifty-odd years."

Clodagh and Rooney locked eyes across the table and Clodagh placed her hand on Brian's forearm urging restraint, but Brian continued, "I've only been in Ireland a few days. The hotel knows my comings and goings. There must be cameras everywhere. Just check. You can see I can account for my time and my whereabouts for almost every moment I've been here. And if you've got cameras in the jacks you'll know what I've done every second. I'm always in full view or with Cate. When would I be able to kill someone? When? Just check the cameras!"

Rooney sighed, then opened the case folder, "You are charged with the murder of Timothy Dooley on the twenty-first of June, 1969."

Chapter 9

When Cate left the garda station she was too stunned and confused to return to the hotel alone. Instead, she walked slowly toward The Green Man. She played over in her head Brian's outbursts of protest to the records Rooney removed piece by piece from the file folder while he made his case. In 1969, Timothy Dooley was found dead in his workshop from blunt force trauma to the back of his head. The original photographs had lightened and lost some of their detail, but still effectively conveyed the murdered man's body in pooled blood. A witness saw Brian leave the workshop hurriedly, and when the body was found the next day, Brian had fled Bunclody and broken all contact. Brian repeatedly insisted he never harmed Timothy Dooley, and Clodagh had a hard time reining him in. Cate struggled to take in all the new information while monitoring Brian's condition. Fortunately, he remained stable.

Clodagh cut off Brian's escalating protests. "As your solicitor, I'm advising you not to speak further. We have the right to discuss the charges privately. Do not talk in front of Detective Sergeant Rooney."

And Cate reminded him, "Brian, let her do her job. Stop talking."

Brian angrily shook his head and hammered both fists on the table once, then tucked them in his lap and glared at everyone in the room. Clodagh and Cate made concerned eye contact across Brian.

Rooney asked again, "Do ye wish to confess?"

Brian stayed quiet and Clodagh said on his behalf, "My client does not confess and denies all charges. We'll need our privacy now."

"Fine." Rooney gathered the evidence and closed the folder. "The charges have been stated. Same as before, in this room you will now be monitored only visually by camera but not recorded." He turned to Cate, "And is your patient currently in physical distress?"

She assessed Brian and replied, "He appears to be stable."

"Then you and I will now leave the accused to his solicitor privilege."

"Oh, okay," Cate realized she was being tossed out. It was an awkward moment as she quickly said goodbye to Brian and Clodagh.

She added, "Remember, Brian. If you have any changes in your breathing, you need to say something right away. Don't wait, okay?"

Rooney held the door for her to exit, then he walked her back to the reception area. He did not extend any pleasantries beyond a simple acknowledgement, "Ms. Jenks."

A moment later Cate was back on the street. Her head was swimming, overloaded, and that was when her steps turned toward The Green Man. As she pushed the pub door open, late afternoon sunlight beamed into the dimly lit interior. An Irish pub smell was like no other and was becoming familiar and comforting. Ash from the fireplace melded with old wooden tables and chairs, joined by a note of hops from the generations of beer poured, drunk, and spilled. But it smelled clean, too.

Alone in the pub, she took a seat at the bar and waited for someone to appear. It wasn't long before John emerged from the back room with his hands full of bar supplies. He nodded to Cate without interrupting his restocking mission.

"John?" Cate said softly, and louder again when he didn't answer, "John?"

"Yeh?"

"Will you talk with me, please?"

He sighed and moved in front of her, "Yeh."

"You know that Brian's been arrested?"

"Yeh."

"You knew it would happen, didn't you? That's what you were going to say this morning. Tell me."

"Tell you what, Cate Jenks? That decades ago Brian took a runner and everything bad that happened in the town was blamed on him? I'm sure he's innocent of the baby, and I'm fair sure that he didn't kill Tim." John looked miserable. "I shoulda warned him."

"I stopped you. Now I'm trying to wrap my head around it, all of this, but truly, I'm just at a loss. Rooney says there was a witness."

John said with a sigh, "Billy saw Brian leave the workshop where Tim was found dead."

"Billy? Billy who?"

"Billy Collins. The other fella who just turned up dead."

"Oh. Oh my God!" Cate began to see the pieces come together. It further explained Rooney's initial visit to question Brian.

John bent forward with his elbows on the bar. He watched Cate struggling to grasp the implications, then he added, "There's more..."

"More?" she whispered.

"Mick Rooney is Tim Dooley's nephew."

"Oh no," she shook her head in disbelief.

"I'm not sayin' he won't be fair, but he's sure to have strong opinions about Brian's history of fathering a child, killing a man, doing a runner, and when he finally returns the only witness is offed. Doesn't look good, no, it doesn't."

"No, it doesn't," she echoed, still trying to absorb the magnitude of what she just learned. She sighed. Her mind was racing and felt numb at the same time. John pushed back to his full height and they shared the moment of despair. Finally, Cate said, "I think I'll have a Jameson now."

"With water?" he asked.

"Yes, please."

John served her drink and poured one for himself neat. Cate sipped, hoping to ease her churning mind. John downed his shot and busied himself behind the bar as the late afternoon regulars began to filter in. Private conversation was no longer possible, and Cate began to feel the attention of the other patrons. She finished most of her drink, left payment on the bar, and made her way back to the hotel.

As she entered the lobby, Rose was behind the desk. Cate nodded politely as she passed by but Rose called to her, "Ms. Jenks, I have a notice for you."

Cate turned back to the clerk, "A notice?"

"Yes, the Taoiseach has issued a notice of travel ban because of the virus. We're to give it to each hotel guest because after tonight no one will be allowed to travel more than five kilometers. Any guests who do not leave must stay for the duration." Rose handed Cate a printed page that outlined stipulations, "I tried to get it to you earlier but you've been out all afternoon."

Cate returned to her room with the page clutched in her hand. She had skimmed it in the lobby, but sat down to read it carefully without distractions. Her mind was overloaded, and she was having trouble absorbing all the facts. What to do? Hastily wrangle a ride to Dublin and leave Brian to sort out his own affairs? Who could she get to drive her to Dublin at this hour? The car service was probably unavailable for an unscheduled pickup under these circumstances. Was "public trans" available, as Arek had called it? Or could she hire one of the locals? How long could a travel ban last? She had three more weeks of sabbatical from work and no commitments at home other than potted plants that needed watering, and Becky would continue caring for them. Money wasn't a problem, considering what Brian was paying her, even if the job only lasted a couple more days and she had to pay her own way after. After Keith died, she had thrown herself into work and constantly picked up extra shifts. The bonuses and overtime piled on top of the extra hours, resulting in exorbitant paychecks and no leisure time to spend the money. Cate's bank accounts had never been so healthy. And one of the best things about her new career in nursing was job security. If the ban lasted longer than her sabbatical and her hospital declined to extend her leave of absence, Cate could have another job lined up before she even landed back in the U.S. Was there any reason to hurry home? She couldn't think of one. She re-read the statement in the printed notice and said aloud, "I guess I will 'stay for the duration.'"

With her mind made up, a sense of peace descended on her as she returned to her comfort zone of handling details. She called the car service and canceled her return to Dublin. The woman who took her call was obviously relieved that Cate wasn't demanding immediate pickup. Cate could hear a great deal of activity in the background. "This travel ban must have created a lot of chaos for you, too." she offered sympathetically.

"You've no idea!" the woman groaned.

"Well, take care and stay healthy," Cate encouraged. "I'll call to reschedule when the travel ban is lifted."

Next, she sent a text to Mags's cell number: *Solicitor Clodagh Walsh representing Brian. He's fine for now. Can I come see you tomorrow morning?* A reply rang through moments later: *Thanks dear yes of course come for breakfast I'll pick you up at 8.* Cate replied: *If it's not raining hard, I will walk for exercise. See you at 8. Good night.* Mags answered: *Cheers.*

Then the time zones, the turmoil, and the Jameson converged into a wave of exhaustion. "I need to sleep," she thought. Her eyelids grew heavier through her bedtime routine. She set an alarm for 6:00 a.m. and was asleep within minutes. It felt like only moments later when her alarm chimed morning's arrival. She quickly readied herself to visit Mags.

The air outside the hotel was chilly, and heavy fog dampened sound in the street. The rising sun set the fog aglow in open spaces, and in the shadows the temperature dropped noticeably. She fast walked across the bridge to warm herself. Within a few minutes she was comfortable in her jacket, and the chill in the air felt fresh on her face. She was wide awake.

"What to do about Brian?" she wondered. Her mind flooded with questions. How long would they detain him? Would they keep him here in Bunclody or move him to another facility? How had he fared through the night? Were they looking in on him regularly? The stress of the arrest certainly would wear away at his fragile state. How did they accommodate him through the night? Did he sleep in a cell? Was he warm enough? Would they release him on bail? Did they even have such a thing in Ireland? And did he kill Timothy Dooley in 1969? Why would he have done it? If he did do it, and had stayed gone so long, why did he come back to Ireland and risk arrest?

Cate arrived at Mags's cottage and raised her hand to knock on the door, but Mags opened it before she could touch the painted yellow wood. Mags's eyes searched Cate's face and she grasped her hands and whispered, "He shouldn't have come back!"

Cate struggled for the right words, "I had no idea there was such a... history. How are you doing?"

"Oh, dear, I've had a lot of time to worry over this. The dread is not new to me. I knew he'd be charged right away. That's why I told him to leave, though it broke me heart to do so. I always prayed he was safe and would stay away. Come in with ye." Cate was shooed through the door and back toward what she was beginning to think of as her seat in the kitchen. The table was already set and Mags urged her to help herself to tea while she finished up at the stove. She then brought two plates to the table loaded with what looked like ham but Cate recognized it as a rasher of bacon, along with poached eggs on toast. There were scones in a small basket. Everything was so fresh and delicious that Cate was briefly distracted from the problems at hand. Irish butter, she had discovered, was so perfectly rich that she was tempted to use it like a frosting on her scone. She realized she'd been quietly absorbed in the meal for a little too long, and with her mouth full she glanced at Mags who was observing her.

When their eyes met, they both froze as if caught doing something naughty, then chuckled apologetically in unison. Cate shrugged, sighed, and leaned back in her chair while dabbing her lips with her napkin. "Did you make these scones?"

"Yeh," Mags said, sipping her tea.

"I'm just going to own up to it now. You'll find at least one missing when I go, because I'm going to put it in my pocket for later."

"Don't muss your jacket, pet, I'll wrap them up for you."

"Thanks, that takes the shame out of it." Cate changed the subject, "I'm trying to get my head around everything that's happened and decide what I will do."

Mags eyed her questioningly, "What do you mean?"

"Well, I can't go home. I got notice of the travel ban last night because of COVID, and now the window to leave has closed. But I'd have felt terrible abandoning Brian anyway, even though I don't know how to help him. The story just keeps getting stranger and stranger. I don't know what to think or do."

Mags asked, "You don't believe he's guilty?"

"Do you?" Cate countered, and watched Mags carefully, widening her senses to gauge any nonverbal subtleties.

Mags paused thoughtfully, then answered, "I have always resisted believing it. No matter how it looks."

Cate said, "I talked to John last night, after I left the garda station."

"Mmhmm?" Mags sipped her tea.

"He told me that Billy Collins was the witness who saw Brian at Tim Dooley's."

Mags sighed and set her teacup in the saucer before her, "Yeh."

"Yeah," Cate echoed. It would be cruel to further emphasize how bad Brian looked.

Mags repeated, "Do you believe he's guilty?"

Cate chose her words carefully, "I was asked to provide medical supervision when Rooney charged Brian yesterday. Brian seemed completely and genuinely surprised. Despite the evidence against him, my gut tells me he's telling the truth, and that he did not murder Tim Dooley. Brian was stunned when Rooney said the murder occurred in 1969. He didn't know Tim Dooley had been killed long ago; he thought they were charging him for a crime that had just happened."

"Oh, my dear," Mags briefly squeezed Cate's hand. "I'm grateful my brother has a friend in you. Everyone here knows the old story and has already formed their opinions. I'm sure he's innocent but he's still under arrest. All those years ago, the people who knew and loved Brian defended him, but he didn't defend himself. He took a runner instead. That was hard to take. It broke our parents. Really broke 'em. It broke me too. I cried for a full year, and even after, too. You see, we had been very close. Brian was my hero. He never treated me like other brothers treated their sisters. He was kind, and fun, and patient with me. I just loved him. He treated me like I meant something to him." Mags's voice broke with emotion. She dabbed her eyes with her napkin, then lifted her face and smiled at Cate, "Your fresh eyes may well help him be treated fairly."

Cate smiled, "Maybe."

"How did you come to know me brother?" Mags rearranged the food on her plate without actually eating.

"We've been neighbors in Florida for years. We are friends, though the friendship was more with my late husband. I went back to school for a mid-life career change to nursing and was buried in the books and then my husband got sick and needed a lot of care, so I haven't had much chance to socialize for a long time. Then I kind of forgot how. Brian was kind enough to check in on me from time to time. I recently took some time off from work, but I don't know what to do anymore when I'm not working. When Brian asked for my help to return to Ireland, I actually felt like he was rescuing me." Cate realized the truth only as she said it and felt immediately embarrassed by her self-disclosure.

"I see. I'm sorry for your trouble, love." Mags's voice softened and her eyes were kind, and for the first time in months Cate found herself on the verge of tears.

"More tea?" Mags lifted the teapot.

"Uh... yes, please."

Mags topped off Cate's cup. "Well, I'm glad Brian offered you the position. Especially as he's needing such a great deal of caring for."

"Yes, he certainly does!" Cate agreed, "But I feel like my hands are tied for the moment." She couldn't think of anything else to add, so she changed the subject. "Have you lived in this house long? It's very nice, and the garden is beautiful."

"Ah, stop it you!" Mags deflected the compliment without energy, then she brightened a little. She explained, "We've lived here more than forty years, moved in right after Liam and I married. We've raised our family here."

"That's wonderful! How many children do you have?"

"Just the four now. We lost our oldest son, Colin, to the sea many years ago. Then there's Margaret, Michael, John, and Padraig's our youngest. He's thirty-two. We're still waiting for that one to settle down." She laughed, "I tell you, you never get over being a mam. Then we have the five grandchildren. They're grown now too. They're in and out of the house often enough. You'll probably meet some of them. If not here, in town."

"I met Patraig just the other night, at the pub. Things were rather tense, but now I know why. I'd love to meet them all. Do the grandchildren help in the garden?"

"Oh, they're not much use in the garden, but they do what I ask of them. You know, they're busy with their own lives. Soon we'll be having some great-grands. Ha ha!"

"Could we go look at your garden? It's a struggle for me to keep anything edible alive in the Florida heat. Everything here is so green!"

"Ah, sure. Let me just get my garden things. Come this way." Mags led Cate into an alcove mud room where she tied a canvas apron over her shirt, changed her shoes, and gathered clippers and a basket, "I never go into the garden unarmed," she grinned. "There's always something needing a snip or a picking."

They made their way out the back door of the cottage, down four steps so narrow that Cate's heels scraped the riser while her toes hung a little over the edge of the tread. She angled her feet to fit securely as she made each step. Beyond the last one was a short walkway paved with rough flat stones set closely together, with seams of short-trimmed grass between them. It led to four neat long rows of mounded earth with rich green cultivated vegetable varieties. Mags guided her through the garden, chatting while she trimmed off a few new peas and placed them in her basket. She clipped some sprigs of dill and added them to the peas, then she deadheaded a few roses in the hedge and casually asked, "Any children of your own?"

"I have a daughter and a granddaughter," she stated simply, "They live in New York so I don't get to see them as often as I'd like to."

Ellie's only interest in school had been art. Keith pressured her to pursue something more practical, so she completed a management degree at UCF then abruptly moved to New York City where she made a fair income between selling her art on the streets and several online markets. She fell in love with a nerdy and creative physical therapist and they had one daughter, Myles. Cate saw her granddaughter several times each year, and they video chatted regularly. During their last visit to Florida, five-year-old Myles had followed her around outside. They repotted plants together, watered them, and filled the birdfeeders. Cate loved observing Myles's silent concentration as she carefully transferred handful after handful of birdseed from the plastic bag to the feeder's glass column. With a young child, everyday tasks definitely took longer, but they were infused with a joyful fascination that filled her heart.

"Ah, family is life's treasure," Mags noted as she snipped a few roses and trimmed them deftly for a bouquet, then laid them into her basket and turned back toward the house. In the kitchen, she placed the roses in a vase, stowed the other trimmings from her basket, then she set about clearing the breakfast dishes. Cate joined in and together they had everything cleaned up in a few minutes, except for their teacups. "Let's finish the pot," Mags suggested, and returned to her seat.

Cate's thoughts went back to Brian's predicament, turning the pieces over in her mind. There was so much she just didn't understand, so many missing pieces to the puzzle, as if she'd started watching a movie in the middle, "Could you tell me more about John?" she asked.

"Like what?"

"I don't know. He seems to care about Brian. He came to see him yesterday, to tell him about Aiden Atley, and he was going to warn Brian about the arrest that would happen too, but I guess I messed that up. Brian got upset about Aiden and had trouble breathing so I stopped John from telling him more. Then Rooney showed up."

"Don't worry yourself about that," Mags said. "It wouldn't have made a difference. Brian and John were fast friends since they were wee lads. John was nearly as hurt as I that Brian disappeared without a word. And so you know about Aiden, then?"

"I learned about him from John, but I met him twice before that. He confronted me in the pub and said something vulgar about Brian. Honestly, he was a little frightening. Later he came into the hotel bar with that garda officer Rowan Ryan. He behaved better then but still made me nervous. Now I understand why he was all worked up, but it was still inappropriate."

Mags shook her head sadly, "He's a hot head. But he hasn't gotten in much trouble for a couple years. Rowan and Arek keep him in line. Those three! If you see one, the other two must be close by. They're good lads, really. But Aiden fancies himself a victim of life. The other two are steady on their feet. They help him see he has options. Now that Brian's back though, Aiden will be all stirred up to eat the head off him. It's a shame to have Brian home and no chance to explain himself. It will surely set Aiden back and fuel his anger."

The situation with Aiden was a whole additional dimension of complication. Cate reminded herself that everyone thought Aiden was Brian's grandson, but they didn't know Brian denied him. She didn't want to be spilling secrets or starting rumors, and she couldn't think of a safe thing to say, so she changed the subject. "Brian said John's family owns The Green Man. Is Addy related to him? She's very friendly."

Mags blinked, then replied, "That she is. She's John's niece, his sister's only daughter. She's a talker too." She laughed lightly. "They call her RTÉ because she's like our own news broadcast service. But with all that, she gets more information than she gives every time. She's a good soul though."

"She was nice to me when it seemed like everyone else wanted to run me out of town."

Mags shrugged sheepishly and set her teacup back in its saucer. "My apologies, dear. I would still send you away right now if you could take my brother with you."

"If only that were an option," Cate replied.

They sat in companionable silence for a few minutes, and Cate was sure Mags's mind was as busy as her own.

"Mags, I met an interesting woman when I was out walking yesterday. Her name is Cailleach?"

"The Cailleach? And she spoke to you?"

To Cate's ear, Mags said the woman's name almost the same as Cate had said it, but with a little throat closure at the end. Cate tried to mimic the sound but couldn't quite get it. After a couple attempts she gave up. "Yes. It was sort of a confusing conversation though. Who is she?"

"Our Cailleach, she doesn't usually have much to say, though I'm not surprised she did approach you, given the circumstances. You'll want to have her on your side, do what she says. Don't go against her."

Confused, Cate shrugged in response, "I guess I did alright? She told me to go back to the hotel and showed me a shortcut, and I took it. How would I go against her?"

"Well, with her, one doesn't always know what one might have done to offend."

"Oh... Then I guess I'll try to behave myself," she replied while thinking "Whatever!" as she set down her empty teacup. Cate's thoughts then turned back to Brian, and she felt she needed to lay eyes on him again. This was the longest she'd gone without assessing him and it almost felt like patient abandonment. The travel alone had been hard on him, and the arrest would have only made things worse. "I'm going to try to get in to see Brian again," she said aloud as she made the decision in her mind.

"I'd feel better if you did," Mags answered.

"Will they allow me to continue monitoring him? I'm very worried about him being detained. He's so frail."

"Our guards rarely lock people up," Mags answered. "Except for Aiden of course. But he's young and strong. I wonder if you can convince Mick Rooney to move my brother back to the hotel. For a house arrest, ye know. It's not as though Brian can run away again. Then you could continue caring for him."

"Hmmmmm... do you think Rooney would go for that?" What an idea! Cate thought. What sort of legal mess would she be getting herself into? Asking to take custody of an accused murderer? However, if Brian stayed in Rooney's custody he might not survive long enough for them to take him to trial. "It does make sense to take him back to the hotel. If they keep him at the station, they'll have to move him to a hospital soon anyway. I guess I'll be on my way to the garda station now. I'm sure Rooney will be glad to see me."

"I'll come along with you to double his pleasure," Mags smiled without humor. "Though I suppose we should go easy on him, as we will be asking a favor. Oh, and don't mention Cailleach to him. She sets him off. I'll give you a lift into town. I could use a bit of breeze in my face."

"That would be great, thank you."

As promised, Mags wrapped two scones in a bit of kitchen paper. And true to her word, Cate tucked the treats into her pocket and patted it gratefully. Mags led her outside to an outbuilding. She swung the barn-style door wide and daylight illuminated a washing machine, a dryer, two bicycles, and a shiny blue Suzuki two-seater scooter. She handed Cate a helmet while she donned one herself. Cate hadn't been on the back of a motorcycle since she was a teenager. The thought was a little scary, but exciting too. "This thing looks fast," she commented.

"Well, it's no rocket, but I do have a little trouble keeping it under ninety. The craic, that is." Mags chuckled conspiratorially and nudged Cate's arm. Cate didn't quite understand what that meant, but she smiled and nodded. Then the older woman hopped on the scooter, started the engine, and rolled outside. "Close the door, pet," she called over her shoulder and beckoned Cate to climb on.

She couldn't stop grinning as she perched on the passenger seat behind Mags, and they accelerated smoothly away. "Mick's probably not even in the office yet. We'll take the long way," Mags called out as she turned away from town.

She steered them on a scenic journey and Cate allowed herself to relax and take in the view. They encountered only a few small cars on the narrow, winding road. In some stretches, tall hedges were crowded close to the edge of the pavement, creating a tunnel effect that exaggerated the scooter's engine noise. Some of the houses they passed were built just steps away from the pavement, and Cate noticed the newer-looking houses were set farther back, with driveways proportioned more like what was normal in the U.S. Most of the time, she had a fine view of rolling countryside that looked like patchwork quilting in varying shades of green with darker hedges and stone fences like stitching between them. The road meandered and Cate had no idea where they were, but the angle of the sun gave her a sense they were headed back toward town. Eventually, Mags slowed and pulled over to the grassy shoulder. There was a scattering of limestone boulders that made it a logical stopping place. The women dismounted and Mags nimbly stepped from stone to stone until her feet were higher than Cate's head. She reached a level spot then waved for Cate to follow.

The climb was like ascending a staircase two steps at a time. Cate was winded at the top, and felt self-conscious of her breathing, trying not to puff too loudly next to Mags who seemed completely unfazed by her own efforts. "Country life keeps her strong," Cate thought. "I'm such a softy!" And then her attention was seized by the view. Before her, the endless green grass fields extended to the horizon, with architectural remnants and clumps of trees here and there. Several small ponds added a bit of shine to the wide green vista. Grazing sheep were dotted throughout. Angled to the west was a huge, castle-like manor house, and beyond it was a solid tree line.

"Oh, this is incredible!" Cate sighed.

"Isn't it?" Mags smiled and gazed out across the land, "Here, one can almost believe all is right in the world."

"For a few minutes, at least," Cate agreed, and they stood in silence, basking in the peace. When Mags finally sighed and changed her position, Cate pointed to the castle and asked, "Whose house is that?"

"It's called Talamh. The Rochfort family has owned it for more than five hundred years, though the house isn't that old. It's only about three centuries."

"Only three," Cate scoffed.

Mags smiled indulgently, "Let's go find Mick."

They clambered back down to the scooter and within a few minutes rolled up to the garda station. The two women entered the reception area and Cate recognized the guard stationed at the desk from the day before.

"Good morning, Lorcan," Mags chirped.

"Hello, Mags," he replied and extended his nodded greeting to Cate too.

"We're here to see Mick. Is he in?"

"I'll let him know you're here." Lorcan typed on his computer keyboard. Moments later Detective Sergeant Rooney opened the door. "Mags, Ms. Jenks." He nodded.

"Mick, we've come to see you about Brian, obviously." Mags looked like a terrier staring down an Irish wolfhound. Her hands were on her hips and her chin lifted.

"Right. Come this way." He led them to his office, a small room with a neatly kept desk faced by two chairs. He gestured to offer seats but Mags cut him off, "Cate needs to look Brian over. How is he? Alright?"

Rooney looked perturbed, "He seems no worse than yesterday."

"Let's have her make sure of that, shall we?"

"Fair enough," Rooney agreed. He led them through the station to a room where a guard sat at a desk monitoring the area that contained two cells. One was empty, with the door open. Brian was in the other.

"You may go in one at a time," Rooney instructed, then to the guard, "Dalton, Ms. Jenks will use the medical kit to examine Mr. Atley."

Dalton handed Cate the bundle that contained the blood pressure cuff and pulse oximeter, then he opened the cell door and she stepped into the small, high-ceilinged room. The walls were white tile and daylight glowed through a high, reinforced window. Brian lay on the low bed consisting of an industrial mattress atop a built-in platform. Cate was relieved to see they'd given him extra blankets. A paper cup half-full of tea sat on the floor by the bed. A toilet and sink finished off the room.

"Hey, Brian, how are you doing?" she called softly.

"Lousy," he grumped, and shakily pushed himself up to sit on the edge of the bed.

"Let me check you out. Have you had trouble breathing?" She slid the pulse oximeter on his finger then applied the blood pressure cuff to the opposite arm.

"Not too much." His voice was hoarse.

"Your vitals seem okay. Are they keeping you warm enough?" Cate paused between questions, but Brian answered with only yeh or neh. "Fed and safe? Are they swapping out your oxygen concentrator batteries on time? Are you in any pain?"

Finally he summarized, "Ah, I'm alright, except I nearly piss myself trying to get to the toilet since they took my cane. I have to get started five minutes before I need to be there, and you know my kidneys don't always give me that much notice."

"That's right, they've taken away your cane," Cate realized, double-checking the cell. "Show me how you're getting up."

Brian scooted to the very edge of the bed, placed his hands on his knees, then rocked back and forth twice to build momentum. On the third forward lunge he heaved himself upward to a standing position, but still bent at the waist with his hands on his thighs. He waited to steady himself, then slowly straightened his spine and finally looked to Cate, his nostrils flaring with effort. "It just takes a little longer this way," he wheezed.

"It won't be long before you end up on the floor without your cane. This is ridiculous." Cate placed a hand under his elbow to stabilize him. "While we've got you up, do you need the commode?"

"No. I just went before you got here and was in the middle of my recovery nap."

"Fabulous," Cate said sarcastically. "I'm going to talk to Rooney about them keeping you in here. This is just not safe. If you're steady enough I'm going to step out so Mags can come in and give you a hug. You know, she only treated you the way she did because she knew you would be arrested for coming back to Bunclody."

"Why the hell didn't she say so?" Brian grumped.

"We'll figure it out, Brian. For now, take some time with your sister. I can tell she really loves you." She stepped back through the cell door. When she placed the medical kit on Dalton's desk, the guard nodded for Mags to enter.

"Is he medically stable?" Rooney asked Cate.

"Detective Sergeant, he needs his cane. He's a tremendous fall risk. Brian needs a balance aid or he's going to fall and break a hip."

"Is he medically stable, Ms. Jenks?" he repeated.

"For now, yes." Cate continued, "I can see why you might not allow a cane in a cell, so can we get him a walker instead?"

"Yes, we will provide him a walker. Mr. Atley's cane has been confiscated as evidence. This morning I will formally charge him with the murder of Billy Collins. You will provide medical supervision while I read the charges, as you did yesterday."

Shocked, Cate barely heard Rooney's agreement to get a walker. "You think he killed Billy Collins too?!"

"There is sufficient evidence."

"And you think he did it with his cane?"

"That remains to be seen."

"I just..." Cate paused and took a deep breath, "I just can't believe it."

Rooney's words brought an abrupt end to Mags' and Brian's embrace and chaos ensued. Mags turned to Rooney and cried, "Ye can't be serious!" Her motion made Brian unstable. He tottered, and Mags barely caught hold of him in time to turn his fall into a hard sit on the bed. The impact forced a fast exhalation that triggered a coughing fit. Brian's face reddened and his eyes watered. Cate found his rescue inhaler on Dalton's desk and hurried into the cell to administer a dose.

As she tended to Brian, Mags flew out of the cell and squared off with the Detective Sergeant. "Mick Rooney, you know better than this! You know he couldn't have done it. What led to these charges?"

"There is evidence and motive," Rooney replied evenly.

"What motive could he possibly have? He didn't even know the man!" Mags sputtered.

"You know yourself that Billy Collins was the sole witness to Tim Dooley's murder."

Cate added, "But then why would he have called Brian to meet with him?"

"We've only Brian's word of that. We know that they spoke by phone, but we don't know what their conversation was."

Brian shook his head as he struggled to catch his breath. "I never..." he finally croaked, barely above a whisper.

"Hush," Cate told him, "Don't say anything else. Concentrate on your breathing and just nod your head to answer me: Do you want your attorney? Your solicitor?"

Brian rolled his red-rimmed eyes and bobbed his head.

"He is asking for his solicitor," Cate informed Rooney.

"I'll call her right now," Mags said icily.

Chapter 10

The file folder Rooney presented for the second murder was narrow, crisp, and new. It contained printouts of digital photos of a man who seemed older than Brian. His white hair was wispy and askew, and the skin on the back of his neck was deeply lined from years of sun exposure. He lay face down, crumpled on the ground. The photos showed little external damage from the killing blow to the back of his head that Rooney described. Brian seemed utterly defeated. He sat quietly as the charges were read. Again, Rooney asked Brian if he wanted to confess, and Clodagh denied his guilt. And same as the day before, Cate reassessed Brian and pronounced him stable, then was dismissed from the room.

When Cate and Rooney rejoined Mags in the reception area, Cate began to advocate for her patient as she had planned, but without expectation of results. "Detective Sergeant, I'm very concerned for Brian's health under these circumstances. He needs close monitoring."

"Mick," Mags interrupted, "Send him back to the hotel and let Cate care for him there. Put him under house arrest. You know staying here will be a death sentence before he ever goes to trial, and you don't want to be guilty of that. Me brother's too decrepit to run again, and there's the travel ban now, so he can't get away even if he wants to."

"Mags, it's not possible!" Rooney shook his head. "I don't have the resources to be setting up private detentions."

"What if Brian can cover the expense?" Cate suggested, "I mean, he paid for my help to get here. He may be able to pay for a guard or whatever oversight you would need him to have to stay at the hotel."

"That's not how we detain murder suspects."

Mags cried, "When was the last time you detained a murder suspect?"

Rooney said nothing, and his expression remained unchanged except for a slight narrowing of his eyes. Cate worried Mags had pushed him too far. "Detective Sergeant, I would like to come back to make my regular clinical assessments of Brian's status. Would it be alright if I continue doing that?"

"Yes."

"Thank you. Mags, I'm going to need a few things since I'll be staying in town a while. Can you give me a lift?" It was just an excuse to get Mags out of Rooney's face. The small woman continued skewering him with her stare as she replied, "Of course, dear."

Outside the station Mags handed Cate her helmet as she put on her own. "We're going to the pub," she announced as she pulled into the street.

No other patrons were in The Green Man, and Mags shouted out to John and Addy, "Mick thinks me brother killed Billy Collins! He's charging him with murder all over again."

"Ah, shite!" Addy hurried around the bar and wrapped Mags in a tight hug. John hung his head and looked miserable. Cate settled herself onto a barstool, feeling out of place in the midst of their despairing camaraderie. John poured four Jamesons and they came together to sip a silent toast. Mags put her hand on Cate's shoulder and gave a brief squeeze of gratitude, then she shimmied onto the adjacent stool and her toes barely touched the support rung. She leaned her elbows on the bar and filled in more detail of what had happened at the garda station. She finished with, "Our nurse is keeping her eye on Brian."

Addy disappeared into the kitchen and returned minutes later with a tray. "Cheese toasties for ye, even though you don't deserve it." She winked as she placed plates before them. A gooey cheese and egg mixture was seasoned with mustard and Worcestershire sauce, melted and browned atop thick Irish soda bread. The simple comfort food worked its magic. As the women ate, several other patrons drifted in and there was no further mention of Brian. Instead, Mags asked Addy, "How are yer wee'uns?"

"Acting the maggot, the lot of them! Where did I get them from, I ask you? Jennifer's on about taking her driver theory test and the car is utterly bajanxed. Your Padraig's to use his computer diagnosis plug-in what's-it to tell us what's gone wrong. If I pray it's nothing serious, then I'll have to pray about Jennifer's driving lessons. There's no end to it."

"There certainly isn't!" Mags laughed.

Addy raised her clenched fists in the air in mock frustration, then moved to the taps to pull pints for newly arrived customers. The two women sat for a time with their private thoughts then Mags commented quietly, "I expect you'll be out of clean pants soon."

"Hmmm? What?" Cate asked, startled.

"You didn't pack to stay in Bunclody, so I'll come round for your washing tomorrow."

"Oh, thanks but you don't have to do that. I can see if the hotel has laundry service, or I'll take it to a laundromat. And I can wash a few things by hand before that."

"Nonsense! I'll take care of it. It's no trouble."

"How about this," Cate compromised, "If I don't get my laundry done this afternoon, I'll bring it over tomorrow and use your machines while I eat more of your amazing scones."

"That'll do," Mags nodded decisively, "We'll have breakfast again at eight either way."

"Perfect. Well, for now I need to go back to the hotel and make some arrangements to stay. My manager will be starting her day so I need to let her know not to expect me back at work anytime soon. I can't imagine the travel ban will last very long, but I'll probably have to quarantine at least two weeks after I go home."

"Oh, dear, will that be a problem for you?"

"Not one that I have to worry about. There's a severe nursing shortage in the U.S., and it gives me a lot of options. If I were still working as a librarian, I wouldn't have dared to vacate my seat long enough for someone else to think about taking it. Not that Brian would have needed a librarian to bring him home. But I've got a very marketable skill set as a nurse, and it gives me plenty of flexibility and security."

"You have reinvented yourself, Cate Jenks, but I can see that flexibility and security are not new to you."

"Actually, I'm like a duck, gliding on the surface but paddling like mad underneath. I'm enjoying getting older though, despite the body changes and hot flashes. I don't worry as much as I used to, and I'm not as concerned about what people think, and that's a very good thing, considering how many people have been giving me the stink-eye for bringing your brother home." Cate vaguely indicated the other patrons in the pub with a roll of her shoulder and eyes.

Mags chuckled, "It's not personal. But it's good you do have a thick skin."

"I'm going to take my thick skin along with the rest of me back to the hotel now." Cate waved her goodbyes to John and Addy. On the walk back, her conversation with Mags played over in her head, especially the part about being a nurse versus a librarian. Nursing had brought her all the way to Ireland, but she never stopped being a librarian at heart. In fact, the two areas of expertise often overlapped in practical application. Cate's research skills had made nursing school easier. Now, since the people around her weren't telling the whole story, this would be a good time to put those skills to use. What could she find out on her own about what had happened all those years ago?

Upon returning to her room, Cate had the strange feeling that she'd been gone a very long time. These Irish days were packed so full of unfamiliarity and upheaval. Her concentration and worry distorted her sense of time. When she stepped into Brian's suite, she became even more uneasy. Clearly, the gardaí had searched the room. Things were still neat, but rearranged, and Brian's suitcases were gone. Then Cate looked her own room over carefully. Did they go through her things too?

Maybe not. All her possessions seemed to be just as she'd left them.

She booted up her laptop while she used her cellphone to call her manager. Linda wasn't thrilled to receive her request to extend her leave of absence, and Cate was reluctant to go into much detail. "They've implemented a travel ban, and I couldn't get out in time. I'll have to stay for now, and I don't know when I can come home." She deliberately left out the part about Brian's murder charges.

Linda advised Cate to file her extension request with H.R., then, in a conspiratorial tone, she asked, "So.... Have you run into Colin Farrell or Aidan Turner yet?"

"No, but I'm keeping an eye out."

"Where are you staying again?"

"Bunclody. It's a little town south of Dublin. I don't think I'll find too many celebrities out this way." The irony was that Brian seemed to be the most famous person in Bunclody or, rather, the most infamous. And she, herself, seemed to be a bit famous by association.

After ending her call with Linda, Cate sent updates to Ellie and Becky, again leaving out the murder drama and blaming her extended stay on the travel ban. Becky cheerfully agreed to continue dropping by Cate's home twice a week to water plants, collect mail, start the car, and ensure the house was in good order. There were no other concerns. No one to miss Cate. No one to return to. She felt a twinge of sadness, paired with an astonished sense of freedom. She couldn't remember another time when she had felt so unencumbered and open to the adventure of uncertainty. "Let's see where this is going to go."

She started her research on the internet, trying to identify if there was a local newspaper that might have covered Tim Dooley's murder in 1969, but she wasn't able to find an answer. "That's the problem with old records," she thought. "Not everything that was ever put on paper was digitized." Then she started to go down a rabbit hole of Irish ancestry records. Dooley was a very common name in Ireland and its meaning implied a dark hero or something burned. The name Atley was of Old English origin and meant meadow. None of this was useful. There were census records available, but most of them were summaries. Other websites required payment to complete Cate's queries, but she wasn't sure she would get exactly what she needed. Her best chance might be looking locally. She checked the Bunclody library's location and hours of operation. It was only a couple blocks away.

The library building was modern, with a rounded cement-and-glass facade. The interior was bright and welcoming with multiple displays that had been diligently crafted by the staff. The children's programming was prominent, and bulletin boards featured library and community events. The library seemed to be well-used. A group of school children was involved in an activity, and there were people of all ages at tables and workstations. Most of the younger adults had wireless earbuds lodged in their ears. There was an assortment of older people too, working, reading, or talking quietly in pairs.

Cate headed to a computer to check for library databases that would give her access to resources she had not been able to find on the internet. She was able to identify a local newspaper that might have coverage. The published issues themselves were not accessible through the computer but the library had record of holdings on microfiche. She steeled herself for any assistance she was going to need to get to the archived materials. The librarian's professional code of ethics required confidentiality about patrons' activities, but other library users would gossip, and if she had to say out loud what she was looking for it would certainly spread as fast as the news of Brian's return. Cate decided to go looking for the microform materials on her own. As she scoped out the stacks, she tried to look like she was browsing without urgency, pausing here and there to pull a book off a shelf. As was becoming normal under the circumstances – though it felt anything but normal – Cate detected the attention of the people around her. She started making her way nonchalantly toward the back of the library, hoping for signage that would show her the way, or to stumble directly upon the microform media itself. A pleasant-looking forty-something woman who seemed like she worked there entered the stacks from the back of the library. Cate seized the opportunity to move further away from other patrons and get some help, making eye contact as she moved closer to the woman.

"Can I help ye?" the librarian inquired.

"Yes, thank you." Cate was relieved by her offer. "I'm looking for old issues of a newspaper on microfiche."

"Ah sure, it's this way." She turned in the opposite direction and led Cate toward the back of the library to an alcove that was the size of a large walk-in closet. It was lined with plain metal cabinets with many short but wide drawer sections. Two workstations were equipped with microfiche readers, and a printed sign over a collection bin encouraged library users to return the microfiche cards when finished.

"Which newspaper are you after?"

"Um, *The People.*"

"That'll be here," the librarian pulled open one of the drawers. "It's a local newspaper so we have every issue going back to its beginning in the nineteenth century."

"That's perfect, thank you," Cate smiled gratefully.

"Have you used a reader like this before?" The librarian switched on power to the closest workstation and the square screen glowed to illuminate the magnified image of its glass plates, empty except for hugely exaggerated scratches and motes of dust, "It takes a little getting used to."

"Yes."

"Let's just get you started with what you're lookin' fer. I'll show you how to place the cards in the reader." The librarian pointed to the cabinet full of microfiche.

"Thank you. Actually, I've used this type of reader a lot, so I'm fine now that I've found it. Thank you for your help. I'm just going to browse for a while." She wasn't about to feed the gossip mill by talking about her research.

"Sorry," the librarian smiled patiently. "I'm protective. It's near impossible to get replacement parts for these machines now, and if a card is improperly filed it's as good as lost. We're not likely to see funds to digitize, so this may well be the only extant copy. For me own peace, I'll trouble ye to let me show how to use it."

Cate laughed sympathetically, "I worked as a librarian for a long time. We once hired a circulation assistant who, it turned out, had a habit of drinking on the job. He was there for only two days and it took three employees a full week to start to repair the damage. Even after all that work we still found quite a few things out of place for a while. I promise to be careful with the equipment, and I'll put every card I pull into the return box so you can reshelve it properly. But you're welcome to show me how to use it if that would make you feel better."

"Once a librarian, always a librarian! I'll trust ye know what yer doin'. What type of library did ye work in?"

"State archives in the U.S. It's been a few years, but back then microfiche was one of the last formats they prioritized for digitizing because of its stability. I haven't kept up though. Standards change all the time."

"That's still true," the librarian nodded and tucked a lock of hair behind her ear. "And I'll be a little bit sorry when we finally do get around to digitizing this collection. I'll miss the vertigo from paging through it." They laughed together.

"Ah, I hadn't thought about that in so long! It makes me dizzy too. Hey, is there a way to print copies of the pages or email them to myself?"

"Unfortunately, no. These readers are ancient and they don't connect to the network. Usually, people just take photos with their phone." The librarian smiled apologetically. "Well, I'll leave you to it then. I'm Fiona and I'll be at the circulation desk if you run into any trouble."

"Thanks, I'm Cate."

"I know," she said over her shoulder as she headed back toward the front of the library.

Cate took a deep breath as she watched her walk away, then she got to work. The newspaper issues were filed chronologically and she was able locate the one printed on June 26, 1969, the first issue published after Tim Dooley's murder. It was front page news. She skimmed the article that began: "THE MAN FOUND MURDERED Friday morning was Timothy Dooley, a 41-year-old Roman Catholic who lived at Bunclody. He was found dead by his 5-year-old son who was sent by his mother to round Tim up for breakfast. Farm hand Billy Collins reportedly saw 19-year-old Brian Atley, also of Bunclody, leaving the property Thursday night. Gardaí have been unable to locate Atley for questioning." The article included quotes from Billy and the distraught widow Anna, who was pregnant at the time with her fourth child.

Cate paged ahead through later issues and found the story was revisited several times with interviews and updates. She took her phone out of her jacket pocket to snap photos of the articles, and discovered the phone's flashlight was on and the battery charge was in the red. As she turned off the flashlight, the phone died completely. She groaned in frustration. She had a charging cable in her bag, but not the right power block that would go into an outlet. It would take a few minutes' charge to get up and running again. With Fiona's neurotic protection of the microfiche, Cate didn't dare leave the machine on and unattended, so she placed the acetate cards back in their protective envelopes and set them in the return box, then she powered off the reader and walked to the front of the library to find an available computer with a USB slot.

She connected the phone and browsed the news on the computer while she waited. It was all COVID-19. The situation in Italy was horrifying and the whole country was locked down, with no nonessential movement allowed at all. People were shut in their homes and struggling to meet basic needs. Additionally, they suffered isolation, anxiety, and grief for the sick and dying. There were beautiful things happening too. Musicians played impromptu balcony concerts for their neighbors. Strangers sang together.

Cate's barely-charged phone lit up with a call from an Irish number. She answered it softly, "Hello?"

"Ms. Jenks?" a man's voice replied.

"Yes. Who's this?"

"Garda Rowan Ryan here. Detective Sergeant Rooney has arranged to move Mr. Atley back to the hotel where he'll remain in garda custody. You're needed at the station to sign an agreement of terms, as you'll continue his medical monitoring."

"Really?" Cate was astonished, "Uh, okay, I'll be there in a few minutes."

Her phone was only up to 10% battery charge, but it would last until she got back to her room if she could avoid bumping the flashlight on again inside her pocket. She would come back for the newspaper articles later; the priority was to get Brian back to the hotel. She gathered her things and thanked Fiona as she passed the circulation desk.

"Did ye find everything ye need?"

"Yes, thanks, I've got to go now but I'll come back later to finish up."

She stepped outside into the cool air and set out walking toward the garda station. She was familiar enough with the streets now not to need GPS to get there. It was straight up the road, so she used a few moments' battery charge to send Mags a text: *Just got call from gardaí. They're moving Brian to hotel. Going to station now to find out more.*

Chapter 11

This time Lorcan didn't make her wait long in the reception area, but the lower half of his face was covered with a disposable face mask. He gave a mask to her too, stating, "You'll have to wear it while you're in the station. It's the only one you'll get so don't throw it out. Supplies are limited." After a few quick taps on his keyboard, he led her to Rooney's office where the Detective Sergeant was at his desk, also wearing a mask.

"Ms. Jenks," he indicated a seat and she settled into it, "The pandemic is creating unusual circumstances."

"It certainly is," she agreed.

"There are new health and safety requirements that require wearing face masks and what they call social distancing. With Brian's health condition, that can best be accomplished by moving him back to the hotel. He'll be detained in his room under guard and his quarters will be monitored by cameras, provided you will agree to continue monitoring him medically."

"Yes, of course I will. But do you think he needs a guard at the hotel? With the travel ban and his mobility issues he wouldn't be able to leave if he wanted to. You could just put an ankle monitor on him."

"He must be under guard at all times. People will know his crime is taken seriously and he will not get away with murder. Additionally, Mr. Atley's return has aggravated old grudges and I won't have anyone in the town take it upon themselves to deliver justice."

"I see." Cate considered the implications. Maybe a guard wasn't a bad idea.

Rooney pushed a printed page and pen across the desktop to her. It outlined the parameters of her involvement in Brian's care, that she would assess him medically and would be video monitored at all times while she was in his room. She was to notify the guard each time she assessed Brian and pronounced him stable, or if his care needed to be escalated. She was not to bring visitors into Brian's room. Anything she took into his room must be cleared by the guard. Upon entry and exit, she would submit to personal search at the guard's discretion. She must wear a mask when providing care to Brian or interacting with the guard. She would remain in Bunclody at all times while the agreement was in place, and it would remain in force until terminated in writing by An Garda Síochána or Cate.

This sounds acceptable." Cate signed her name and Rooney added his signature beside hers. "Can I get a copy of it for my records?"

"Certainly," he answered then stepped out of his office to make the copy.

When he returned, Cate took the sheet of paper from him, folded it in half and placed it in her bag. "When will Brian be moved back to the hotel?"

"We'll need the afternoon to set up cameras in his room. Mr. Atley will be transported to the hotel this evening. Be there by five to receive him."

"Thank you. It's very compassionate of you to consider moving him there."

Rooney's voice was without emotion, which Cate found more unnerving than if he spoke angrily, "Mr. Atley should remain locked in his cell. I'm only doing it to keep him from taking a hospital bed that will be needed by someone else."

"Well, that's a good reason too," she replied, and left. She said goodbye to Lorcan as she stepped out into the cool Irish breeze, and removed her mask to breathe in the fresh air.

She made her way down the street in the direction of the hotel, but stopped at a low masonry wall and sat on the cold stone top of it, glad that her jacket provided padding and insulation. She texted Mags: *Brian will be at hotel at 5 & kept under guard.* A few moments later Mags texted back: *Thank God!*

Cate couldn't think of anything she needed to do to get ready to have Brian back at the hotel. She didn't really want to be onsite while the police were setting up their camera system, so there was no reason to go there right away. She would stop in at the Eurospar on her way back and pick up more mineral water and maybe a couple snacks. She would also address her laundry situation, and either locate a laundromat or plan to go to Mags's. With Brian back at the hotel she would probably spend more time there and less time out and about. However, he didn't need a babysitter, and the guard would have eyes on him at all times. She just needed to check in every few hours. As long as he was stable, she would be free between those times. But she would have to remain in town, for who-knows how long. She would see if she could buy a deck of cards at the Eurospar. Maybe the guard would allow her to put them in Brian's room so they could play cards to pass the time. With nothing else on the agenda now, she could return to the library and charge her phone enough to take photos of the articles about Tim Dooley's murder.

She retraced her route back to the library. When she was less than a block away, Aiden stepped out from its entrance onto the sidewalk, heading in her direction. His eyes narrowed and his steps slowed but he didn't acknowledge her, and he quickly crossed the street to avoid her path. His anger was palpable and unnerving as he stalked away. Cate reminded herself of trauma-informed nursing basics: when inclined to ask "What's wrong with you?" change the question to "What happened to you?" The habit creates empathy and seeks understanding of behaviors. However, it didn't mean she would let her guard down. Mags had mentioned that Aiden had been in trouble frequently, but not much lately. He'd even been locked up in the past.

She glanced back up the street to be sure Aiden was still heading away from her before she entered the library. She returned to the computer she had used earlier and plugged her phone back in to charge. One of her work friends had tagged her with a vulgar but hilarious nursing meme that made her struggle not to laugh out loud in the quiet environment. It felt good to have something to laugh about, so she clicked on its source and went down a rabbit hole of internet silliness to give her mind a break. She was almost giddy by the time her phone had reached 50% charge, then she unplugged it and went to the microforms alcove at the back of the library. The microfiche cards had already been removed from the return basket, so she opened the file drawer to retrieve them.

She aimed roughly for the place where she'd found the dates she needed, then let her fingers flip through the beginning of 1969, January, February, March, April, May, December... Wait, where was June through November? She backed up and scanned through the cards again. Five months of newspaper issues were missing, and she had only taken out June through September during her prior visit. She remembered that October was on the next card in the drawer. Cate flipped through the section of the drawer again, double-checking what she saw. Then she closed the drawer to re-check its label. This was indeed the correct drawer. She looked back to the return basket and verified it was empty. The cards she used earlier may have been misfiled, but what happened to the other ones she had seen and left in the drawer? Microfiche couldn't be checked out of a library, so they must be here somewhere. Cate made a quick search in the adjacent drawers where they were most likely to be misfiled. No luck.

She sighed and resigned herself to having to ask for help again. She made her way back to the circulation desk but Fiona wasn't there. A middle-aged man was checking out materials for a short line of patrons and there were no other staff members in sight so Cate waited her turn, dreading the idea of explaining what she was looking for and the problem of the missing microfiche to this man in front of everyone in the library. To her great relief, Fiona reappeared, emerging from the stacks with a young woman who had several books in her hands. Cate made a beeline toward the librarian as the two said their goodbyes and the patron moved to check out her items.

"Hi again," Cate gave a little shrug and wave.

"Howya?" Fiona smiled.

"Actually, I need more help with the microfiche."

"Sure sure," the librarian headed toward the microforms alcove with Cate in tow, "What's the trouble?"

"Well," Cate stalled a few seconds until they were out of earshot of other patrons, "I've come back to finish up what I was reading but can't find the cards. They're not in the drawer and not in the return basket where I put them. Do you put them somewhere else before they're reshelved?"

Fiona stopped and turned to face Cate, "No, I was going to reshelve them and the basket was empty. Thought you must have put them up yourself, even though I said I'd do it."

"No, I left them in the basket. Did another librarian move them?"

"Scott's been at the circulation desk all afternoon, and it's just the two of us today. Let's go have a look."

They returned to the microforms alcove and searched without results. Fiona looked almost as upset as Cate felt, but for different reasons. The integrity of her collection was compromised, but Cate felt personally targeted. Had Aiden been watching her? Did he take the microfiche? And why would he do that? What was in the newspaper stories that he didn't want her to see? Why would he care what the articles said? He was born decades after Tim Dooley's murder.

"Someone else must have used them and put them away wrong," Cate suggested. "I guess I can read the files for a bit and try to find them. Do they get used often?"

"Rarely," Fiona replied, "Are you sure you didn't accidentally pick them up with your own things?"

"I'm positive," Cate reassured her.

"Would you mind checking before we spend hours searching?"

"Certainly." Cate placed her bag on the table with the microfiche readers. As she removed the items inside, she suddenly felt nervous that the missing cards might be there. It was the same apprehension she always felt at the security checkpoint at the airport, as if there was a chance she had accidentally packed explosives in her carryon luggage. When everything was out of the bag, she almost wished she had found them there. That would mean there was no uncomfortable coincidence of someone else using the same materials she was reviewing. Fiona said the microfiche was rarely used, so Aiden probably took the cards because Cate had been using them. And that meant he was spying on her and deliberately interfering. Why? And how far would he take it? Was he just trying to frighten her, or was he dangerous?

"Someone must have put them in one of the other drawers," Fiona said.

"I have a little while before I have to go," Cate checked the time. "I'll look for them until then."

They worked together, starting with spot checks of the most likely filing mistakes. Then they moved on to one-by-one reading of the whole collection. Cate started with the drawer where the cards belonged, Fiona took another drawer. They chatted lightly.

"What made you want to be a librarian?" Cate asked.

"Ah, me gran was the librarian here before me. I grew up helping her. Me sisters and brother were outdoorsy types, but I've always preferred to be surrounded by the books. There's nothing else I ever wanted to do. And yerself?"

Cate shrugged, "Most of my career choices have been accidental. My undergraduate degree in English studies was fascinating; I loved every minute of college. But that particular degree qualified me for just about nothing professionally, so I took a library assistant job after graduation. After working there for a couple years I thought I'd better move on or move up, so I went to grad school. The moving up part went fine until it didn't. The state archives got downsized when the economy tanked and my position was eliminated. So I did what I do best: I went back to college again, this time for a recession-proof career in nursing. So you've lived in Bunclody all your life?"

"Yeh," Fiona finished a drawer and opened another one. "Except for my uni years."

"Where did you study?"

"Dublin Business School."

"Did you like living in Dublin? I only spent one day there and just scratched the surface with exploring."

"Yeh, the city's loads of fun, but expensive. And my family is here."

"Bunclody seems to be a lovely town, but I've found it a bit complicated so far."

Fiona smiled without looking up from her work, "I would imagine so." After a few minutes' companionable silence, she announced, "I have to relieve Scott at the desk now, but I'll continue the search later. Which drawers are ye going to read?"

"I'll finish this one then I have to go too."

A short time later, Cate gave up searching and left the library. As she exited the building she paused to look in all directions, in case Aiden was nearby, but she didn't find him there. So she made her way down the street, past the hotel to the Eurospar. She had remembered to pack a reusable shopping bag in her things, so it was easy to gather up and carry her purchases of mineral water, playing cards, and four Tayto cheese and onion crisps sandwich kits. She had read that the flavored potato chips were an iconic Irish snack, and they were often enjoyed between buttered slices of bread. The kits each contained two slices of bread, two pats of butter, a single serving bag of Tayto crisps, and a knife to spread the butter.

She returned to the hotel about four, stowed her purchases, and stretched out on her bed to contemplate the bizarre circumstances in which she found herself. Just a few days ago she was home in Florida, at loose ends and wondering what to do with herself. Now she was across the Atlantic, surrounded by people she barely knew, eyeballs-deep in two murder investigations and a generations-long community scandal, acting as an ad hoc corrections nurse, in the middle of a global pandemic. She spoke aloud to the universe, "Be careful what you wish for, right? This is plenty, thank you." Then she wished she could pick up the phone and call Keith to tell him about all the craziness of the situation. She would like to talk to Keith of three years ago, before he got sick. He was a good listener then, readily laughing at her jokes and sharing her wonder or outrage. He was her constant encourager. Cancer and toxic medications and depression simplified him in the final year of his life. He wasn't able to follow complex concepts. He lost interest and energy for doing more than watching TV and napping, and his sense of humor grew crude and a little bit mean. In some ways, Cate had been grieving his absence long before he actually died. She reminded herself that medical innovations of recent decades have changed the way people live and die, and that most people will experience several years of declining health. Cate pondered how Keith's final year played out and how the end of Brian's life was going. What's important? What makes it a life well-lived? What would happen to Brian? Was he going to spend his last days, months, or years in prison? Deep in thought while lying down, Cate drifted off to sleep.

She awoke to firm knocking on her door. "Ms. Jenks," she recognized Rooney's voice on the other side.

"Coming," she called as she sprang out of the bed and quickly checked herself in the mirror, smoothing her hair and clothes in one sweep, and placing the mask on her face.

Rooney awaited her in the hallway while Garda Ryan and another older uniformed officer escorted Brian into his room. Brian was using a simple front-wheeled, aluminum frame walker and he looked older and smaller than ever. He was the only person not wearing a mask, and he was huffing and puffing as usual.

"Hello, Detective Sergeant," she greeted Rooney.

"Ms. Jenks," he nodded. "Mr. Atley will be confined to his room. You may tend to him using the adjoining door, but if he crosses into your room he will be immediately returned to a cell at the station."

"I understand. Thank you, that will make it easier for me to keep an eye on him."

The older guard stepped back out of Brian's room. "Howya" he nodded as he crossed the hallway and used a key card to open the door of the room opposite of Cate's. He pulled a chair and small table into the hallway and seated himself behind the table with his back to the hotel room. The arrangement faced Cate and Brian's doors while allowing space for other traffic in the hallway. Cate was reminded of the guard's desk outside the jail cells at the station.

Rooney said, "This is Garda O'Malley. He will be monitoring Mr. Atley's quarters at all times with video surveillance. Be aware that the toilet is also monitored."

"Thanks for the warning," Cate suppressed a nervous giggle and committed to memory never to use Brian's bathroom herself.

Garda O'Malley arranged a tablet on the desk and tapped its surface. "It's working," he told Rooney.

"Good," Rooney replied, then turned to Cate, "Please examine Mr. Atley now and confirm that he is stable."

Cate entered Brian's room from the hallway, passing Rowan as he held the door. Brian was seated in the blue wingback chair and Cate felt a wave of relief to see him in what had so quickly become his regular spot. "Hey, Brian, welcome back."

"Hello, Cate," he croaked.

She placed her hand on top of his and gave a reassuring squeeze, "You looked pretty good using the walker. How's your breathing?"

"Fine," he said, though he was still noticeably winded from his efforts. He turned his hand under hers to grip back, and he held on for an extra beat before releasing her hand and shrugging his shoulders.

Most of Brian's belongings had been returned by the gardaí and they were set neatly on the room's tabletop. Cate plundered one of the bags and located her blood pressure cuff, pulse oximeter, and thermometer. She squirted hand sanitizer in her own hands and Brian's, wiped her equipment down with sanitizing wipes, then she took Brian's vital signs.

"Are you having any pain?"

He shook his head, "My back's tweaked by that jailcell bed, but it'll work itself out."

"I can give you something for it. A dose of Tylenol might let you rest easier," she said.

"Nah, I don't need it."

She checked the battery level on his oxygen concentrator then pronounced him stable. Rooney and Ryan left, and Cate and Brian were alone. She was acutely aware that O'Malley was watching from the hallway. She glanced around trying to figure out where the cameras were placed and spotted one in a corner near the ceiling which must give a full view of most everything. The door to Cate's adjoining room was open on this side. She would need to re-enter her room from the hallway then open it from her side too.

She sat down in the chair opposite Brian. "We'll need to order you some supper. Is there anything else you'll need tonight?"

"No," he answered flatly.

"I'm glad they've moved you back here."

"Yeah." He was avoiding eye contact, staring at the floor, then he shook his head slowly and sighed, "There's not much to be glad of, so the little things will have to do."

"That's the spirit," she encouraged softly while opening the menu, "Want to try the cottage pie again?"

"No. It's too much."

"What did you have for lunch?"

"I don't remember."

"Then you'll need something for supper. You could eat just a little bit. It's okay not to eat it all, but you do need food."

"No, it will sit too heavy and I can't get comfortable. Guess I'm off my feed again."

"Is there anything else that sounds good?" Cate read the entrees from the menu. "There's a piri piri chicken, a red curry, a steak sandwich, a cod fillet, bangers and mash, or chicken mash. And there's tagliatelle pasta with mushrooms and leeks in a light cream sauce. There's a seafood pie, if you're in the mood." She glanced at his face, "No? How about soup or a salad? There's tomato and roasted red pepper soup served with brown bread. Oh my God, I'm drooling." She looked to Brian again to see if he was as enchanted as she was by any of the offerings.

His eyes were closed and he was shaking his head, "No, Cate, it's all too much. I have no appetite."

"Well, I'm worried you will get ill if you don't eat at least a little. You're under a lot of stress, and you have to put some fuel in the tank or you'll find yourself in a crisis. Tomorrow I'll see if I can get you some meal replacement shakes. But for now... hmmmm.... Oh, how about a Tayto crisp sandwich? Have you ever had one of those?" Cate remembered the sandwich kits she had purchased earlier.

"Hmmm? Tayto?" Brian's eyes sprang open and he blinked as if waking, "Cheese and onion? I haven't tasted them in years!"

"Wait here," Cate popped out of her chair and stepped toward the door then realized the irony of what she'd said, "Uh, of course you'll wait. Sorry. I'll be right back."

To avoid startling the guard, Cate opened the door carefully and announced herself, "It's Cate. I'm coming out,"

"Hello, I can see that," he answered.

"Is there anything you need me to do when I come out of the room?"

"Like what?" he sounded amused, though the facemask he was wearing hid all expression except a deepening of the crow's feet by his eyes.

"Like, do I need to tell you I'm coming out?"

"Nah, I can see when yer comin'." He indicated his tablet screen.

"Okay. I just wanted to make sure. I'm going to get Brian a sandwich. Do you want to see it before I give it to him?"

"I'll need to have a look at anything before it's taken into his room."

"That's what I thought. I'll be right back." Cate returned to her room and opened the door into Brian's, but then she gathered a bottle of mineral water and two of the Tayto crisp sandwich kits, and returned to the hallway to show everything to O'Malley.

His eyebrows rose as he inspected the snacks, "Ah, so it's a three Michelin star service!"

"That's what I hear," Cate laughed. "We don't put chips, I mean crisps, on our sandwiches in the States so it seems a little strange, but I'm looking forward to trying my first Tayto crisp sandwich. Since I promised to keep my mask on when I take care of Brian, I'll be eating in my own room, but this one is an extra and I thought you might like it."

"A bribe? And we've only just met," he chuckled.

"Is it that good?"

"When you try it, you'll be sorry you gave one away."

"Now I can't wait. The mention of a Tayto sandwich is the only thing that caught Brian's interest. He seems nostalgic about it. How long have Tayto crisps been around?"

The guard tilted the tablet so he could view its video clearly while they talked, "As long as I remember, we've had crisps, but until the sixties they were all plain and imported from the UK. A fella named Joe Murphy opened a factory in Dublin to make crisps in Ireland. And he put a twist in. He flavored 'em with cheese and onion, and salt and vinegar. All of Ireland fell in love with 'em. That mascot pictured there is Mr. Tayto and he is dear to all," O'Malley tapped the logo on the package. "He ran a campaign for the 2007 general election, and has published his official biography. And would you believe he has an amusement park in County Meath, with a wooden roller coaster?"

"I can believe it," Cate replied. "In the U.S., we have theme parks dedicated to all sorts of food and drink."

"Fair play. Now, I can't tell you who did it or when it happened, but the Tayto sandwich came into being and has become a national staple. To do it right, use Brennan's bread, slather it with Kerry Gold butter, crush some cheese and onion Tayto crisps on it, slap the bread together and you've got yourself a Tayto sandwich. And now me mouth is watering."

"So is mine!" Cate laughed, "Thanks for the Tayto education. I'm going to give this to Brian and go enjoy my own."

"Cheers!" O'Malley raised his sandwich pack in a toast as Cate entered Brian's room.

"Look what I found at the Eurospar, Brian. It's a kit with everything you need for a Tayto sandwich," she held the package out and he took it with more enthusiasm than she'd seen in him since the start of their trip. He turned the package this way and that, squinting at its contents and cheerful printed instructions.

"Do you want me to put it together for you?" Cate offered.

"No, I believe I can manage," he chuckled. "Have you tried one yourself?"

"I'm going to. Mine is in my room. I have to wear a mask when I'm with you so we can't eat together, but we can leave the door open between our rooms and try it out at a distance."

"Ah, yes," he answered quietly. "That will do."

Cate returned to her room through the adjoining door and they prepared their sandwiches. Brian coached her when it came time to put on the crisps.

"Do I crunch them up into little bits first?" she held up the packet.

"No, leave them as they are, but give it a good smash straight down when you put on the top slice," he demonstrated then waited for her to follow suit.

"Okay, got it. Ready?"

They held their sandwiches up and bit in unison. The unassuming snack was a sensuous melding of textures between the soft sweet bread, the salty velvet of the butter, and the delayed and muted crunch of the even saltier crisps with their pungent umami from cheese and onion. Brian slumped back into his chair with his eyes closed, chewing slowly.

"Oh my God, this is so good!" Cate held her hand in front of her mouth, talking through her food. Then they indulged in their sandwiches silently, except for their crunching. Brian was a slow eater and Cate didn't want to distract him in any way that would interrupt his meal, so she had keep herself from wolfing it down. When he finally finished, she asked, "Why haven't I had one of these before now? I mean, we may not have Tayto brand in the U.S., but we have all kinds of flavors of chips... crisps. They would all be delicious on buttered bread."

"It wouldn't be the same."

"Yeah, maybe not," she conceded, "But maybe close enough to get myself in trouble eating too many of them. Are you still hungry? I have another sandwich kit."

"No, this was plenty," Brian waved his hand over the now-empty packaging.

"Okay. I'm glad you were able to eat a real meal."

"I think it will help in the long run, but now I feel full and tired." He shifted back in his chair.

"Is there anything you need?" Cate offered.

"No, thanks. I'm just going to watch a bit of TV and take a nap sitting here."

"Okay. I'm going to leave my door just a little bit open. Call out if you need anything. I may go out for a bit later. If I do, I'll let you know. Unless you're sleeping, of course, and you can always call the guard if you need help."

Brian nodded sleepily, "Thank you, Cate," then he pressed the TV remote.

Cate pulled the door nearly shut and sat down on the chair at the desk. What a day it had been! And what should she do next? She should address the laundry situation, having packed lightly for what was supposed to be only a week away from home, including the flying time. Now there was no way of anticipating how long she would be staying in Ireland. Brian had packed more clothing than Cate, but he would eventually need laundry done too. The easiest solution might be to use Mags's washing machine, even though Cate would have to carry the laundry on foot or ask Mags to pick her up on her scooter. She would have to carry it on foot to a laundromat too. She just felt a little awkward about imposing on Mags for such a personal issue. However, she reminded herself, she was already beyond personal with Brian and his family, and it would be much more pleasant to get her laundry done while being treated to more Irish fare.

She settled her decision, tomorrow she would do her laundry at Mags's, then go back to the library to search for the missing newspaper articles. She felt restless now. It was too early for bed and she needed something to do.

She scrolled through some novel recommendations but couldn't decide what to choose. She had the same problem with streaming services. Unless there was something she specifically wanted to watch, she would spend tons of time reading synopses and rejecting them. She didn't particularly like TV, but she found it easier to just watch whatever was on than to choose something. Tomorrow she would go back to the charity shop and pick a couple novels from whatever they had in stock. It never seemed to be a problem to make a selection from tangible books that were physically in front of her.

She advised Brian she was going out and headed to the hotel bar. It was a small place with eight stools, four on two sides. The L-shaped bar itself was finished in light oak, and the floor was a similar tone with inlaid designs. A handful of small tables were spaced neatly along the outer walls. The ceiling was lower than that of the hotel lobby, and it was finished with oak paneling that contrasted with the old stone masonry wall behind the bar. The light fixtures were modern, bringing warmth to the natural textures. The place was cozy, clean, and inviting.

She found the Polish bartender there again, alone. "Hello, Arek," she greeted him as she seated herself.

"Ms. Jenks," he nodded.

"Call me Cate."

"What is your pleasure, Cate?" His Eastern European accent sharpened the consonants and softened the vowel so her name sounded exotic when he said it.

"How about another of the Prince's martinis? And a mineral too, please."

While he readied her drinks she asked, "How's your family?"

"Grand," he replied automatically.

"Are your Polish relatives keeping healthy?"

"My aunt has a heart condition. I called my mother today, she said she has been sick but she cannot see her because they are not allowed to leave their homes in Warsaw. You know, they have had quarantine there."

"I'm sorry to hear that. I hope he has a complete and quick recovery."

"Thank you." Arek cast his gaze downward and his deep-set eyes were hooded beneath his prominent brow.

Cate changed the subject, "How is Aiden doing?"

His gaze bounced back to hers without moving his head, giving a strong side-eye. "Grand," he said simply.

"I know he's a friend of yours. I'm asking about him because he came up to me in the pub the other night and was very aggressive. I've seen him around town a few times since, and he seems so angry. I heard about who Brian is to him, so I know why he's upset, but... I don't know... A couple people have said he's been in trouble in the past, and that you and Rowan are a good influence on him. I'm not trying to get you to speak badly about him, but do you think there's a chance he might hurt someone?"

Arek didn't answer immediately, then stated, "Nah."

Cate wasn't expecting Arek to betray his friend. Rather, she was sending a message that she had seen Aiden and wouldn't hesitate to turn attention to his behaviors. She was certain Arek would tell Aiden about their conversation, and perhaps rein him in. The result would only improve things, and make Cate a little safer. "Well, every time I've seen him, he seems like he's about to blow up."

"He is an intense person," Arek stated with a hint of a nod.

"Does he ever crack a smile? Laugh? Or relax?"

"This is a therapy session?" he replied blandly so it wasn't clear if he was being funny or caustic.

"No," Cate laughed as if there was nothing uncomfortable between them. "I'm just trying to get a sense of what's normal for Aiden. Some people are naturally intense like that, for whatever reason. Or is he so upset with Brian, and maybe me too, that I need to be careful of him? I'm asking because it seems like he turns up a lot, and I expect I'll see him again."

"You do not have to worry about him," Arek stated firmly.

"Is he married? Or is there a girlfriend?"

"Are you interested?" Arek's eyebrows shot up and his chin tucked down. He was definitely teasing her now.

"What? No!" Cate raised her palms in protest. "I'm just trying to learn a little more about him as a person, beyond his anger." She stopped herself from saying, "As Brian's grandson," because Aiden believed it but Brian denied it, and that bombshell hadn't exploded yet.

"His grandfather's return has set him off a bit, and then there's everything else that Brian has done. Aiden will calm down in time."

"I hope so, and that he stays out of trouble."

"Like his grandfather?" Arek suggested with an arched eyebrow.

"Ouch!" Cate sputtered as she sipped her martini, "Jeez, take me to the burn unit."

Arek nodded once as if to say 'exactly,' then cracked a smile. "Ah, do not cross the street to be offended." He placed a snacking plate of peanuts before her then excused himself, "I have to clear the taps now."

Cate was left with her drinks. She checked her email and read a disturbing update from her daughter Ellie. New York City would be enacting "shelter in place" orders because of spread of COVID-19. Several New Yorkers had died from the virus in the last couple days. Officials were concerned that huge numbers of patients would soon overwhelm the hospital system that was unprepared with supplies and staff, so they were attempting to "flatten the curve" of contagion by ordering a lockdown. Schools were already closed for spring break and would be converting to distance learning for the remainder of the term. Childcare for Myles would be no trouble, though, because Ellie and her husband Peter were both considered non-essential workers and would stop going to their workplaces. Cate remembered that, fortunately, they had acquired a car two years ago from a friend who was downsizing. She texted Ellie, encouraging her to leave New York immediately and move her family into Cate's house. She barely noticed time passing during their back-and-forth messaging. Finally, Cate urged *Get out b4 they ban travel there like Ireland. U will have the place to urself. No idea when I can come home.* Ellie replied, *Talking it over w Peter.*

Cate knew it would be hard for Ellie to return to the house where her father died. Their personalities were similar, and their relationship had always been a little bit volatile but very close. In her preteen years, Ellie had started calling Keith "Daddy-o," with a fake jazz musician voice. Over time the nickname got shortened to just "O."

Cate's thoughts turned to Keith's final days. For weeks, he had been sleeping in a hospital bed in their home office because he couldn't climb the stairs to their bedroom. His pain had been difficult to control and he resisted recommendations to increase his medication, except for adding on medical marijuana which he smoked on the lanai while watching cloud formations, wearing a hoodie in the Florida heat. He had remained independent enough that Cate could leave him alone while she worked her hospital shifts, and he was adamant about not having anyone stay with him. He used a walker to keep himself steady and wore a medical emergency call button necklace. He was eating very little food, except for yogurt and meal replacement shakes that she stocked in a mini-fridge in arm's reach. Mostly he watched TV from his bed or the chair beside it, or he slept in his smoking chair outside.

On a Wednesday evening with five days off work ahead of her, Cate had gone upstairs to get a few hours sleep. She awoke in the middle of the night to the sounds of Keith's voice talking to someone. Downstairs, she found him sitting on the floor next to his bed, staring at something she couldn't see.

"What are you doing?" she asked.

"Resting," he kept his eyes focused on the distance.

"Did you fall?"

"No, huh uh," he shook his head.

"Are you hurt?"

"No," he scoffed as if the question were ridiculous.

Cate looked him over for injuries. "I want to make sure you're not hurt. Look at me." But he would not follow direction. She checked his blood sugar and oxygen saturation. Both were fine, but she still turned on the oxygen he had recently started using during sleep and placed the cannula in his nose. He did not appear to be in acute pain and was not bleeding or bruised anywhere she could see. "Keith! You're going to get cold on the floor and then you won't be able to get up, so you have to help me get you back in the bed or I will call the fire department to do it."

"They said they would take me home."

His words gave Cate a chill, and she automatically answered, "We're already home. Who told you that?"

Finally his eyes came back to hers, and he answered confusedly, "The... nurses?"

"Come on, you have to help. I can't get you up by myself." Actually, his flesh had withered so much that she could lift him alone, if he cooperated. But if he resisted, they might both go down. For now, he followed her instruction and she was able to counterbalance enough to raise him into an embrace, then they did an awkward slow dance to the bed with Cate firmly directing Keith when to move his feet. She sat him on the mattress then pivoted his legs and tucked him in, and he never got out of that bed again. He was too weak even to stand and turn to the bedside commode she had ordered from hospice. She called Ellie the next morning, "Your dad's not doing well. I think you should come now if you want to see him." Ellie got on a plane right away and arrived even before Keith's family came from south Florida.

Cate opened the front door to Ellie and they hugged hard, then broke it off quickly before either could start crying. She led her daughter to the office and they stood together in the doorway regarding Keith sleeping peacefully. Ellie's eyes widened and Cate compared the small man before her to the image of Keith in a family photo on the desk: more than seventy pounds lighter, with his sallow skin deeply creased and hanging loose. His nose and ears looked too big for his head, and his glasses were owlishly large now too. Ellie's last visit was more than two months ago, and the most dramatic changes had occurred since then. Cate indicated the chair beside the bed. As Ellie sat down, Keith's eyelids fluttered open and he startled.

"Hey, O," she soothed.

"Honey!" his voice was thin and raspy and he raised his arms reaching for her. She hugged him carefully, struggling against tears.

The three together were normally very vocal, joking and laughing and talking about anything. They were an industrious family, always with multiple projects underway, and any time together was an opportunity to share the latest ideas, foods, news, or stories. This event of Keith's dying took away all their words. He had no energy for expression; he and Cate had spent every day of the last year living an extended goodbye. And now Ellie's heart was breaking before them. Cate sat beside her and the two women watched Keith recede into sleep again.

She gave an update, trying to make Ellie more comfortable, "I think his pain is under control now. When I ask if he's hurting he keeps saying no. I've been giving him the morphine drops when he seems to struggle to breathe, or if he looks like he's in pain. You know, moaning or grimacing. He wouldn't swallow this morning, and he turned his head when I tried to put yogurt in his mouth."

Ellie searched Cate's face, "But he's going to get dehydrated. Should he get IV fluids or something?"

"He is going to get dehydrated, yes. If we place an IV it will just prolong this process. It's not that he can't drink, it's that his body doesn't want it anymore. That's normal at this stage. But you can offer him something. Maybe he will take it from you."

"I believe you," Ellie said softly, "But I'd like to try anyway. Is that okay?"

"Of course," she kissed the top of Ellie's head as she got up to go to the kitchen. She returned with Keith's favorite strawberry yogurt and a cup with a straw that she handed to her daughter.

"O," Ellie rubbed his shoulder, "Wake up, Daddy-o. I've got your lunch here, you better eat it before it gets... warm?"

Keith's eyes opened, "Huh?"

"I've got some yummy yogurt for you, O. Have a bite!"

She pressed a small spoonful to his lips, and he softly said, "No."

"Don't be like that, O. Did you ever play 'here comes the airplane' with me when I was little? Now it's your turn. Open wide, here it comes."

Keith stated firmly, "No," then closed his eyes.

"At least drink some water then," she tried. "Mom says you didn't drink anything yet today."

Keith barely shook his head and did not open his eyes or his mouth.

Cate touched her shoulder, "It's okay, El. His body just doesn't want it."

Ellie set things down and sighed, "Then I think I'm going to cry."

"That's okay, too. I do it all the time. I've got tissues," she pointed to a box on the table beside the bed. "He can't talk much now, but he hears everything we're saying. I'm going to go cry in the other room and try to tidy things up. The Sweets will be here in a couple hours."

"Oh, God," Ellie moaned and laughed at the same time. The Sweets were Keith's oldest sister Anne and her husband Bob. "Hear that, O? Your favorite brother-in-law is on the way." Bob Sweet was a six-foot-nine giant of a man with a booming voice and an ironically bad case of diabetes. He and Anne lived in their RV, of which Anne had become the full-time driver since Bob's below-the-knee amputation, even though he was getting around pretty well on a prosthesis. Anne was nearly as loud as her husband and always made a grand entrance in a swirling cloud of perfume and oversized accessories. She was twelve years older than Keith and called him her first baby.

The Sweets brought an extraordinary amount of KFC takeout with them, and the smell of fried chicken filled the house. "You gotta keep up your strength!" Bob rumbled as he deposited a double armload of bags and boxes onto Cate's kitchen counter. Then he went to the office to say goodbye to Keith and comfort Anne who had been unusually quiet during her time alone with her brother.

They kept their visit short. After the Sweets left, Cate and Ellie clung to each other in the kitchen. "What are we going to do with all this chicken?" Cate sighed.

"I'm going to put a dent in it now," Ellie served herself a hugely mounded plate with light meat, dark meat, mashed potatoes, gravy, coleslaw, and a biscuit. Cate served herself a more modest amount and they sat at the dining room table with Keith's place empty. It felt simultaneously familiar and strange, and they both picked at their food without appetite. After a while they gave up and returned to Keith's bedside.

The hospice nurse made her daily visit and offered bland reassurance that Keith's decline was progressing, that everyone was doing great, and that she was available if they needed anything. Then she retreated to her car while Cate and Ellie exchanged sidelong glances. The whole visit took less than fifteen minutes. "I wonder what she'd do if I said I needed something," Cate pondered, and Ellie giggled too much. Cate could see the stress was getting to her.

She encouraged Ellie to get some rest but the young woman insisted on staying by Keith's side, so Cate took a break instead. After a three-hour nap, she returned feeling somewhat refreshed. As she approached the office, she heard Ellie talking to Keith in soft tones. Cate found her with her forearms braced across the bedrail and her chin on her hands, talking about the trip they had made to North Carolina during Ellie's senior year of high school. She described their hunt for garnets in an old mine and the trail ride they had taken. As Cate sat beside her, Ellie elbowed her mother without pausing her story, "Remember, O, how that guy helped Mom up onto her horse? He put his shoulder under her butt and lifted her up and then he said, 'Ma'am, I'm going to need my hand back.'"

The women laughed through the memory. "I wasn't expecting him to do that!" Cate gasped, "That horse was so tall, there was no way I could get up by myself. I went up like an elevator, and then his hand was stuck between my leg and the saddle. I was just so proud to be up there without falling off the other side, I didn't even notice." Keith's face remained neutral but Cate could feel his attention, his listening.

Keith died in the night. Cate and Ellie were sitting with him, then Cate went to the kitchen to make some tea and Ellie went to pee. Ellie returned first and found him gone. He'd stopped breathing and the color had drained from his face. As is common in dying, he'd stepped out of his body when no one was looking. Cate's only regret was that Ellie had found him, and the anguish in her voice crying, "Mom!" replayed in her ears at the strangest times.

When Cate saw her dead husband, he simply seemed gone to her. Finally and fully gone, instead of half-gone as he'd been all these months. She brushed back the hair on his forehead, then gently held his eyelids closed and caressed his cheek. Then she and Ellie held onto each other and everything was blurred with tears. When the enormity of the moment began to ease and they looked at each other like "what's next?" Cate instructed Ellie to open all the windows in the house while she called hospice. It was a clear breezy night and the house almost felt as if it were breathing. The on-call nurse arrived and called the doctor to pronounce the death, then an aide showed up. Together they did post-mortem care which resulted in Keith looking neat and peaceful in freshly arranged linens. The aide stayed at the bedside for several hours until the funeral home came to take Keith's body. Cate and Ellie sat on the lanai sipping tea in the dark. At four o'clock they were both ravenous and ate cold fried chicken straight from the refrigerator. At six, Cate started sending text messages and making phone calls to family about Keith's passing.

Ellie flew back to New York the next day. Her usually wide, round eyes were swollen and red. She said she just couldn't sleep there because she kept seeing her father when she closed her eyes. Time helped. She seemed to be coping better the next time she visited Florida with Peter and Myles, but when Cate was restless in the middle of the night and came downstairs to get a drink she found Ellie in the office, huddled in the chair with her heels tucked against her butt and her arms wrapped around her knees.

"How do you stay here?" Ellie asked, "Doesn't this place make you miss him all the time?"

"I've been missing him since before he died," Cate admitted, "It's called anticipatory grief. He was different and slipping away for a long time. The disease, the pain, the medications, the depression. It all affected his personality and his ability to interact with me. In some ways I was lonelier while he was here than I am now that he's gone. Now I know he's at peace, and I guess I'm at peace here too, though I don't actually spend that much time at home. I'm changing jobs at the hospital. It will have a steep learning curve but more money too, and I'll stay even busier." She sighed, "Everyone walks their own path with grief. There's no right or wrong way to feel. But you know your father always wanted us to be happy. He would want us to celebrate and remember the good times, and also move on to make new memories. Every day I'm here without him becomes more normal."

"I don't want it feel normal that he's gone." Ellie hugged her knees and her eyes were luminous with unspilled tears.

Cate pulled herself back from the memory, and focused on the present-day complications caused by the pandemic. It would definitely be hard for Ellie to return to the Florida home, but Cate feared for her and her family if they stayed in New York during a lockdown. Their apartment was tiny and they spent most of their time out in the city. There wasn't even room to store extra supplies; they bought most of what they needed day-to-day. How would they fare if they were quarantined for weeks or months? Cate mentally urged Ellie to go to Florida, though she knew not to press further. She was relieved to receive her daughter's text: *We will go thx. Will update u from the road.*

Cate exhaled a breath she didn't know she was holding and took too big a gulp of her martini. Her eyes watered as she tried not to have a coughing fit. Arek saw her struggle and checked on her, "You are okay?"

"Yes, I am," she choked, smiling. "I just got good news from my daughter."

"Congratulations."

"Thank you, and thanks for the drink."

Though it was still early, Cate's relief left her suddenly extraordinarily sleepy. She acknowledged it might not be just from her relief over Ellie's safe exit from New York. That was combined with the constant stress of this bizarre journey that was unfolding one crisis after another: two murder charges, amidst the pandemic travel ban, in a foreign country where everything was at least a little bit different from everything as she knew it. It was a relentless onslaught of change and adaptation. Even though she'd been in Ireland only five days now, it felt so much longer. She was tired. In fact, her legs felt almost too heavy to make the trip back upstairs. It took concentrated effort to push through the sudden lethargy, but the idea of her warm bed was calling. She hurried through her assessment of Brian and gave the camera a thumbs up signaling O'Malley that he was okay, then she gathered clothes Brian needed washed into one of his small travel bags. She cleared it with O'Malley then took it to her room to carry with her tomorrow. Just before she fell asleep she remembered to set her alarm for the next morning.

Chapter 12

Cate awoke before the alarm with thoughts of the day vying for attention. There were several things she needed to do and her now rested but anxious mind was over-rehearsing because she was concerned she would forget something. She switched on the light and jotted down a to-do list: Brian assessments q4h, Check on Ellie, Notify Becky to drop off key, Laundry, Articles @ library, Charity shop for book.

What else? There was something she was forgetting. Oh, Mags! Mags was going to feed her breakfast, but that was planned before Brian had been returned to the hotel. Maybe Mags had something else in mind now.

Cate showered and dressed, then peeked in on Brian. He was still asleep, so she returned to her room and texted Mags, *Good morning are we on for breakfast?* Brian's sister replied, *I'll bring it to ye both.* Cate wasn't sure about visitation to Brian. Rooney had stipulated that Cate was not to bring anyone to visit him, but could other people come on their own? They could when Brian was held at the station, but that might be different at the hotel. She called Mags.

"Good morning, pet," she answered on the first ring.

"Good morning, Mags. I can already taste those scones."

"Don't eat the stale ones there, dear. Today I'm putting in blueberries, but they're far from ready for the oven yet."

"I'll wait if I can," Cate laughed. "So, about you coming here to see Brian... Do you know if Rooney has okayed that?"

"What's there to okay? He's me brother and I've a right to see him. And he has to eat."

"Of course. It's just that Brian being moved to the hotel is an unusual arrangement. Yesterday Rooney made me sign conditions, including that I would not bring visitors to see him. He made it clear that Brian would be moved back to the station if any of the terms are broken, so I just want to be sure I don't mess anything up. I'll check with the guard to find out if you can visit. Also, I do need to do my laundry."

"Mick can have his shite if he thinks he'll keep me away."

"Well you know more than I do about how things work around here. I just don't want to make anything worse for Brian or for you."

"Fair play you," Mags cooled her ferocity. "I'll come pick you up on the Burgman. Liam's already taken the car to the Murphys. See you in twenty? That gives me time to put the scones in the oven and we'll be back here before they're done."

"Perfect. See you soon."

Cate gathered her clothes that were most in need of washing and stuffed them into her reusable shopping bag, then she pocketed her to-do list and gathered her essentials for going out. Before leaving her room, she looked in on Brian again. He was still sleeping peacefully. When she stepped into the hallway she was surprised to find a different guard sitting at the makeshift monitoring station.

"Good morning," Cate said to the woman who paused her pen over a newspaper that was folded to frame a sudoku puzzle.

"Ah sure," she answered without interest, only briefly glancing up at Cate before writing a number into an empty square.

"I'm Cate Jenks."

"Maudy Doyle," she answered with a brief wave of her pen.

"It's nice to meet you. I guess Garda O'Malley has gone home?"

"I've no idea where he's gone," she wrote another number in a puzzle square.

"I meant that his shift has ended." This one was a real peach. "Just letting you know I've checked on Brian and he's still sleeping. I'll do my full assessment later when I come back. Is he allowed to have visitors?"

"No visitors." The middle-aged woman shook her head as she marked another number and pushed her glasses further up her nose with the other hand.

"Thanks," Cate said without meaning it. She strode down the hall to the elevator. As she waited, she turned back to look at Garda Doyle who glanced up from her puzzle only for a brief second. Cate remembered another item for her to-do list: grab a few more Tayto sandwich kits since Brian seemed to enjoy them. As she stepped into the elevator she slid the bags of laundry onto her forearm, withdrew a pen from her shoulder bag and her to-do list from her pocket. If she didn't write things down she would forget them and it would drive her crazy knowing there was something she was supposed to do but couldn't remember. The elusive item would return to her brain as soon as it was sufficiently inconvenient. There must be a law for that, like Murphy's Law or the Peter Principle. If it wasn't already named, it could be called Jenks's Jinx.

The elevator doors opened, Cate stepped forward and fumbled her pen, knocking it around with her wrist and upper arm like a crazy hacky sack. She was trying to keep it from falling down the crack of the elevator shaft which was known for its ironic gravitational pull. At work, Cate had once dropped her ID badge into it and had to spend the rest of the shift manually keying in her computer credentials and asking coworkers to let her through doors. H.R. charged her twenty dollars for a replacement, and the engineering guy retrieved her old badge as soon as it had been deactivated and replaced.

Cate's pen went flying away from the elevator doors into the hotel lobby, spinning and careening across the marble tiles. The toe of her shoe caught in the formidable elevator gap as she followed the pen, and she chased her balance by taking several lunging steps. She tried to make it look like an intentional reach for her pen and ended up with her shoulder bag and the laundry all sliding forward down her arms. Then she overcorrected into a collision course with three people who were engaged in conversation with their backs to Cate. Her shoe kicked the pen further away, her bags flopped to the floor, and she came to a screeching halt before actually making contact with the startled trio.

"Damn it!" she hissed, feeling her face flush with embarrassment. At least she hadn't actually fallen, or taken anyone else out. The three people leapt in response, pulling each other aside and then they turned toward

Cate. She brought herself upright with all her things in a heap on the floor, and found herself facing a male hotel employee whose nametag read Hughey, another man who looked familiar, and the woman who had yelled at Brian in the hotel lobby the other day.

"Oh, excuse me! I'm so sorry!" Cate hunched her shoulders.

Cate and the hotel employee asked simultaneously, "Are you alright?" The two people with him remained silent.

"I'm fine," Cate was the only one who answered. There was a flurry of activity as Hughey and Cate reached for her things and dodged back to avoid colliding again. Then Cate made herself stop, muttering, "Sorry." Hughey picked up her bags as Rose hurried over from the reception desk, bringing Cate's pen which had traveled almost all the way there. The other woman's face was stony as her dark eyes drilled Cate, and her companion looked on with a distasteful expression. Where had Cate seen this man before?

"I'm sorry, really," Cate offered, with her palms turned up, feeling utterly mortified. Like the time she forgot that the night shift nurse had reported a patient had double leg amputations. Cate was chattily conducting her head-to-toe assessment and went to check pedal pulses, shifting the covers around, saying, "I can't find your feet." The second it came out of her mouth she remembered, and there was no way to recover from it. Cate had that same feeling again, wanting the floor to open up and swallow her.

Hughey said quietly, "No harm done," but he was also clearly aware of the awkward confrontation that was occurring. He handed Cate her things, then turned back to the other two, "If you can just re-send that invoice we'll get it cleared up right away. Sorry to add to your troubles."

Cate hurried out the lobby doors into the morning air and moved down the sidewalk to wait for Mags away from the hotel entrance. Her face was still hot with embarrassment. That woman she had nearly plowed into, Cate remembered was Anna Dooley. Dooley, as in Tim Dooley, the man Brian was accused of murdering before he fled Ireland. Clearly a relative.

Cate decided to focus her attention anywhere but on the hotel doors so she wouldn't risk another face-to-face with Anna Dooley when she emerged. She moved further down the block, just past the hotel but still in clear sight for Mags' arrival. With her back to the building, she examined the sky, the parked cars, and the trees lining the center of main street. A truck rolled from the alley and came to a brief stop before turning left onto Main Street. The couple from the hotel were in its cab, with the man behind the wheel and Anna Dooley in the passenger seat. Anna was glaring at her and when Cate realized it, the corners of Anna's mouth turned down in blatant disgust and she abruptly aimed her eyes forward. The box truck was painted with a company name in flowing script: Dooley & Sons Farm to Table. Its diesel engine accelerated away with the characteristic knocking sound and sulfurous whiff of exhaust fumes.

When the truck was finally out of sight, Cate took a deep breath to try to release her tension. It wasn't enough, so she rolled her shoulders and hung her head, tilting her ear toward her shoulder, then chin to chest, then the other ear to the other shoulder. Her neck movements sounded crunchy inside her head. "That was just awful," she said to herself.

Minutes later, Mags rolled up on her scooter. "Good morning, pet," she smiled as she dismounted. She detached some cargo netting that was holding a spare helmet on the back of the bike and beckoned to trade the helmet for Cate's bags of laundry.

"Good morning, how are you?" Cate replied, holding the helmet in her hands while Mags opened an under-seat storage compartment and stuffed the laundry bags inside.

"Grand." She sat back atop the scooter and waved her hands at Cate, prompting her to get moving, "The scones will be tough if they bake too long."

Cate didn't move. "Um, who is Anna Dooley?"

Mags paused, sighed, then answered, "That's Tim Dooley's widow. Did you meet her?"

"Not exactly. I almost knocked her down a few minutes ago." Mags's eyebrows flew up, so Cate added, "Accidentally, of course. Like, literally almost knocked her down being clumsy. And this was the second time I've seen her in the hotel. She came right up to Brian and yelled at him the first day we got here. Right after we saw you. He didn't know who she was."

"She supplies the hotel restaurant. You were bound to cross paths."

"That's horrible." Cate felt sick.

"The Dooleys are prolific. Go anywhere in County Wexford and you'll be sitting next to one of them."

"Great," Cate sighed.

"Hop on, now. Before the scones are ruined."

Cate secured the helmet on her head and climbed behind Mags who called out, "Hang on!" and accelerated briskly. On the few short straightaways she drove exhilaratingly fast and they both were laughing giddily by the time they paused outside the little detached garage next to Mags's cottage.

"Would you get the door, pet?"

Cate dismounted and opened it as Mags eased the scooter inside. Mags helped with getting Cate's laundry started in the machine, then they made their way to the house. Delicious aromas were wafting toward them even before they reached the door. Cate could smell the scones baking, and something else that was savory and rich.

"Oh, Mags, what are you cooking? It's heavenly!"

"Gwan with you! It's just a coddle I threw together from the bits and bobs in the fridge. Let's wash up and tuck in. It'll just take a minute to wet the tea." Mags started tea steeping, and in no time she had removed the perfect scones from the oven and nestled them into a cloth-lined basket on the table which was already set with two kinds of jam, clotted cream, and butter. Then she lifted the lid of a burbling pot on the stovetop. Steam curled upward and the intoxicating aroma grew even more concentrated.

"That's the coddle?" Cate asked as her mouth watered.

"Yeh," Mags drew back a bit to avoid steaming her glasses.

"I've never heard of it. What is it?"

"Every coddle is different. It starts with potatoes in whatever stock is at hand. Then you throw in everything else you've got leftover and let it all bubble until it's stew. Sorry, pet, it's not fancy. We've got some beans, sausage, cabbage, carrots, bacon, and onion in this one. There's a bit of cream too because that's how my mother always made it, and I forget the rest." She shrugged mysteriously and brought the brimming bowls to the table. The coddle was so velvety thick that there was not even a chance of sloshing during transport.

"You're spoiling me," Cate warned.

They chatted lightly as they ate, not talking about Brian or other serious things. For what had promised to be a trip to Ireland with a small amount of work and a lot of relaxation, it had instead been packed with non-stop worry and complication. Cate was grateful for the respite in Mags's cottage. Nearly an hour passed and they were down to just sipping tea but Cate didn't want the meal to end. She would have been happy to stay well into the afternoon not worrying about anything, trading stories and jokes with this country woman who was like her scooter – quick, efficient, adorable, and a bit fierce. Just as Cate was beginning to feel the pull of responsibility to get back to check on Brian, a knock sounded at the cottage door.

John's tall frame filled the doorway and Mags beckoned him in, "Join us. Cate and I have had our coddle and there's plenty left for you."

"No, Mags. I don't want to put ye out."

"Go on, then! Just a taste with your tea."

"I won't trouble ye," he passed Mags and took a seat at the table.

"Go on! Even though you don't deserve it." She moved to the stove and began filling a bowl from the soup pot.

"Alright, it'll be lovely," he finally relented as Mags was already placing the steaming bowl and a mug before him.

John's multiple verbal refusals contradicted his body language the whole time, and it reminded Cate that she'd read it was Irish custom to repeatedly offer and refuse. She'd read that sharing tea was such a deeply ingrained custom that it was normal for workers to be served tea and biscuits when they came to do maintenance in an Irish home. She wondered, how often had she seemed rude, or maybe just foreign, during her time here? She thought back to a story that a colleague described years ago about his time in an Asian country where the colloquial greeting was "Have you eaten?" The polite answer was always "Yes," no matter whether one was full or starving. Her friend accidentally replied literally to an acquaintance, "No," and the shocked man immediately bought him food. Her colleague said it was the most awkward and excruciating meal he had ever eaten, and he blushed furiously as he told the story even years after it happened. When she planned this Irish trip, Cate assumed she would eat in a few restaurants, take a taxi ride here and there, walk around, then head home. She never expected she would be in and out of houses of the locals or navigating complex social situations. Irish etiquette was something she should study more in her free time, since she was going to be here a lot longer than she expected. She needed to learn how to hang out with the Irish without committing faux pas. And since an Irish Miss Manners would probably advise not to travel with an accused murderer, she was starting out behind the eight ball.

John took a taste of coddle and nodded appreciatively to Mags, then prompted, "What's the story, Cate, how's Brian faring?"

"It's been a trying couple days, but he's stable. I don't know if that sounds reassuring, but stress tends to make his condition worse and the travel, the accusations, being arrested... It's a lot. I know I'm not telling you anything that's surprising. For now, he's hanging in there."

"Hanging in there," Mags echoed. "Go way outta that he came back at all! And that he's been arrested for two murders. Two! How anyone could see Brian and think that he could kill a person. It's just absurd. Mick Rooney must know that."

"Mick is doing his job," John frowned, "And he's a Dooley. The pressure's on him from all sides. But he moved Brian back to the hotel, and we might give him some credit for that."

"I will yeah," she scoffed, "And he got after Aiden again yesterday. Told him to mind himself and that he has an eye on him. As if the lad needs any more doubt heaped on. He's done right these last years, he doesn't need his nose rubbed in it when he hasn't done anything."

"Are you sure he hasn't done anything?" Cate asked cautiously.

"What do you ye mean?"

"Well," Cate said nervously, wanting to balance her safety concern with maintaining her relationship with Mags, "It's just that Aiden came up to me in the pub the other night and kind of sounded threatening about Brian. I didn't know who he was then, but he was so intense that I felt a little scared. Maybe other people heard him too and thought the same thing?"

"Nonsense!" Mags protested.

"You know him much better than I do, so I value your opinion." Cate chose her words carefully, avoiding the confrontational use of the word 'but,' "And, everywhere I go, Aiden seems to be there. And he is very angry. Maybe Rooney is concerned about it."

"Aiden's following you? I'll put a stop to that right away! The lad just needs time and understanding, not threats from the gardaí. He's been through so much that wasn't his fault. Since Brian has returned, with time, I pray Aiden will get the chance to come to peace with his grandfather."

John and Cate made brief eye contact then both looked away deliberately. John busied himself digging into his coddle and Cate touched her teacup.

"What?" Mags demanded, her gaze darting between them. "What's going on? You two are having a conversation with your eyes. Tell me!"

Cate looked to John, but he didn't speak.

"I'm telling the two of you right now, if you don't say what you're sneaking about, you'll never eat another of me scones. Tell me!" she demanded again.

"Alright!" John conceded, "I went to see Brian before he was arrested. He denies being Mary Margaret's father, so he can't be Aiden's grand-da, can he?"

"What do you mean, he denies being her father? Claire named him. She would know."

"He's not Mary Margaret's da, Mags," John said softly. "Brian kept Claire's secret of who the father was, and I kept her secret too. He never knew that Claire named him after he left."

"But she was like a sister to me, and Mary Margaret was my niece! Why didn't she tell me?"

"Claire was older than you and in a bad spot. She couldn't risk her secret coming out."

"But Mam and Da took her in when her own family sent her out on her own. Did they know?" Mags pressed her palm against her chest.

"I don't think so," John said gently.

"They were so broken by what Brian did. I suppose they needed to care about his child," Mags recalled.

"But, Mags," he reminded her, "Mary Margaret is not Brian's child. This I know."

"Then why didn't you say so, John?" she wailed.

"And who would have believed?" he asked. "Claire named him. There was nothing I could make right by saying different. Your mam and da cared for Claire and for Mary Margaret. They needed that."

"Oh, dear God! Dear God in Heaven! What a mess," Mags whispered, gazing into her memories, reevaluating all she knew. Then her eyes cut to John's, "So you know who Mary Margaret's father was."

"I do."

"Go on, then."

"Now, Mags," he shook his head, "It's not mine to tell. And I don't think the story coming out now would help the current situation."

Realization dawned in her expression and she cried, "It was Tim Dooley, wasn't it?!"

John swallowed hard, "I never told you that."

"There, you didn't have to," she nodded decisively and then thought further. "Ah, sure and that doesn't help our Brian at all."

The three shared the silence, each with their own thoughts racing. Cate excused herself to move her washed laundry into the dryer. When she returned, Mags and John were clearing the meal. They all finished the job together.

"Will you take some scones with you?" Mags offered.

Cate tried out her Irish manners, "I don't want to trouble you."

"Ah, go on," Mags replied automatically.

Cate couldn't bring herself to decline again, "Thanks, I'm glad you insist. Today's scones are even better than yesterday's but I got too excited about the coddle to do them justice."

Mags had a care package already made up in a brown paper bag. John offered to give Cate a lift back to town as soon as her laundry was dry, folded, and packed in its bags. Their drive back to the hotel was quiet again, but not because of the tension of secrets. This time, it was the quiet of shared concerns. When John let her off at the curb in front of the hotel, he didn't hurry away. He looked her directly in the eye with gentle gratitude, "Thanks for looking after Brian. Will you be needing anything?"

"Thank you, but no, I can't think of anything right now."

"Then I'll give you my mobile so you can call if you do."

Cate entered his number into her contact list and sent him a text message so he would have her number: *Thank you.* She gathered her thoughts as John pulled away from the curb. She would assess Brian, put their clothes away, then start working through her to-do list. Soon it would be late enough that she could send messages to Becky and Ellie without waking them up. Hours ago, Ellie had messaged that she, Peter, and Myles were en route to Florida and had stopped overnight at a hotel off the interstate. Becky would need to leave a key for them hidden outside the house.

And Cate needed to buy Tayto sandwiches for Brian. She had forgotten to add that to her list this morning. She reached into her pocket to retrieve the paper but couldn't find it, even after checking her pants and jacket pockets. "Okay, what all did I have written on there?" she asked herself as she headed up to her room. "I know I'm going to forget something. Jeez."

In the hallway, Cate placed her mask over her mouth and nose. Garda Doyle looked as if she hadn't moved the whole time Cate was out. In fact, she appeared bored and sleepy. She came alert as Cate approached.

"Hello again," Cate said as she passed her table.

"Howya," the guard replied.

"I've got clean laundry to put in Brian's room. Is it okay if I take this through to him?"

She showed her the clothes and the guard palpated the bag while peering inside. She rifled quickly through the folded laundry without disturbing it much and nodded to Cate, "Yeh sure, go on."

"Thanks. I'll be going in to do my medical check on him in just a minute. Do you need anything? A cup of tea?"

"No, thank you," the guard seemed a little surprised.

Cate tried out the Irish re-offering, "I've got these lovely scones Mags O'Connor served at breakfast. They might still be a tiny bit warm."

"I won't hold you up from seeing to your patient."

"It's no trouble. How do you take your tea?"

"With just a bit of sugar, thanks." A slight smile was evident in the corners of eyes.

"I'll be right back." Cate let herself into her room and returned a few minutes later with a cup of tea and a scone she had warmed just a few seconds in the room's microwave. She placed the refreshments on the guard's table.

Garda Doyle peeked under the napkin that was wrapped around the sweet, "I haven't had one of Mags's scones in donkey's years."

"Enjoy," Cate offered and returned to her room. A while ago she doubted Garda Doyle would ever warm up to her. Tea and scones are magical, she decided, or maybe the guard was just not a morning person.

Cate proceeded to Brian's room, knocking softly on the adjoining door. "Hey, Brian. How are you?"

He was dressed and sitting in the blue wingback chair with the walker parked beside him. "Hello, Cate." A room service tray sat on the tabletop with a partially eaten bowl of porridge.

"I'm glad to see you've had some breakfast! How did you sleep?" She sat down in the chair near him and leaned forward to look and listen.

"Better than the night before. It's good to be back in a real bed."

"I can only imagine. Are you having any pain?"

"Nah."

"Let's check your vital signs," she said as she gathered the equipment. Brian's breathing and oxygen saturation were a little better than yesterday. Cate was relieved the stress hadn't pushed him into a crisis. Yet, she amended... he wasn't having a crisis yet. Just wait until he heard the latest.

Cate gave a thumbs up to the camera, then she sat back down. "I did our laundry at Mags's place today."

"Did you, now." The question sounded more like a statement.

"She made me breakfast too. She called it a coddle. Have you ever had it?"

"Ah, yes. Our mam could make a coddle out of rocks and sheep piss."

"That's not what it tasted like," Cate chuckled humorlessly, then continued, "John dropped by too."

"Why are you torturing me with a party I wasn't invited to?"

Cate sighed. "Mags figured out who Aiden's grandfather really is."

"Ah shite! What do you mean, figured out? Did John tell her?"

"No, but she put it together. Apparently, Aiden's been in a lot of trouble through the years, and he's been thrown off by you coming back, enough that it's causing some concern. Rooney's got an eye on him and Mags is worried. She was hoping that making peace with you, his grandfather, would help. John kind of had to set her straight that you are not related to Aiden. Then she figured out on her own who his grandfather really was."

"Jaysus! And you know it too?"

"I do."

Brian's hand was shaky as he rubbed it over his eyes, down his face, briefly covered his mouth, then he dropped it back to the arm of the chair. He stared despairingly at Cate, "I never would have come back if I'd known Claire named me as Mary Margaret's father. I wish I'd left this all alone. How can I possibly set such a mess right?"

"When things are really bad," Cate said carefully, "The truth is usually what's best for everyone. It may not be the easiest way, but it's what makes space for understanding, healing, and even forgiveness."

Brian's expression flattened and he did not shy away from her gaze, "I agree with you. Aiden probably needs the truth. Why do I feel like you're talking about more than that?"

"Brian, I'm your friend, not your solicitor. And we really haven't had a chance to talk since you were arrested. I'm not going to ask whether or not you... you killed those men. I just want to say that I will be very disappointed if you did."

"Cate, I could never, ever kill anyone."

His words hung in the air and sounded believable. Cate thought, "That's the problem, though. How many lies do we hear every day and never know we've been deceived? Lots of people get so much practice telling lies that it doesn't stress them out at all and they seem perfectly natural." She wasn't particularly cynical, but she had taken care of plenty of patients who said things with absolute conviction that just didn't add up to what she observed while tending to them over time. She had no way of knowing for certain whether Brian was lying or telling the truth. She decided to cautiously believe him unless new information proved otherwise.

"I'm glad to hear that," was what she said out loud, then she changed the subject. "I'm going to run a couple errands today. I thought I would pick up more of those Tayto sandwiches. You seemed to enjoy it last night, and they'll keep so we can have some on hand for you to eat anytime. Is there anything else that sounds good to you?"

"Nah, that'll be grand."

"Well, let me know if you think of anything. Oh, and I have something else you might like. I have to go back through my room to get it and then show the guard so I can bring it in to you."

Having eaten one of Mags's scones herself, Garda Doyle readily approved the snack and sealed playing cards for delivery to Brian's room. Brian actually looked excited about the scone and began munching on it while Cate broke open the deck and they negotiated what game to play.

She said, "I know how to play Gin Rummy, King's Corners, Go Fish, War, Five Card Draw... uh... I think that's it,"

"Gin Rummy it is, then," Brian reached for the cards and slowly began to shuffle.

"Are there any Irish card games?"

"Ah, yeah. My parents would play Spoil-Five at home and everyone played it down at the pub."

"Can you teach me?"

"I'd need a refresher course myself."

"What's the main objective of it?"

Brian looked pensive. "It's a trick taking game. There's a trump suit, and it's called Spoil-Five because the Irish word cúig means both five and trick. You want to take at least one trick, or three of five, or, if you can, take all five tricks. But, of course, everyone else is trying to prevent that by taking at least one, which is why it's called Spoil-Five. The red and the black suits are ranked in opposite orders. And there's robbing, jinking, and rejigging."

"Wow, that doesn't sound like something I could learn in one sitting."

He began dealing for Gin Rummy, "Neither could I."

They played three hands before Brian said he'd had enough. "Quitting while you're ahead?" Cate harumphed at his fifty-point lead.

"It's the one single way I am ahead," he replied, gathering the cards and squaring them up.

Cate frowned sympathetically. "Alright, then, I'm going to make like a baby and head out." She hoped the little joke would cheer Brian up, but he only winced. She continued, "I'll run my errands and see you in a while. It'll be at least a couple hours, so go ahead and get the guard to order room service when you get hungry."

"Right. Thanks, Cate."

In her room, she received a text message update from Ellie. They were on the road and expected to arrive at Cate's house in the evening, which would be well after midnight in Ireland. Cate texted a reply to Ellie and an update to Becky, then rewrote her to-do list, tucked it in her pocket, and left the hotel. She started out with a brisk walk for exercise, looping through the streets. This took her by the charity shop where she bought the juice glass. She perused the books and selected two paperback novels that were being sold four for one euro. This was only her second cash purchase in Ireland and again, she felt distinctly foreign because the money was unfamiliar and required extra attention. She rarely used cash at home anymore, and almost never had coins on hand except for a couple quarters she kept in the console of her car to use for the shopping carts at Aldi.

The single European euro existed in coin form only, rather than paper, and felt as strange to her as using a dollar coin would in the U.S. She had to look carefully at the coins she had with her to make sure of what she was handing over to the shopkeeper. The euros she pulled from the pocket of her shoulder bag had numbers printed on one side and images on the other. The image was selected by whichever European Union country had minted the coin, so that side of the coin didn't help her to know what the denomination was. The one-euro coins had a silver-colored center surrounded by a gold-colored ring. The two-euro coins were slightly larger with an opposite arrangement of a gold center with silver outer ring. Using cash in Ireland, she realized, was one more thing that she had to think about consciously rather than do on autopilot as she did at home. Those types of little attention demands gave her a fresh view of her surroundings, but they were cumulatively tiring. The shopkeeper took Cate's euro and gave her back a fifty-cent coin that was almost the same size as the euro, but all gold in color. It seemed counterintuitive and Cate realized her own value system expected gold colors to indicate higher values than silver, even though she knew the coins weren't real gold or silver. With American coins, it was size that indicated value. The bigger the coin, the more it was worth, except for dimes. Dimes always disturbed her sense of order for that reason. They were like Mercury, the smallest planet if you didn't count Pluto, though Pluto definitely deserved planetary status and she still had hurt feelings about its demotion. And dimes had a Mercury head design in the first part of the twentieth century, which seemed fitting for this unexpectedly small coin. Her musings about coins were the types of thoughts her mind played with when she wasn't preoccupied by life and death issues of murders, pandemics, and nursing care.

Cate found she'd wandered several blocks not paying much attention to where she was going. She changed course and headed back toward the library. As she passed through its doors, she was pleased to see that the Bunclody library was truly thriving. It was even busier today than yesterday, and a group of elementary school-aged children was engaged by Fiona in a glass-walled activity room. Cate returned to the microforms section and perused the drawer that should hold the articles she wanted to read. The cards were still missing. She flipped through the adjacent microfiche cards again, as if she and Fiona both might have repeatedly missed spotting them slightly out of place. No luck, of course. Cate inhaled the familiar scent of the library as she sighed, wondering what to do next.

She pulled a small stack of microfiche cards from the issues of *The People* newspaper that were still in the drawer and seated herself at the reader to scan the local news in the months following Tim Dooley's murder. National and international political articles splashed across the front page of each issue. Most other content described happenings in Dublin, while small-town local news was printed toward the back of each issue and she found the unfamiliar place names challenging. She scanned rapidly, trying not to get distracted as she looked for any references to the murder, but she found nothing. She sighed as she placed the cards in the return basket, then she randomly took out a few more cards to spot check late 1970.

Cate placed one of the new cards in the reader and shifted the pointer to the index image. The movement on the screen caused her a mild wave of dizziness and she smiled at the strange thrill of it. She thought, "This gives me everything I could ever want from an amusement park ride. I have no use for roller coasters. Just give me a quiet corner of the library with last-century tech and I'm a happy nerd."

A name caught her attention in her distracted scanning: Jack Dooley. She backed up to the beginning of the article and read about 21-year-old Jack Dooley from Gorey being arrested in Dublin for the "serious offences of armed robbery, kidnapping, and assault." On his way home late at night, Dublin publican Donal Clarke was attacked, beaten, and left seriously injured. The article indicated that two other local business owners had recently met with similar misfortunes.

Gorey was only a few miles from Bunclody, and this Jack Dooley would be about the same age as the Jack Dooley who bought her a drink in the pub. Could it be the same person? If so, was this a family with criminal ties? Had the gardaí ever considered a suspect other than Brian for Tim Dooley's murder? If Billy reported seeing Brian flee the murder scene, and Brian then disappeared, maybe the gardaí never even looked for anyone else. Cate snapped a photo of the article with her phone's camera then began to scan later issues looking for follow-ups to Jack Dooley's arrest.

She was interrupted by her cellphone vibrating in her pocket. Mags's contact information displayed on the screen. No other patrons were close by so Cate answered it softly, "Hi, Mags."

"Hello, dear, what's the story? You don't sound yourself."

She kept her voice low, "I'm being quiet because I'm in the library. Is everything okay?"

"No worse than before. I'll meet you and we'll go to see Mick. Aiden must be allowed to see Brian. I'm just at the pub. It will take a few minutes to get to you and we'll walk to the garda station."

"Um, okay. See you soon." Well, if Aiden was allowed to see Brian it might give Cate a chance to bring up the missing microfiche.

As she disconnected the call, she considered how she could keep these microfiche cards from going missing too. She looked around her carefully. No other patrons were in sight. "If I leave these cards in the return basket, they have a good chance of disappearing," she thought. "So, do I put them back where they belong, or do I put them where I know I'll be able to find them next time?"

If she squirreled them away for safekeeping, they were as good as lost – to everyone but her. She felt almost unbearably naughty for doing it, but it seemed like the best decision. She gathered the cards she had used, plus the next two years of issues and placed the whole stack behind a group of old books on a nearby shelf. She used her phone to take a photo of the shelf and edited it to draw a highlighted circle around the hiding place.

She checked around again to see if anyone might have witnessed what she did, then she sat at one of the workstations for a few minutes to calm down and give Mags time to make her way to the library. She tried to distract herself from her guilty feelings by reviewing new messages from Ellie and Becky. Her sweet friend had left a spare key to Cate's house for Ellie and stocked the fridge with some basics so the road-weary travelers wouldn't have to worry about a grocery store run right away. She had also sent Cate a photo of a beautiful flower arrangement she left on the kitchen island as a welcome.

You're amazing! Thank you so much! Cate texted Becky, followed by three heart emojis. Then she gathered her things and made her way toward the exit to meet Mags. As she neared the circulation desk, she noticed the middle-aged male librarian from her last visit and was shocked to also recognize him from the hotel this morning. He was the man who was with Anna Dooley, the one who had looked familiar to her when she almost ran into them. Fiona had said his name... Scott. Was Scott a Dooley? He was with Anna this morning and they seemed to be taking care of some business together. Mags said Anna supplied the hotel restaurant, and the company name painted on her delivery truck was Dooley and Sons. Was Scott her son? It was possible. He was the right age. Cate felt a dropping sensation in her stomach and her cheeks flushed hot. What if she had happened to ask Scott for help with the microfiche instead of Fiona? How incredibly uncomfortable that would have been!

Cate passed the circulation desk just as Scott finished helping a library patron whose departure cleared the line of site between them. Cate felt the jolt of eye contact, and she struggled to maintain a neutral expression as she hurried on her way. Out of the corner of her eye she saw his expression change again to anger and distaste.

As she reached the sidewalk, she realized she had been holding her breath. She let it out then drew in several deep, calming breaths as Mags arrived.

"You alright, pet?"

Cate rolled her eyes, "One of the librarians, a guy named Scott. He was with Anna Dooley at the hotel this morning. Is he a Dooley too?"

Mags nodded, "Yeh."

"The company name on Anna's delivery truck is Dooley and Sons. Is he one of them? Her sons?"

"O'course, o'course," Mags shrugged.

"Well that's uncomfortable." It suddenly occurred to Cate that Aiden might not be responsible for the missing microfiche. What was in those missing newspaper articles that would make Aiden or Scott want to keep her from seeing them?

Mags said, "I told you the Dooleys are all over County Wexford. Reach out in a pub and you'll touch one. Leg it now, dear, Mick's expecting us."

"Speaking of the Detective Sergeant," Cate looked carefully around to ensure no one was close enough to hear, "If you're going to convince Rooney to let Aiden see Brian, you're going to have to tell him that Brian is not Mary Margaret's father."

"Yeh."

"But Brian is conflicted about letting that be known. He only just learned that Claire named him and he said he doesn't want to make her known as a liar."

"That's why I'm going to tell Mick. The time for secrets is over. I do love my brother dearly, but Aiden has suffered his whole life because of a lie his granny told. In my heart, he will always be my own great-nephew, and he deserves to speak to Brian, to hear truth from him even if it's a more painful tale than the lie itself. If we delay, I fear it might happen that we would lose Brian, and Aiden would never know the truth from him. He is so frail!" Mags's voice became breathy as she stifled tears.

Lorcan greeted them inside the garda station with a mask on his face. He gave one to Mags as Cate took her own from her pocket and put it on.

"What's this about?" Mags frowned.

"Protection from the virus," Lorcan replied.

"It was one of the terms I agreed to in taking care of Brian," Cate reassured her. "All around the world now, healthcare workers, police, firefighters, pretty much anyone who provides care to the public is wearing masks to try to slow the spread. And it will help keep those people well so they can continue taking care of others."

Lorcan led them to Rooney's office. The Detective Sergeant was sitting behind his desk with a number of paper file folders strewn before him, but he was tapping on his keyboard. He closed the files as the two women entered and placed a mask on his face while motioning them to sit, "What is it now, Mags?"

"Mick," Mags settled herself into the chair and launched right in, "It's just become known to me that Brian is not the father of Mary Margaret Atley, and that means he is not Aiden's grand-da."

Rooney straightened his spine and lowered his chin to look at her over his reading glasses. "And how did you acquire this information?"

"I sussed it out meself from a conversation about Aiden."

"A conversation with whom?"

"That I cannot tell you now."

His eyes narrowed, "Would it be your brother?"

"Oh, Mick, you know Brian's incarcerated. I haven't seen or talked to him since he was here in the station."

The two women waited and watched while Rooney weighed the information then asked, "And what is it you want from me?"

Mags replied without hesitating, "We want to take Aiden to see Brian so he can tell him the truth himself."

Rooney sputtered, "What in God's name!... Brian is a murder suspect in custody, not a visiting celebrity taking tea with his fans."

Cate saw his words land with physical force, tightening the lines around Mags's eyes and twitching up the tension in her shoulders. Then her eyes glistened with tears as she softly said, "Mick, I know it's asking a lot, but all of us are suffering now. Myself, Aiden, Brian, even poor Cate here being dragged into all this misery. If we can clear up just one part of it, it would help us heal. Won't you let us try?"

Rooney shook his head without meeting her eyes. Instead he turned to Cate, "You've seen the anger in the lad. I know of your dealings with him. It's not safe to allow Aiden near Brian. It's not safe!"

"Oh, Mick," Mags stifled a sob, lowered her head in concentration to pull herself together, then faced him again. "You've known me all your life, and both our families have suffered deeply. It's your job to find the truth in all this, and this is a part of it. I'm asking you to please let that truth be known. We don't know how long Brian will..." her voice trailed away again, overtaken with emotion, and then she cleared her throat and said plainly, "Me brother's health may not hold."

Rooney leaned back in his chair. He let the silence build discomfort while he took his time considering, then he said, "Here is what will happen. Ms. Jenks, you will return to your patient. I will find Aiden. If he agrees to see Brian, I will bring him to the hotel. Mags, you will go home, or wherever you like, but this is not a family reunion."

"Maybe Brian should have his solicitor there," Cate suggested.

"No," Rooney replied immediately, "Brian is not being questioned. He is a detained suspect who is being granted the privilege of a visitor and as such has no right to privacy. Same as if he were in my holding cell. Everything he says will be monitored. I have your mobile, Ms. Jenks."

"Thank you, Mick," Mags sagged with relief. "We're truly grateful. Come on, Cate." She stood abruptly and urged Cate out of Rooney's office as if she feared he would change his mind.

Cate paused.

"Cate?" Mags beckoned from the doorway. "Let's let him get on with his day."

"Detective Sergeant?" Cate began carefully, "I've been reading old newspapers from when Timothy Dooley was killed, and I was wondering about the investigation that occurred."

"What of it?"

"Well, like, I was wondering who else was considered a suspect, in addition to Brian?"

Rooney's eyes narrowed, "Brian Atley was the only individual witnessed at the scene of the crime, and he fled. He made himself the prime suspect and remained so throughout the investigation."

"Yes, but why would he have come back if he was guilty? And, um… well, I read an article from 1970, just a year later, about a man from Gorey who was charged with armed robbery and kidnapping. Isn't Gorey close by?"

"What would that have to do with Tim Dooley's murder?"

"The man who was arrested was named Jack Dooley. Is there any chance he was a relative of Tim Dooley's?"

Rooney's expression was tight, "Jack Dooley is Tim Dooley's cousin. His criminal history is well known and unrelated to the murder that occurred in Bunclody. Ms. Jenks, do you think you're starring in an American movie? Do you think that the whole Irish investigation has only needed your remarkable reasoning skills to finally break this case?"

Cate flushed with embarrassment, "No. And I don't mean to come off like that at all. It's just that Brian seemed so genuinely surprised by the charges that I can't imagine it's an act. So, I wondered if other possibilities had been considered." Fearing she was jeopardizing Rooney's decision to let Brian meet with Aiden, she added, "I'm not questioning the competence of the investigators."

"You must be taking the piss, Mick." Mags stepped between them, "Don't give out at Cate. If you're so sure me brother's guilty, go find Aiden so we can at least get him settled."

Rooney held his ground before sighing and shaking his head, "Go on then, Mags."

Wide-eyed, Cate didn't say another word until they were outside the station. As they removed their masks she exhaled sharply, "Oh shit, Mags. I'm so sorry. I was trying to help, really."

"You are helping, dear."

"By insulting Rooney? I don't think so."

Mags put her arm across Cate's shoulders and gave a squeeze, "It does my heart good to hear how you care for my brother."

Cate was unaccustomed to hugs these days and leaned in awkwardly to mirror the affection. "Do you think this is a good idea, though? Brian talking to Aiden in front of Rooney without Clodagh there?"

"It can't be helped," Mags sounded certain and squeezed Cate's shoulders again before releasing her, "Go to Brian and talk sense to him before Mick and Aiden get there. You will have to make sure he doesn't make things worse for himself. I'm sorry, pet. I wish I could be there, too. And now, I've got to go talk to Aiden and make sure he'll go with Mick."

"No pressure," Cate thought to herself.

Chapter 13

Brian was dozing in the blue wingback chair. Cate started her assessment without disturbing him. His coloring was pale, especially his lips, but his breathing was not unusually labored. She woke him gently, calling his name then patting his forearm softly as she spoke continuously, increasing her volume until she broke through his sleep, "Hey, Brian, it's Cate. I need you to wake up so I can do your medical check. Wake up, okay? We need to do a few things, Brian. Hey, Brian."

His eyelids snapped open and his eyes rolled in alarm, "Whuh?" His startled hands flapped tremulously and Cate pulled her own hand away until he became fully alert. Even the mildest people might wake up swinging their fists, and it only took getting clipped by a patient once for her to become permanently careful of this moment.

"Hey, it's Cate. I need you to wake up."

"I am awake." He rubbed his eyes, "What time is it?"

"It's after three." She checked his vital signs and prepared his breathing treatment. "Listen, some things have happened, and I need to bring you up to speed." She used the few minutes his mouth was blocked by the nebulizer to tell him about Mags revealing to Rooney that Brian denied fathering Mary Margaret. As expected, Brian disengaged the mouthpiece to shout a protest but Cate cut him off, "Brian, don't! You've got to stay calm. I don't know how long it will take for Rooney to find Aiden and get here. Let's assume it could be any minute now. Mags is very worried about Aiden, and she's worried about you too. So she got special permission from Rooney for Aiden to visit you and finally know the truth. The thing is, it's not going to be a private conversation. Rooney is going to be here too, to supervise and make sure Aiden doesn't get violent."

Brian scowled but kept the nebulizer in his mouth.

"You will need to be very careful about what you say because Rooney is going to be listening. I already asked if you could have Clodagh here, but he won't allow it since you're not being questioned."

Brian nodded and his shoulders slumped a little.

"Listen," Cate advised, "You can turn Aiden away. You don't have to talk to him. I didn't feel like I could tell Mags what a bad idea this is, but I am telling you."

The whooshing hum of the machine continued. When the medicine in it ran out, Cate shut it off. Brian rinsed his mouth before speaking. He was unusually calm as he stated, "I will see him."

Cate signaled a thumbs up to the camera indicating to Garda Doyle that Brian was medically stable, then she disassembled and cleaned the nebulizer while she considered how to respond. "What you say could make things a lot worse for you."

"But I could make some of it right for Aiden, at least. All these years, his whole life, he's been thinking I abandoned his granny and his mam. He's got my name, for God's sake, and I never knew he existed. He needs to know that I didn't get Claire pregnant."

"So," Cate replied carefully, "If you weren't responsible for Claire's pregnancy, and you didn't kill Tim Dooley, why did you run?"

Brian's expression changed, and he looked stubborn again, "I had my reason and it had nothing to do with any of this."

She spread her hands, palms out, in a gesture of peace, "Look, you don't have to tell me, but that answer certainly doesn't make you sound innocent."

"Cate, I knew my leaving hurt people and I came back here at the end of my life to make amends, to try to heal old wounds, not to make new ones. I had no idea of all the stories people made up against me while I was gone. I'm not Mary Margaret's father, and I didn't kill Tim Dooley or Billy Collins, plain and simple."

Two quick knocks sounded on the suite's door as Rooney called from the other side, "Coming in!" The door opened immediately to reveal the Detective Sergeant with Aiden a step behind him, masks covering the lower halves of their faces. Cate glimpsed Rowan Ryan in the hallway behind them as Rooney entered the room and held the door for Aiden to follow. The young man's eyes flashed as he glared angrily at Brian. Rooney pulled a visitor chair from its place at the table and positioned it halfway across the room from Brian.

"Sit there," he commanded Aiden who reluctantly lowered himself onto the chair. "Ms. Jenks, you will monitor from your room." Cate stepped through the doorway but maintained a clear line of sight to Brian and Aiden. Rooney left the suite's door open behind him and remained standing.

Cate thought, "He's controlling the space and keeping it safe, putting himself and me at the exits so neither of us will get stuck in there if one of them gets rowdy. Brian is exposed, but Rooney and the other two gardaí will be able to stop Aiden if he attacks him."

"Aiden Atley," Rooney began, "This is Brian Atley, the man you have been told is your grandfather. Brian, here," he pointed with an open, flat hand, "Says that is not true. As you know, he stands accused of the murders of Timothy Dooley and Billy Collins. I have granted this special visitation today so that he can tell you his side of the story. Both of you will keep your tempers in check or you'll find the meeting over."

"O'course," Brian replied. Aiden did not speak; he stared malevolently at Brian who cast his eyes downward and began, "Well, ah.... you may not believe me, but this is all very sudden. I have only just learned that Claire, er, your granny named me." He finally raised his eyes to Aiden's, "But there is no possibility that I am your grandfather. She and I were never together that way. I hope it will ease your anger to know that."

"Is that it?" Aiden spat back, "That's what I came here for? To hear me murdering, lying grandda call me granny a liar? How would that 'ease my anger,' as you say?"

"It's the truth."

"Jaysus!" Aiden gasped, "You take me for a feckin' eejit. Why would she ever have named you if it weren't true? What could she have gained by it?" He put on a mocking falsetto voice, "Oh, me oul' one's knocked me up and kilt the neighbor and now run out in me time of need."

"You're no eejit, and neither was your granny," Brian sighed. "She must have believed that naming the true father would have been worse for her and her child."

Aiden's expression of contempt faltered and surprise flickered for a moment before he gathered his rage again. With fists clenching on his knees he challenged Brian, "So, she's dead and gone now with no chance to defend herself. You can puke lies all over her memory. Go ahead now, who really was my grandda?"

Brian remained calm and, to Cate, his voice sounded sad, "Your granny told me of her troubles. We were dear friends. I was only ever her friend, and she swore me to secrecy. I will keep her secret because it's not mine to tell."

Aiden looked dangerously explosive, "Fookin' shite hawk! You're tryin' to make me into a murderer to follow in yer footsteps." He rocked back and forth in his seat as if beginning to spring up, then changing his mind, then starting again.

"Leave off, lad!" Rooney warned. Aiden glared at him, then hunkered down in the chair with his fists clenched.

Brian coughed and raised a palm begging a pause as he turned up the dial on his oxygen concentrator. He took several breaths and exhaled through pursed lips, then continued, "I only tried to help her. And after I was gone, I suppose she named me so that my family might step in. Truly in that way, you and I are related. We just don't share blood."

Aiden's tone was sarcastic again, "It's a heartwarming tale. You come off all honorable, with my granny long dead and unable to say otherwise. How convenient! If you're innocent, why did ye run?"

Cate thought, "Be careful, Brian." She wished Clodagh was here to step in. She could see Rooney's laser-sharp attention as he observed the interaction. This was a completely legal interrogation by proxy.

"Why I left is my own business," Brian coughed again, paused, then continued, "I never killed anyone, and I am not your grandda. I'm not going to beg you to believe me, but I promise I've told you the truth. It is also true that I finally came home to make amends to the family that I hurt by leaving, and I realize I had no understanding of the many wounds that occurred while I was gone. I don't have much time left, and I doubt if I can fix anything before I die. I do hope that hearing the truth will help you somehow, someday, even if you can't accept it today."

"Gobshite," Aiden sneered.

"Um, it would be easy to prove," Cate offered from the doorway of her room. All eyes were immediately on her. "DNA testing. It doesn't have to be anything fancy. You can use one of those genealogy websites. If you both register and submit a sample, the results will show if you're related or not." She realized she was painting Brian into a corner. If he was telling the truth she was helping to exonerate him, but if he was lying she was forcing his hand. "We can collect both your samples here, with all of us witnessing so everyone knows it's done right. You know, with chain of custody intact. Brian, if you'll pay for expedited processing, we should be able to get an answer in just a few days."

She was watching Brian's face, but her eyes flicked momentarily to Rooney when he made an appreciative noise, "Huh."

Brian didn't look uneasy at all. "Of course!" he replied eagerly, then broke into a fit of coughing. Cate felt her knees weaken in relief as her confidence in her friend recovered significantly. When his coughing eased, Brian asked Aiden, "Will you do it, lad?"

"Yeh," he muttered, with his eyes still narrowed suspiciously.

"I can find a DNA service now, if that's alright with everyone," Cate suggested.

"Garda Ryan will assist you." Rooney motioned Rowan to enter the room, and the young guard walked briskly past Brian and Aiden into Cate's quarters. She booted up her laptop and together they searched and identified a prominent genealogy site that would provide service to their location. They created accounts for both Atley men.

"There," Cate announced after typing in the account number from the credit card Brian had given her for the trip. "We should receive the collection kits tomorrow. We can overnight the specimens back and they guarantee results in three days or less."

"Then we're done here for today," Rooney announced, and Cate and Brian were soon alone in his room.

Cate flopped into a chair feeling quite exhausted. "Man! I've been all over this town today and I never made it back to the Eurospar for snacks. We'll have to order room service for your dinner. Is there anything that appeals to you tonight?"

Brian was deep in thought and seemed startled by her question, "Hmm? Oh. Well. Now that you mention it, I think I could eat some bangers and mash."

"Really?" Cate was surprised he had an appetite and an opinion about what he ate. It told her his mood was improved after meeting with Aiden. "I'll place the order. So, how do you think things went? I know you kind of got blindsided by Aiden's visit, but you seem to be doing better than I've seen you in days."

He didn't reply right away and Cate gave him silence to consider. Finally, he said, "It is good to be able to do something. Thank you for your idea about the DNA test. At least that will get sorted out."

"You're welcome. I'm glad..." she was searching for the right words, "I guess I'm relieved you're willing to take the test."

He looked at her directly and acknowledged, "I know you have no reason to trust me when everyone else says I've done these terrible things. Thank you for entertaining the possibility that I'm innocent."

She smiled wryly as she picked up the room service menu, "Yeah, so please don't make me regret it."

Now that Brian had mentioned it, bangers and mash sounded wonderful and Cate ordered the same for herself. When the food arrived, a knock sounded on the door, then it opened and a man's voice called, "Your dinner's here."

"Hello, Garda O'Malley," Cate stood and received the tray he passed to her.

"How are ye keeping? There's a second tray out here for ye, too."

"Good, thank you," she placed Brian's tray on the table beside his chair, then retrieved the other from O'Malley's station in the hallway. She carried it through to her own room then returned as he was addressing Brian, "How are ye, Mr. Atley?"

"Grand," he replied flatly.

"Glad to hear it. Enjoy your dinner," and to Cate he reminded her, "I'll be here overnight. Do keep me informed of your medical checks so I can record them."

"Of course. Can we order you some dinner too?"

"Ah, thanks but no, I've already had mine."

She remembered the Irish manners and offered a second time, "Something sweet then? There's a bread pudding on the menu."

"Ah, no, truly, I couldn't."

"Then some tea?"

"Maybe later, thank you."

Cate was relieved. One of the last websites she had reviewed about Irish etiquette stated that if the third offer is declined, she didn't have to push it further, and the hot bangers and mash on Brian's tray smelled so good she only wanted to get to her own room to enjoy hers. Brian turned on an Irish news channel, so she pulled the door between their rooms almost completely shut and turned on some music.

She settled herself in her chair and uncovered her plate to behold the steaming, fragrant comfort meal awaiting her. There were two sausages, the bangers, nestled into a mountain of mashed potatoes. A brown onion gravy pooled across it all, and a scattering of green peas brightened the plate opposite the bangers. Cate anchored one of the sausages with her fork. As the tines pressed into the its skin, she heard a cracking sound and glistening juices flooded out into the surrounding potato. She trimmed off the end of the sausage, used it to scoop up a bit of potato and gravy, and put the whole forkful into her mouth. It was exquisitely soft, rich, and salty. "How am I not going to eat all of this?" she wondered aloud.

Thirty minutes later, she had managed to restrain herself a little. Almost half of her meal was still on the plate but she hadn't stopped picking, just one more bite even though she felt full, and then another. "I have to stop," she laid the silverware down, covered the plate, and moved the whole tray off to the side.

She took out her phone and called Mags, who answered immediately, "What's the story, dear?"

"Hi, Mags."

"Yeah go on, and don't skimp on the details."

"Well, when Aiden arrived, he was wound so tight I thought there was going to be trouble, but Rooney warned him to settle down. Brian was calm. Actually, he did very well. You know, he's a bit of a hot head too, and I was worried he was going to say something that might incriminate himself. But he told Aiden that he was not his grandfather and that he and Claire had been loyal friends. He suggested that was probably why Claire named him, so that the Atley family would help her. He was also quite kind to Aiden, and said that while they were not related by blood, they are part of the same family. I'm probably not quoting him exactly right, but that was the gist of it. We're going to follow up with DNA testing from a genealogy service to prove whether or not they're related. I don't know if the meeting was helpful to Aiden, but it certainly seemed to help Brian. I'd say it gave him peace."

"Oh, Cate, you're a dear one to help sort this mess. You've brought peace to me too. And I think it did help Aiden. He seems doubtful now of his granny's story."

"You've seen him?"

"O'course! I was waiting when Mick turned him loose."

Cate chuckled, "I shouldn't be surprised."

"No, you should not. Aiden needed someone to be with him, and he's still my great-nephew, no matter what. The truth of his parentage doesn't change it. He needs family now more than ever."

"Mags, you are a treasure."

"And so are you, pet. Now, you haven't told me that Brian named Mary Margaret's father."

"He did not."

"Did Aiden ask?"

Cate thought carefully, "Yes, but Brian said he had promised to keep the secret. Also, Aiden asked Brian why he ran, and he wouldn't answer."

Both women reflected in concerned silence, then Mags said brightly, "Well, it can't be helped. Let's all get some rest and see what the morning brings."

"That's an excellent idea. Good night, Mags."

"Good night, dear."

Cate ended the call and scrolled through her text messages and emails. She was beginning to wind down when Brian cried out to her from the next room, "Cate! Come here!"

He'd never called to her like that. She hurried, slipping the mask on her face as she darted through the doorway, "What's wrong?"

He was staring at the television, "They're shutting down the whole country."

"What do you mean?"

"It's because of that virus. They're shutting everything down. Listen."

Together they watched the news report that showed excerpts of the announcement from the Taoiseach, the Prime Minister. "We need to flatten the curve and suppress this virus. So, I am asking you to stay home if at all possible. That is the best way to slow the virus, ensure our hospitals are not overwhelmed and buy us the time we need to build more capacity for testing, contact tracing, beds, ventilators. So, you should only leave home to go to work if you can't work from home and your attendance is essential. You should only go to the shops for essential supplies, out for medical or dental appointments, to care for others or to take physical exercise.

"We are in this for long haul. This could go on for weeks or months and we need to maintain our humanity, we need to see our families and loved ones and look after our mental and physical health. And we can do it if we maintain a physical distance of two metres or more."

A female news anchor appeared and described that additional restrictions would take effect the following day, then the video cut back to the Taoiseach's announcement, "No unnecessary travel should take place within the country or overseas, now or over the Easter break. All theatres, clubs, gyms, leisure centres, hairdressers, betting shops, marts, markets, casinos, bingo halls, libraries and other similar outlets are to shut. All hotels are to limit occupancy to essential non-social and non-tourist reasons. All non-essential retail outlets are to close to members of the public and all other retail outlets are to implement physical distancing; essential shops have been identified. All cafes and restaurants are to limit supply to take away food or delivery. All sporting events are cancelled, including those behind closed doors. All playgrounds and holiday and caravan parks will close. All places of worship are to restrict numbers entering at any one time to ensure adequate physical distancing. All organised social indoor and outdoor events of any size are not to take place."

"Wow," Cate was stunned, "That changes everything."

"For me, not so much, but for you and everyone else," Brian shook his head. "I'm sorry I've trapped you here, Cate."

"The travel ban started two days ago. I had already decided to stay and notified my work, but I didn't think it would last very long. Didn't he just say it would be at least until after Easter? And now they're going into full lockdown."

Brian's eyes grew glassy with tears and he choked on his words, "Ah, Cate, you stayed to help me." Then he cleared his throat, "Of course, I'll continue to pay you as long as you're stuck here."

"Brian, that would become very expensive."

"The only thing I don't have to worry about is money. I told you, I've saved all my life and now I don't have much time left to spend it. Besides, my needs are limited. What I do need is you. You looking after me for a while longer, and I'm just so damn grateful you decided to stay." His voice disappeared into a silent sob, and he covered his eyes with his hand. Cate patted his shoulder then retrieved a handful of tissues for him. Brian collected himself, blotting his eyes, snorting and honking into the tissues, then glanced at her indirectly, "Sorry."

"What's a little snot between friends," she joked. Brian sputtered involuntarily and laugh-cried into the tissues even more. Then they sat quietly, listening to the news program that repeated the headline story with additional details. She mentally inventoried their needs and current supplies. The only food they had was a couple aging scones, one Tayto sandwich kit, some cashews, and mineral water. It sounded like they would be able to get takeout meals from restaurants, and food stores would be allowed to remain open. Cate was familiar with supply chain interruptions caused by hurricanes, but those were quite localized, compared to a pandemic. When a hurricane barreled across Florida, whole swaths of the state might be heavily damaged, but there were always fleets of utility trucks deployed from across the nation to clear fallen debris and restore power. Water and groceries were delivered to those in need. But with a global pandemic, who would be left unaffected and able to send help? Everyone would suffer similarly and simultaneously, so individuals or small groups might have only themselves on which to rely. Fortunately, there were a few people in the town who had good will toward Brian, and Cate by extension.

As the news coverage began to repeat itself, she decided to go do some scouting. She crossed back into her room and prepared to go out. In the hallway, she checked in with Garda O'Malley, "Have you heard the Taoiseach's latest announcement about shutting things down?"

"Ah, sure. We had early notice."

"That makes sense. I'm going to go out for a bit. Do you think it will be safe?"

O'Malley's eyebrows rose, "Er, yeh, you're dressed warm enough, I suppose."

"I mean, do the gardaí expect trouble with the lockdown starting tomorrow? Is there any concern about looting or rioting?"

O'Malley chuckled, "Rioting in Bunclody?"

"I guess not, then." Cate felt heat rising in her cheeks and was glad to have the mask covering her face, "Where I come from it's a reasonable question. I just didn't want to unknowingly walk into a bad situation."

O'Malley's expression shifted subtly, and as Cate realized the irony of what she said her face flushed even hotter, "Another bad situation. Jeez." She threw her hands in the air in exasperation, "I'm going to stop talking now."

He chuckled again as she stalked toward the elevator, tucking the mask into her pocket. Downstairs, the lobby was empty except for hotel staff. Rose was placing a strip of painter's tape on the floor several feet away from the reception desk. "Hello, Rose," Cate called.

"Good evening, Ms. Jenks," the young woman replied as she stood then moved behind the desk. "Please remain behind that line. It's one of the new rules for distancing."

Cate backed up so that her toes were fully behind the tape. "It looks like I'm going to be staying on in Bunclody as long as the travel ban lasts. And I just heard the announcement on TV about the lockdown within Ireland. The hotel will remain open, won't it?"

"Yes it will, thanks to Mr. Atley being moved here, and you staying with him. That makes the hotel an essential non-tourism service. We'll be running a skeleton crew since there won't be the same comings and goings as usual."

"Oh, I see." Cate had a heavy feeling this was the very beginning of rapid change, "Will the restaurant serve meals?"

"That has not been determined yet," Rose replied, wide-eyed. "Management will be meeting in the morning. It's a sure thing there'll be no table service, but takeaway is still allowed so we may be able to do room service too."

"Good." Cate was relieved. "Can you let me know when a decision is made?"

"Certainly."

"Thanks. Also, I'm going to need to do laundry now and then. Does the hotel offer laundry services?"

"Normally yeh but that will stop tomorrow due to the new health and safety guidelines. There's concern of contagion. But there are two launderettes on Main Street you can use as long as they stay open. There are also self-serve machines outside the petrol station."

"Okay, thank you."

Cate made her way to the hotel bar. Its stools had been moved into a corner of the room so there was no seating directly at the bar, but there were chairs at the tables. Aiden's tall friend was shifting things around and cleaning. There were no other customers, so Cate projected her voice from the doorway, "Hello, Arek."

"Hello, Cate." He seemed cheered to have someone to talk to, "What can I get for you?"

"Are you still open?"

"Only for tonight," he waved her to come in. "What can I get you?"

"A mineral, thanks."

"Are you sure? This will be the last time I will be able to serve you anything. After close, I do not know when the bar will open again."

"I heard about the shutdown. And you make a good point: this will be my last chance for a Prince's martini for a while. I'll take both then, the martini and the mineral."

"Right," he poured the mineral, brought it to her table and placed it before her then returned to the bar. She watched the tiny streams of shimmering bubbles rise to the surface while he prepared her cocktail. Cate wondered what would happen to Arek if the lockdown lasted for an extended period. "Do you only tend the bar here?"

"Only?"

"I mean, I know that they're shutting so many services for the public. Is tending bar your only job? Or do you have other duties that will continue?"

"Nobody knows what is going to happen," he shrugged as he brought the martini to her.

"Ain't that the truth," she took a sip. "I'm going to miss the Prince's martinis, and this bar." Cate looked around, only just now realizing how true her statement was. He nodded in agreement then shrugged again, and she could tell the uncertainty weighed heavily on him. She reflected with her drink for the next half hour, during which time no one else entered the bar except for Rose with hotel business. Then with the martini warmth in her cheeks, Cate left the hotel and strolled the streets of Bunclody.

"It really is a sweet little town," she thought. There were a few people in sight, and she felt safe now that Aiden had been addressed and was simmering down. She also felt toasty, bundled in her coat, and maybe a little toasted, she admitted to herself. Her thoughts wandered while her feet crisscrossed the streets. The air was cold and carried a faint tang of smoke. Maybe it was from a peat fire warming someone's house with the traditional fuel, though she wasn't sure what a peat fire would smell like. The idea didn't sound particularly appealing because peat was compressed vegetation cut from bogs. In Cate's experience, wet decomposing stuff usually didn't smell good, but the Irish had used dried peat instead of firewood for centuries. She circled her route back toward the hotel with a plan to stop in the Eurospar, but found it locked up with a hand-written sign on the door notifying that it had closed early to prepare for the new restrictions that would begin tomorrow. The lights were on inside and the employees were still at work.

"It's gonna be okay," she told herself. Then, "How on earth is it going to be okay?" She felt her mood shift as she stood on the sidewalk in the deepening darkness. What was she thinking, to not go home when they first announced the travel ban? Now access to necessities was going to be limited and here she was a stranger in a small town, in a culture that was new to her, knowing no one. Well, not no one. She knew Brian, the infamously accused murderer and absentee father. She hoped she knew him, anyway. And she knew Mags a little, and John, and even Rooney who seemed fair enough that he would help her if she needed it. And she had met Arek, and Addy, and Fiona the librarian, and Cailleach the old woman at the faery circle, and the other guards, and even the man from the car accident, who all might think of her kindly enough to help her out if money alone couldn't buy what she needed. "Don't borrow trouble," she reminded herself, as her mother used to say. It even sounded sort of Irish. "Don't borrow trouble," she thought again as she turned toward the hotel.

The stretch of sidewalk in front of the Eurospar parking lot was lighted well enough but empty of people, and the back corner where Billy Collins died was deep in shadow. Someone had killed him, and if Brian didn't do it, who did? And why? She kept her eye on the spot as she came to it, but when she passed it, she got a full-on case of the heebie-jeebies as if the killer were waiting at the scene to come running up behind her. "Don't borrow trouble," she repeated. She had had this instinctive response all her life. As a kid, if she had to go outside at night it was no problem with the lighted house at her back, to go get her shoes or the toy that had been left out. But the moment she turned to go back inside and the darkness was behind her she felt like prey. The hairs on her arms and legs would stand to raise goosebumps and she'd scamper back at full speed, feeling hands or jaws or claws flying up behind her. When she was safely inside with the door closed, the threat evaporated and left her giddy. "Act like a grownup," she chided herself. "You're going to walk back to the hotel." And she did walk back, but rather quickly.

As she came off the elevator, Cate placed the mask on her face. Garda O'Malley sat at his station with the monitoring tablet on the tabletop before him. "Ms. Jenks, what's the story? Did you join in any rioting?"

"I looked but couldn't find any. Thought I probably shouldn't be the one to start it, though," she rolled her eyes and he chuckled. "Call me Cate," she added.

"Pat," he replied.

"Seriously though, Pat, I just tried to pick up a few things at the Eurospar, but they're closed. The sign says they're getting ready for tomorrow. What's going to happen?"

"They'll be limiting the number of people allowed in at one time, so everyone'll be queuing and waiting."

"What about supplies? I guess closing early kept the store from being cleaned out."

"Yeh, that too. It wouldn't hurt to go early tomorrow if you hope to do the messages."

"Uh," Cate wasn't quite sure what he meant, "Do the messages?"

"Yeh," he nodded.

"What kind of messages?"

"Any kind you need."

"Sorry, I don't understand." What bureaucratic requirement was she going to have to take care of now?

He said slowly, as if she were a little dense, "Go to the shops and buy what you need. The shopping. That's going for the messages."

"Oh, I've never heard anyone call it that!" Cate was relieved, "Going for the messages is shopping?"

"Yeh. And what do Americans call it?"

"Uh, just shopping. Grocery shopping specifically, but any other kind is just... shopping. So I would like to do the messages in the morning. What time does the Eurospar open?"

"Eight. But go early," Pat advised.

"Thanks. Now I'm going to do Brian's medical check and get to bed."

"Right," he nodded.

"I think I'll settle in with a cup of tea. Can I bring you one too?"

"I wouldn't trouble you," he shook his head.

Irish manners, Cate reminded herself, second offer, "It's no trouble at all."

"Don't put yourself out."

Third offer, "I've got one of Mags O'Connor's homemade scones left over, too. It won't be as good tomorrow, so I'll bring it with your tea."

Pat's eyes crinkled with a smile only partially hidden beneath his mask, "That'll be grand!"

A thought occurred to her, "So, you and Garda Doyle are doing twelve-hour shifts?"

"Yeh," Pat answered.

"Who relieves you for breaks?"

"There's no relief needed, except from boredom," he laughed. "The work's not exactly strenuous. I've got this room for the jacks," he gestured behind him, "And I keep me eye on this tablet the whole time."

"That makes sense. I'll be back in a few minutes with the tea."

She wetted the tea, as the Irish say, completed her medical check on Brian while it steeped, delivered Pat's snack, then got ready for bed. As she snuggled under the duvet, her cell phone chimed a message from Ellie that they were only a couple hours away from Cate's house.

She texted back, *Good. Going to bed now knowing ur safely there. Love you.* Ellie texted back three heart emojis.

Chapter 14

Cate's alarm woke her in plenty of time to get to the Eurospar before it opened. She checked on Brian who was stable but glum again, and still touched by Cate's willingness to stay in Ireland to care for him. His resulting manner was quiet and apologetic, seeming almost on the verge of tears, and twice during her assessment he patted her hand affectionately. Then he agreed to let her order him porridge for breakfast, without any protest or substitutions. She found this docile version of him unnerving, but then he perked up a little after a few bites of food.

As he ate, Cate swept the curtains open to reveal a dense gray fog beginning to glow with morning light. She told him, "I'm going down to the store to stock up on some snacks... I mean, to do the messages."

"Listen to you, puttin' on the Oirish. It's too early for the messages. How about a couple hands of Gin Rummy instead, and I'll give you a chance to win back your money?"

"I'll take you up on that later. With the lockdown there are new restrictions on how many people can go in the store at one time, so the guard said I should get in line early. I want to have a little something for us in case there are shortages, at least a few of those Tayto sandwiches you like. Is there anything else I can bring you?"

"Nah, go on then," he huffed, and Cate was relieved he was pouting again. Just before she stepped back into her room, he said, "Bring me a newspaper when you come back. Since they won't let me have my computer, at least I can read what's what."

"Okay."

In the hallway, she greeted Garda Doyle, "Good morning."

"Howya, Ms. Jenks?" she was friendlier now.

"Please call me Cate. Brian's doing fine this morning, and I'm on my way to the Eurospar. Last night, Pat said there would be quite a wait to get in, so I might be gone a while. Is there anything you need before I go?"

"You can call me Maudy, and no, thanks, unless you happen to come by more of Mags's scones."

"I'll bring you one if I do," she promised, then made her way downstairs. She was careful exiting the elevator, feeling haunted by yesterday's stumbling confrontation with the Dooleys. She stepped deliberately over the gap between the elevator car and the floor, and checked her balance while looking all around the lobby. There were no Dooleys to plow into, just the hotel employees Moira and Hughey working behind the reception desk. Cate waved to them as she left the hotel.

The walk to the Eurospar was shorter this morning because there was a line of customers that extended all the way up the block toward her. Pieces of tape on the sidewalk indicated where they should stand so that everyone kept two meters distance between them. People were chatting loudly to accommodate the extended spaces. She took her place at the end of the line. A middle-aged woman was turned backwards, chatting with the sandy-haired man directly in front of Cate. He was speaking quickly and Cate didn't understand what he was saying, but the woman nodded while overtly looking past him and said, "Howya."

"Good morning," Cate replied.

The man then turned, looked surprised, and grudgingly greeted her, "Howya." Then the two were quiet. Others near them didn't fall completely silent, but they became noticeably less animated.

Cate wasn't sure if she could get used to this kind of attention. It felt as intensely uncomfortable as her nerdy self not fitting in in junior high school. But in this instance, people really were looking at her and judging her. She wondered, "How many of them are team Dooley and how many are team Atley? Team Atley is probably pretty small."

Two women several spots ahead were talking and gesturing at the place where Billy Collins's body had been found. Cate heard people join the end of the line behind her, but she just didn't have the nerve to turn around. The only good thing happening here was that the line was moving. Just as she was debating whether or not to stay in the line, John Kelley came into view, his long strides steadily covering ground on the other side of the street as he headed in the direction of the Green Man. He nodded, waved, and responded to greetings from almost everyone in the line. When he spotted Cate, he crossed the street to her, and she felt immense relief, though his recognition earned her even more attention.

"Howya, Cate?"

"Good morning, John."

"I can see ye've heard the news of the lockdown."

"I guess it's not too surprising. It's happening all over. My daughter lives in New York, and they're doing the same thing there."

"Well, it'll only be that much harder seeing you're away from home. Stop by the pub at lunchtime and I'll fix you up with takeaway."

Irish manners, she remembered, "Oh, thanks, but I couldn't impose."

"Nonsense, it's no trouble."

Her mind was scrambling for a second way to turn him down, "I'm sure you already have your hands full with all the changes going on today."

"Yer lunch will be packed and ready for you at noon. Don't let it get cold."

"Yes, sir," she formally accepted.

John patted her shoulder in a fatherly gesture and ambled away. The energy around her shifted to curiosity, and while no one spoke to her directly, conversation normalized. She tried not to let her relief show but inside she felt like someone had poured honey down her spine. The rest of the waiting time before she got in the store was much easier. Just before she got to the entrance, a store employee called out instructions to those within earshot, "You will have ten minutes to get what you need then you must pay up and get out. We are not allowed more than ten customers in the store so there's barely pissing time. No visiting nor lollygagging. I'm talkin' to you, Brandon." Good-natured laughter rippled through the crowd.

Soon, Cate passed through the shop's doors. Ten minutes went by all too quickly, but she ended up with a few nonperishable items that would make hearty snacks in case food supplies were limited. Since she had no stove, she chose almond butter, crackers, instant porridge, peanuts, some chocolates, a bag of apples, and a newspaper for Brian. There were no Tayto sandwich kits left. In fact, the store's shelves were already noticeably depleted. Cate made her way toward the checkout and took a spot at the end of the line, setting her feet on the tape mark that portioned out two meters' distance from others. Three registers were in use, but a single queue was structured to send the person at the head of the line to whichever register was being vacated by a customer. It took only a couple minutes for her to reach the head of the line, and a Eurospar employee directed her toward the register where a man with his back to her was walking away while maneuvering his bags and replacing his wallet in his back pocket. In his distraction, it took several tries of sliding the wallet against his hip to catch the fabric edge, and the up and down motion loosened a folded piece of paper from either the wallet or the pocket. It fell to the floor without him noticing, so Cate picked it up and called out, "Excuse me, you dropped this."

Looking down, what she found in her hand was her own to-do list that had gone missing yesterday, and the man who turned in response to her voice was Scott Dooley. A double-jolt of surprise coursed through her, first as she recognized the paper, and then when their eyes met. Dread chilled her stomach as Scott simply turned away without further acknowledgement.

"Next!" The same clerk from her first visit to the store was waiting for her to place her items on the conveyor belt. Cate wavered, looking to the clerk, then back again at Scott who in just a few steps was out the door. She was so rattled she couldn't think straight. Her groceries were rung up and she used her credit card to pay because she couldn't even begin to count out Euros. What to do with the to-do list? It felt contaminated by

Scott Dooley's possession, so she couldn't bear to put it in the pockets of her clothing. She stuffed it into the side pocket of her shoulder bag, then gathered her groceries into her shopping bag and left the store feeling incredibly exposed as she crossed to the other side of the street to make her way back to the hotel. At least there were plenty of people watching her.

How had Scott come to have her to-do list? She must have dropped it when she stumbled out of the elevator. She couldn't remember having it after that unfortunate incident, though she didn't notice it was missing until later. Why didn't he just give it back to her when she dropped it? Maybe he didn't notice it on the floor until after she had exited the hotel. Clearly, he had anger toward her so it made sense he wouldn't have bothered to help her by returning it. Everything made sense, except the fact that he kept it.

Cate kept a watchful eye on her surroundings as she walked back to the hotel, but she was burning to review the list. What did it tell Scott about her plans? It was basically an itinerary for her whole day yesterday. Is that why he held onto it? It was just so creepy that he had it. At least she had it back now.

At the hotel, Moira and Hughey were still at work behind the reception desk. Cate asked if they'd had an answer if room service would continue during the lockdown. "I'm sorry to say no," Moira informed her, "Our restaurant will be closed beginning tonight. There are only a few guests in the hotel, and it's not enough to warrant staffing and supplying the kitchen."

It seemed Cate and Brian would become heavily dependent on John's takeaways from the pub. Cate took the elevator back up to her floor and showed her purchases to Maudy. "I bought a few things to snack on, plus a newspaper for Brian. I'll store most of it in my room, but can I carry things through to Brian as needed?"

"Yeh. Just take 'em all out here so as I can see everything."

Cate removed each item from her bag for Maudy to inspect, then put it all back in. She unpacked it again in her room, creating a neat cache of goodies on the small shelf next to the tea kettle, then she carried the newspaper through to Brian. He was dozing in his chair, so she placed it on the table next to him and went back to her room. She sprawled into the chair and took the to-do list out of the side pocket of her shoulder bag. Holding it with both hands, she pinched just the corner edges between her thumbs and forefingers to avoid touching its surface. She felt icky about Scott carrying it around in his pocket, and it felt as though physical contact with the list might contaminate her further. Why did he have it in his pocket? Why not just throw it away? What did he know about her from this list? Brian assessments q4h, Check on Ellie, Notify Becky to drop off key, Laundry, Articles @ library, Charity shop for book.

If he understood medical notation he would know that she was assessing Brian every four hours. If he didn't understand it, he was a librarian so could be counted on to look it up. She assumed then that he could predict where she would be at those intervals. Her list also confirmed her interest in the articles at the library, that she would be going to a charity shop, and that she would be dealing with their laundry. Did it put her in any danger for someone who might have ill will toward her to have any of this information? Probably not, but she suddenly saw a silver lining to the cloud of being under guard.

Should she tell the guards about this strange incident? It wasn't as though Scott had stolen her to-do list. She probably dropped it in the lobby when she stumbled. But there was also the missing microfiche in the library, where Scott happened to work. It was more likely that Scott, rather than Aiden, had done something with the cards. In fact, she hadn't seen Aiden at all while she was in the library. She only saw him leave it when she was on the way back there from the garda station, but Scott was there all along. Fiona said he was at the circulation desk all day, but that didn't mean he'd been glued there the whole time. And since it turned out he had a special interest in Cate, he could easily have identified what she was researching. Two coincidences were too much. She decided she would inform Rooney, just to be safe.

She felt uncomfortable making the call, having the very human response of not wanting to make a scene, mentally talking herself into believing that she was exaggerating the threat. But, she reminded herself, "You have to listen to your gut. If it's telling you something is wrong, you have to speak up or you might end up regretting it." Alternatively, if she alerted Rooney and nothing came of it, worst case scenario was that she'd get a reputation for being a scaredy cat. "I can live with that," she reassured herself.

Rooney took her call after only a brief hold, "Ms. Jenks."

"Good morning, Detective Sergeant. I have a concern. Do you have a moment?"

"Yes, and that's all I have."

"Thanks," she forced herself not to use the wheedling words that undermined the validity what she meant to say. like 'I just...,' 'It's probably nothing...,' 'Sorry to bother you...,' Instead, she said, "I have had two unusual encounters with Scott Dooley and I want to make you aware."

"Go on."

"As I mentioned yesterday, I was researching Tim Dooley's murder at the library. The microfiche cards I was using disappeared before I could review them all. I later learned that Tim's son Scott is a librarian there. Also, yesterday I lost my handwritten to-do list. Then this morning Scott was in line in front of me at the Eurospar and dropped a piece of paper. I picked it up to give it back to him and he wouldn't speak to me, then I realized what the paper was. It was my list. I'm pretty sure I dropped it in the hotel lobby yesterday, but I'm uncomfortable that he kept it and then refused to speak. I mean, I can understand why he wouldn't want to speak to me, but I don't know why he would have kept my to-do list."

"Noted. Thank you," Rooney stated.

She could hear him shuffling file folders on his desk. He might have been blowing her off, but there was also a good chance he was overwhelmed with lockdown duties. Cate banked her irritation and asked, "Do you believe he might be dangerous? Should I be worried?"

Rooney paused, then replied, "Scott Dooley does not have any history of violence. However, he's never before been forced to suffer the return of his father's murderer. I cannot offer you further reassurance, and there are bigger problems at hand. You have a guard stationed outside your door at all times. If you feel unsafe, stay inside. That's all I can do for you now."

Was he still ticked off about her questioning the investigation? Maybe. However, Cate knew very well what it was like to juggle multiple conflicting priorities and try to maintain professionalism while one's adrenaline surged, so she cut him some slack, "I can hear how busy you are. Thanks for taking my call."

"Bye, then." He disconnected before Cate could do it herself.

"Okay, well at least he knows about it," she thought. She didn't want to stay cooped up in the room. Despite Scott being creepy, he had not threatened her person in any way, and he did not have a violent history, according to Rooney. It was understandable that he wouldn't be friendly. But unfriendly is different from dangerous. No, she was not going to imprison herself along with Brian. She was going to go out for some fresh air, just as she had each day she'd been in Bunclody with no harm done. She would take a nice walk then pick up lunch from John on her way back.

Brian was still napping so she informed Maudy of the lunch plan. "Can I bring something for you too?"

"No, thanks, I've got my lunch already with me."

Irish manners, offer number two, "I've only eaten at The Green Man a couple times, but it was excellent. Are you sure you wouldn't like a cottage pie or cheese toasty?"

"Ah, you twist my arm but I must resist," Maudy protested.

"It's no trouble, I'll just bring it along with ours." Cate wasn't used to begging people after they'd already said no.

"If I eat Addy's cooking I'll never stay awake to the end of my shift," she laughed.

"That's true," Cate agreed. "I'll definitely need a nap after lunch."

She made her way out of the hotel, again being extra careful stepping out of the elevator. There were no Dooleys in sight. Outside, a light drizzle was softly starting and Cate congratulated herself that she was beginning to get used to this Irish weather. She didn't even consider postponing her walk. Like the locals, she pulled up the hood of her water-resistant jacket and continued on. A new route seemed like a good idea. Besides, the non-essential shops were all closed now. She started away from Main Street on Church Street. As she walked, the rain began to taper off and the drips falling from the edge of her hood became less and less frequent.

St. Mary's Church was constructed from gray stone. Its pointed arches and steep rooflines contrasted with its subdued color pallet. Cate wondered how old it was as she wandered into the graveyard looking at birth and death dates on the headstones and plaques. Her footing was a little slippery on the wet path, so she went slowly and carefully, taking time to pause now and then and breathe in the rain's chill. The relative humidity made her exhalations hang in the air in visible clouds that swirled away before they disappeared. She wondered where Tim Dooley was buried. And Claire Fitzpatrick. Would they have been laid to rest here, or were there other cemeteries in Bunclody? She hadn't really intended to come to the graveyard, but when she started thinking about all the deceased people everyone else was thinking about, she decided she probably didn't need to be seen hanging out here.

She walked back to Main Street and decided to return to the faery circle, if she could find it. On the sidewalk just past the hotel, a woman walking in her direction slowed as she came near. Rather than pass by, she made eye contact and asked, "Cate Jenks?"

"Yes?" Cate thought, here we go again.

"I'm Margaret Murphy, Mags O'Connor's daughter."

"Oh, hello," Cate greeted, relieved she might have met an ally, "It's nice to meet you. I do see a family resemblance." Margaret was a larger, younger Mags.

"Yeh, people say Mam's the fun size, I'm regular."

Cate laughed and felt she might end up liking Margaret as much as she liked Mags. "Well you do look alike."

"I was hoping to run into you," Margaret chirped. "Would ask you to sit but the park's a bog now. Can we walk together instead? Where are you headed?"

"To the river," Cate didn't want to share the faery circle. They covered the distance in a few minutes and leaned their elbows on the railing to watch the water flow below them.

"Padraig said he'd met you, and I pumped him for information about our uncle Brian, but he said he hadn't even asked you. Men. I knew I'd have to get answers for meself."

Cate laughed, "What do you want to know?"

"Mam only told us good things about Brian from her memories growing up. But, of course, we knew the other stories more. I never met him, but it was almost as if he was always here in some way because of all the stories. I want to know of the real man. So what can you tell about me uncle?"

Cate was caught off guard and unsure what to say. What did she really know about Brian? Her own memories of their neighborly relationship were so different from the temperamental, scandal-embroiled, terminally ill man she had become acquainted with in the last few days. "Let me think." Then she offered, "He's kind. Intelligent. And in ill health."

Margaret made a scoffing sound, "Not like that. That's not what I'm asking. I want to know is he all Mam thinks he is? Or is he going to disappoint her again?"

"That's a pretty big ask, and I don't know if I can really be of much help. I understand you want to protect your mother, but I can only tell you what I know, which isn't much. My late husband knew Brian better than I did. They were dog-walking friends. You know, they visited when they both happened to be outside. I really only know things that Keith told me through the years, and there were instances when Brian was generous and caring. He donated a van to an organization that helps children who age out of the foster care system. It helps get them to and from their jobs so they can live on their own. And he served on the board of an organization that helps blind people. I know about that because he gave us tickets to a fundraising dinner where we dined in total darkness to learn what it's like to be without sight. SWAT officers served the meal using their night vision goggles. It was an incredible experience. That night, Brian received an appreciation award because of his volunteer work. And he's always been kind to me. When my husband was ill, he checked on me. He seems genuine." Misty rain began to fall again, making light ticking sounds on Cate's hood.

"Do you think he's guilty of the murders?" Margaret asked.

"When he asked me to help him return to Ireland, he said he wanted to make amends. I never had a sense that it was for anything criminal. It's hard for me to imagine him killing anyone. But it also seems he's going to need a strong defense."

Margaret nodded as she stared across the water, "Thanks for that."

"I hope it helps ease your mind."

"It'll have to do, won't it?" she pushed away from the railing and began to walk back toward town. Over her shoulder she added, "Mam likes you."

"I like her too," Cate smiled at Margaret's back. She waited a few minutes longer, then she walked in the opposite direction, crossing to the other side of the River Slaney and found the footpath off the paved road. The rain increased and she decided to layer her poncho over her jacket. After all, water-resistant didn't mean water-proof and the edge of her hood was beginning to get saturated. She dug into her shoulder bag but couldn't find the slim plastic package that held her as-of-yet unused poncho. She cursed inside her head, remembering that she had set it aside when she organized herself to go for the messages, and she had forgotten to put it back in her bag.

She debated whether or not to turn back, then growled, "Oh, it'll dry." She continued walking and was glad of her decision because the rain began to let up within just a few minutes. She pushed back her hood and with her other hand moved her humidity-curled hair away from her forehead. Her boots made squelchy noises with every step. When she paused to listen, she also heard dripping leaves, the occasional breeze, and bird song. She crossed the pasture then reached the trees beside the stream. The faery circle would be on the other side of the next hill, if she remembered correctly. Just past the crest of the hill, she would have a fine view of the tree ring in the middle of the field. As it came into sight, she found a fallen log that made a perfect bench except for its sheen of slowly evaporating rain. "My pants will dry too," she told herself. "Wait, my trousers will dry... and my pants too, I suppose." In doing her laundry at Mags's house, she had learned that Irish trousers are what Americans call pants and Irish pants are what Americans call underwear. She relaxed and thought about the whirlwind of the last few days.

After some time, someone else's squelching footfalls sounded behind her and she turned to find Cailleach on the path. As before, her socks were pulled up over the cuffs of her trousers, and her gray hair was plastered against her scalp. The long braid hung dark and heavy with humidity.

"Cate Jenks," she stated.

"Cailleach," she knew she was mispronouncing it.

The old woman joined her on the log without asking, and they sat for a few minutes in silence. Then Cailleach asked, "Are ye prepared?"

"For what?" Cate felt strangely unpressured and peaceful beside this weathered woman.

"Fer what's to come."

"Can you be more specific?"

"To stay in Ireland donkey's years," Cailleach answered.

"I don't really know what that means." Cate felt no urgency to understand. "Maybe you mean a long time, with the lockdown. No, I'm not prepared at all. I was supposed to be on my way home already. At least, that was the plan before it all went sideways. Things have become pretty dramatic."

"That they have," Cailleach chuckled. "You'll be the better for it though."

"Why? What doesn't kill us makes us strong?" she rolled her eyes.

"Are you needed in the States?"

"Well, no, I guess not. Not anymore."

Cailleach nodded once, "But ye are needed here, and will be fer a spell. Brian still needs ye, now more than before. Mags needs ye too. Ye bring healing to the Atleys who have suffered. The plague's coming, so there will be dire need of every healer. And ye've yer own hero's journey to complete."

"That's a lot." Cate didn't bother to question Cailleach's assignment list for her.

"Indeed," she patted Cate's hand. "You'll do, Cate Jenks. You'll do."

"Thanks," Cate said quietly. Then Cailleach stood and began walking back the way she'd come. "I have a question," Cate called after her and the old woman paused and turned around. "Is that a faery circle?" Cate pointed to the ring of trees.

"Aye."

"Is it okay to go inside it?"

"Ye know it's not," Cailleach deliberately winked one button eye, then she turned and ambled away. Cate giggled and a shiver traced her spine. There was no way in hell she was ever stepping inside that ring.

As she watched Cailleach reach the crest of the hill, a hedgehog emerged from the underbrush, nosing its way through the grass. Cate felt surprised to see both Cailleach and the hedgehog at the same time, realizing that she had half-believed the wrinkly, cryptic old woman was the hedgehog. She watched the adorable creature go about its business and when it finally disappeared from her view she had no idea how much time had passed. She stayed longer, sinking into the feeling of being part of nature. Halfway to the faery circle, a small hawk dive-bombed some unfortunate prey in the grass. She noticed the hawk's legs covered with reddish feathers and thought, "That bird looks like it's wearing shorts." She watched it alternate shredding bites of its meal with careful surveying for danger, turning its head this way and that. When it flew away, she decided it was time for her to go too.

She took the long way back, retracing the path she had come rather than the shortcut on the boreen that Cailleach made her use last time. It brought her back into town right on time to pick up lunch from The Green Man. An older teen was stationed at a table on the sidewalk in front of the pub with several takeaway orders stacked before her. She looked like Addy, but thinner, and with a nose ring and bars pierced through the cartilage of each ear. "Howya?" she asked disinterestedly.

"Hi. Do you have an order for Cate?"

"Hang on." She opened the pub door and called, "John, she's here!" Then to Cate she said, "Gwan in."

The interior of the pub was changed. All of the barstools and chairs were crowded together off to the side, in compliance with the Taoiseach's order to suspend table service. There was no one in sight. Cate leaned her elbows on the bar and put her foot on the railing. She could hear activity in the kitchen. Moments later, John emerged with a paper package of food. "Howya, Cate?"

"Grand, and yourself?"

"Grand. You're beginning to sound Irish."

"I might be getting the hang of it. I was wondering what you were going to do with the pub with lockdown ordered."

He nodded slowly, "We'll be able to stay open for takeaway, but we can't let anyone in."

"You just let me in," she teased.

"You're not just anyone," he replied sincerely.

"Awwww," she put her hand on her heart. She was genuinely touched by his comment. "Seriously, will you be able to keep business going on takeaways?"

"People need food, and we have to make a living. I'm going to hire Aiden to make deliveries. With Addy and her Jennifer cooking full time, we may be able to make up in food for some of our losses in drink. Besides, I can't let my cooks go or I'd starve."

"I could tell that was Addy's daughter out front. She's her mini-me. So you don't cook?"

"Not as such. I really don't care to eat what I can make, and no one else would want it either. Our town is used to good food coming from our kitchen, so I wouldn't want to disappoint. My talents lie in pulling pints."

"Will you be able to serve any liquor for takeaway?"

"Likely yes. The law allows it, as long as the drink is taken a minimum distance away from where it's sold. There's concern about congregation and contagion. I wouldn't want to be the reason people get ill, so I'll work out a system before we start serving again. That system may just be, 'You don't have to go home, but you can't stay here.'"

"I applaud your caution. This virus can bring a horrible death. We all need to be careful. The gardaí are all wearing masks now, and they require me to wear one when I'm near them or taking care of Brian."

"I know," John sighed, "I had to wear one too when I visited him today."

Cate was shocked, "How did that happen?"

"Mick granted my request. I reminded him that Brian and I go back to childhood together, and that prisoners are allowed visitors."

"Good point. And how was your visit? Did Brian manage to stay calm?"

"Ah yeh, he was grand. He is worried about Aiden, as am I. Hiring him for the deliveries serves more than one purpose, eh?"

"I suppose it does. Well, I'd better get back to Brian for his medical check. What are we having for lunch?"

"Meatloaf and boxty."

"It smells delicious. What is boxty again? I've seen it on menus but haven't tried it."

"It's a humble potato pancake, but Addy makes it special. 'Boxty on the griddle; boxty on the pan. If you can't make boxty, you'll never get a man.'"

Cate was startled by the sing-song cadence of his statement, "What?"

"It's an old Irish rhyme," John laughed.

"Well, the first time I came here I asked Addy about specials, and she told me nothing was special. It sounded like an existential statement."

He nodded gravely, "If everything is special, how can anything be special?"

"How very philosophical of you. Now I'm going to go ground myself in worldly pleasure by eating this lunch."

"See ye, Cate."

"Bye, John. Thanks for looking out for us."

She picked up the surprisingly heavy paper bag that held warm containers nestled together, and the aroma that wafted up to her face reminded her that she'd skipped breakfast. Cate hurried back to the hotel. Checking for Dooleys in the lobby had become part of her routine, and she was relieved not to find any this time. She pondered how many uneventful trips through the lobby she would need to experience to stop expecting something to happen with the Dooleys there. At least this was one more uneventful experience.

The elevator doors opened onto her floor and Maudy was looking bored at her station. She perked up as Cate came closer, "Howya."

"Actually, I'm starving, and John packed us lunch from the pub. How did your morning go?"

"I'm all wore out," she yawned dramatically as if just waking. "If John Kelley made your lunch, I hope he put in some Calcichews with it."

"Don't worry, Addy made it." Cate unloaded the bag and the aromas intensified. There were six small containers, with three servings of meatloaf under brown gravy and three paper clamshells with two potato pancakes each. "Oh, and he put in too much! There's no way Brian and I could eat this. Can you help me out?"

Maudy laughed, "I told you before, it will put me to sleep. Keep it for yourself later."

"But it will never be as delicious as it is right now. Please take it." Cate pushed one of each item toward Maudy and stacked the remaining containers back into the paper bag.

"Ah, but I've packed meself a ham sandwich," Maudy protested.

"It will keep for tomorrow. Please, help me with all this food!"

"If you insist," Maudy surrendered with mock reluctance.

"Thank you." Cate continued into her room. She set the food down then knocked softly on the door to Brian's suite, opening it carefully to see if he was awake. Surprisingly, he was standing at the window, gazing out on the street below.

"Brian?" she called to him, "Are you okay?"

"Yes, Cate, I'm okay," he braced himself on the handgrips of the walker, then scooted it twice to turn toward her. "I'm more okay than I've been since we arrived."

"I'm glad to see you up. Have you already done your breathing treatment?"

"No, not yet."

"Let's knock all that out at one time then." She gathered her supplies while he made his way to his chair. By the time he sat, the pulse oximeter showed an unusually low oxygen saturation with a high and irregular heart rate, moreso than she liked to see even with his physical effort. She assembled the nebulizer but kept watch on Brian from the corner of her eye. He didn't seem particularly over-taxed. A nurse looks at the numbers but also looks at the patient and he seemed stable. "How are you feeling? Are you light-headed or dizzy?"

"No more than usual."

His heart rate and oxygen saturation were both improving a little. "These last few days have been hard on you."

"That's an understatement," he agreed.

"I think we need to be extra careful going forward. I'd like to get a doctor to check you out."

"Whatever you say," Brian waved a hand and nodded.

He wasn't resisting, and yet he didn't seem sick. Something was different about him. "I heard you had a visitor earlier today."

"Ha!" he snorted, "We are indeed in a small Irish town. News travels faster than the speed of light."

Cate laughed with him. "Actually, I got it straight from the source. John told me himself."

"Oh? And what did he tell you?"

"Only that Rooney allowed the visit. And he said you were concerned about Aiden, but I already knew that."

Brian shook his head sadly. "Yeah, poor lad's been fed a false story his whole life. He's probably naturally hotheaded anyway with Fitzpatrick and Dooley blood in him. He's had reason to be angry all his life, and only just now learned he was betrayed differently the whole time. I hope he will control himself and not do anything rash. I almost believe I understand how he feels, except instead of having false stories told to me, I had false stories told about me."

Cate replied, "Those two things are kind of different. And, since you weren't here to hear the stories, it was probably a very different experience for you." She had continued to monitor his vital signs while he talked, and they were within normal range for him. He just seemed different to Cate somehow. "Is something changing?" she asked herself. "He is fragile and has been under so much stress, but he's not running a temperature, and he is fully alert and oriented."

He conceded, "Oh, I wasn't without some of the blame, for leaving like I did. I'm just saying I can imagine how hard it must be for him."

"Well, John's going to help Aiden by hiring him at the pub during the lockdown."

"As what? A bouncer?"

Cate smiled. "That's probably not a good fit for him. He has too much scrappy energy that revs people up more than calms them down. No, John can't have people in the pub so he's planning to do takeaway with his niece Addy and her daughter Jennifer doing the cooking, and Aiden making the deliveries."

"That's creative." Brian coughed and Cate gave him the nebulizer. While he took his treatment, she gave thumbs up to Maudy's camera then tidied the room to avoid talking to him. She'd been guilty in the past of talking to patients right after she started their nebulizer. It felt strange to stand silently for those minutes, doing nothing, so she would find herself making conversation and creating awkward moments when the person normally would answer a question, and then she'd remember they couldn't talk. They either interrupted their treatment, or they rolled their eyes and waved their hands trying to answer without talking. "I'm as bad as a dentist," she thought. It was just better to do something else for a few minutes.

The newspaper she had brought Brian earlier in the day was disassembled and folded in various arrangements. Several pages lay on the table beside the chair, and others were on the bed. She gathered them all up into one stack, squared their edges, and folded the whole thing into a narrow rectangle that she placed back on the foot of the bed so Brian would have room to eat at the table. Then she noticed there were hand-drawn circles marking some of the real estate ads, and it made her sad. By the time Brian would get through a trial, assuming he might manage to get two not-guilty verdicts, his health surely would be too far gone for independent living.

As his treatment ended she told him about lunch. He rinsed his mouth and she brought his food from her room, set it up for him, then she retreated to her own room where she could take off her mask and eat. Brian was delighted by the meatloaf, and Cate was enthralled with the boxty. In the end they agreed they should have had double portions of their favorites instead of one of each. When she came back to his room to clean up, she found he had finished nearly half of the meatloaf serving.

He leaned one way, then the other in the chair, groaning, "Oh, I shouldn't have eaten so much."

"Here, rest your elbows on the table so you can expand your lungs." She helped him position for better breathing. "How's that?"

"I'm going to have to stay this way a while," he moaned. "But it was so good. I can't wait to meet Addy and thank her for the meatloaf... If it doesn't kill me first."

She sat in the chair beside his, again feeling sad that he would probably never meet John's niece under normal circumstances. There would be no chance to drop by the pub for a pint in the afternoon. It seemed a particularly cruel twist that Brian had come from so far away, and then was halted literally only blocks from reuniting with his family and friends.

"What is it, Cate?" he asked, watching her. Even though the lower half of her face was covered, her eyes must have given away her sadness.

"Oh, Brian..." Pressed, she hunted for the right words. "How are you going to get out of this mess? You said before that you left Bunclody for your own reasons. If that's true, why won't you save yourself?"

He patted her hand, "I've been sussing it out, Cate. I'm going to talk to Rooney soon."

"I'm worried about your health, and I'm worried you will run out of time."

Brian wheezed a little laugh as his eyes hinted tears, "I am worried about that too."

Then silence held space between them, and they kept their own thoughts. Finally, Cate ventured, "You'll need to have Clodagh with you when you talk to Rooney. In fact, you should talk with her privately first. Why don't I call and ask her to come by today?"

"Let me rest on it, Cate." He closed his eyes as if exhausted, but she had seen this maneuver before. He was avoiding the subject.

"Brian, don't talk to the police without representation. That's just about the worst thing you can do when you're under arrest."

He opened one eye, "You've been arrested too?"

"Of course not!" Her chin tucked involuntarily with indignance, then she straightened her shoulders and added quietly, "But I have watched a lot of *Law and Order.*"

"Ah, shit!" he barked laughter that disintegrated into wheezing. Cate sat by, waiting for him to recover or need rescuing.

"But, seriously," she started when he settled down, and that only set him off laughing and coughing again. "Okay, fine, my recommendations come from TV shows, but there's too much at stake not to have your attorney with you... your solicitor. I'll put it this way, it won't hurt to have her there, but it could hurt a lot not to have her there."

He chortled and wheezed again.

"If you won't do it for yourself, please do it for me. I don't like surprises, and we've had way too many on this trip."

"I agree," he finally said, still giggling. "Ah, Cate, I think you just tried to kill me."

She sneered as if smelling something bad. "Now that's in poor taste. Besides, if I were trying to kill you, don't you think I'd be better at it?"

"Yes, yes I do," he patted her hand. "You're good at everything."

"Ugh, flattery!" she scoffed, but she sandwiched his hand still on top of hers, then let go and stood up. "Okay,

I have two choices: a nap or a walk. If I lie down now I'll just get heartburn, so I'm going to try to walk off some of that lunch."

"It'll be a nap for me, thanks. Would you pass that pillow and the TV remote?"

Cate got him situated with his arms resting on the pillow on top of the table, and the remote in easy reach. "Want a blanket too? When you're not too full, you can put the pillow behind your head and lean back in the chair for a snooze."

"You're brilliant," he happily accepted.

She returned to her room and put on her jacket to go out, then she spoke with Maudy in the hallway, "You were right about lunch. I want a nap so bad right now! I'm going to try to walk it off."

"Good for you, and leave me here to fend for meself."

"Yeah, sorry about that," Cate chuckled. "Kind of sorry-not-sorry, I guess. I would have eaten all those boxty potatoes myself if you hadn't taken some. How long have you been a garda?"

"Only about ten years. Well, active for ten years."

"What kind of training did you have to do?"

"I had to apply and get accepted at The Garda College at Templemore. It was a long time ago, and I joined quite late, actually. I was the oldest member of me class."

"Are there many female gardaí? Were there other women in your class?"

"O'course! About a quarter of us are female, give or take," Maudy answered.

"I think that's quite a bit more women in policing here than in the U.S. What made you want to become a garda as late as you did? Sorry for drilling you with questions, but I'm curious about how you got to it. I became a nurse just a few years ago, so I like hearing about other women who make career changes later in the life. You were a lot younger than me when you made your change, though."

Maudy spoke softly, "Well, Fergal and I lost our son."

"Oh, I'm so sorry to hear that," Cate said, immediately regretting that she'd asked.

"Thank ye. It was an accident and such a terrible thing, so unexpected, but it brought me out of meself too. I suppose I became bolder and eventually decided to do what I'd always dreamed of doing."

"I cannot imagine the pain you must have gone through, losing a child."

"There's no other like it," Maudy nodded in a businesslike way and inhaled deeply, then exhaled to close the subject.

Cate followed her lead, "Did you say your husband's name is Fergal?"

"Yeh."

"Fergal... Doyle?"

"That's right. My Fergal's the one you sugared up when he decided to park the car on top of a brand new Škoda Octavia. I'll get even with ye for that," she shook her head dramatically and laughed.

"Yikes," Cate laughed too and held up her hands. "I couldn't help myself. Just doing my job. How's Fergal doing now?"

"He's much better, and he may finally take his condition seriously. Would you believe he's talking of starting a gym membership?"

"Oh, no... I mean... that's great, but now all the gyms are closing with the lockdown."

"That's alright, he's just talking of it. Do ye have children of yer own?"

Cate thought, she's letting me know it's okay to talk about children. "I have one daughter, and one granddaughter. They live far away from me so I don't get to see them often."

"Where do they live?"

"New York City. But they've just arrived at my house in Florida because of the virus lockdowns. It would be much harder for them to stay in their tiny apartment in New York than it will be in my house. And here I am all the way in Ireland."

"Perhaps you will be able to go home before they do," Maudy encouraged.

"Thanks, I hope so. Well, I am going to go take that walk, so you will have to try to stay awake on your own. Can I get you a cup of tea before I go?"

"Thanks, I'm well provisioned here," she waved over her shoulder toward the hotel room behind her, "I was just going to start the kettle meself in a moment. Can I pour you a cup instead?"

Dueling tea service? Cate had no idea what the etiquette was for making or receiving a counter offer of tea in Ireland. How would she even Google that? She decided to do a runner instead, "Thanks, but I'd better get moving."

The lobby was still Dooley-free so Cate passed through without delays. As she stepped onto the street a text message from Mags vibrated her phone. She walked slowly as she texted her reply that both Brian and she were doing fine and didn't need anything. As she put her phone away and began to pay attention to her surroundings, she found Fiona the librarian walking toward her. "Hi, Fiona!"

"Howya, Cate?"

"I heard the announcement last night that the library would be closed, along with everything else."

"Yes."

"Did you happen to find the missing microfiche?" Cate asked, feeling guilty about the cards she had hidden.

"No," Fiona shook her head and tucked her hair behind her ear, "I wasn't able to search for them again."

"I looked too, but didn't find it. Did you ask Scott about it?"

"I did. He said he had not reshelved anything in that area."

Cate wanted to probe further about Scott but wasn't sure how, so she changed the subject. "So, what will you do with the time off from work?"

"I'll be overseeing online schooling for my wee'uns, of course. But I'll have plenty of time to fill with other activities."

"Oh, that's right, they've closed the schools, too, haven't they?" Cate asked.

"They have."

"What else do you do with your time? I've been in town just a few days and now everything's closed. What kind of outdoor activities are there for those who don't golf?"

"There's always walking," Fiona pointed out. "Mount Leinster makes a lovely day trip, and the views are inspiring. Or perhaps you could try Douentza Garden, or Newtownbarry House gardens."

"What kinds of things do you like to do?" Cate asked.

"A little of this, a little of that," Fiona smiled, "I do fancy a bit of music, but with the pubs closed it will be happening in people's gardens."

"I'll be staying in Bunclody until the travel ban is lifted. The live music in the pubs has been great. I'm really going to miss it," Cate hinted for an invitation. She had already crisscrossed the streets many times, and would soon run out of things to do. It would be nice to connect with someone new.

Fiona paused uncomfortably, then said, "Give me your mobile number, and I'll ring you if we get something going."

"That would be great, thank you." Cate dictated her number and the librarian put it in the contact list of her phone but she didn't offer her own or send a confirmation text. It was a clear "don't call us, we'll call you." The two women had seemed to have some things in common, but maybe Fiona had only been professionally helpful and pleasant. Cate admitted she was more likely to be anti-Atley than pro-Atley. She might even be a Dooley herself. As Cate felt the sting of rejection, she thought, I will need to get used to being persona non grata with most people around here.

They parted ways as it began to rain again. Cate pulled up the hood of her jacket then remembered her poncho. She had not put it back in her bag. She groaned inwardly, "Do I want to go back for it? No. Should I go back for it? Yes." She was only four blocks away from the hotel. "It's not like I'm running late for an appointment," she reminded herself. "It will be better to stay dry, especially since there won't be many public places open to get out of the rain, if needed." She just hated re-doing things. She had lots of patience for detail work, double-checking, and revising, but she had zero patience for starting any task over again from the beginning. Maybe it was the stress of the whole circumstance of this trip and the lockdown that then magnified her frustration. The hood of her jacket was sagging into her face and kept sliding down when she pushed it back, obstructing her view again and again. She was suddenly over-the-top angry, and while she realized it was probably because of the overwhelming stress of the situation, she just couldn't calm it down.

She stomped her way back to the hotel and threw her hood back as she barged through the lobby doors, finally getting it out of her way. Then her hair flopped back into her face. Her aggravation burned and her heartbeat thundered in her ears. "Damn! Damn! Damnit!" she growled as she jabbed the elevator button over and over again. She saw her soggy self reflected blurrily in elevator's shiny exterior doors and her frustration ignited into rage. Then she realized that she was going to cry. Yes, that was it. Tears were coming, and she had a very short window of time to get back to her room before they were going to burst out.

Cate wasn't usually a stress-cryer, but when pressures really built up, that safety valve sometimes just blew. When it happened, it wasn't just a couple tears to blot. It was a full-on ugly cry that took its time, producing copious amounts of snot, flushed skin, and puffy, bloodshot eyes. It was the kind of cry that worried people because Cate looked like something was terribly, terribly wrong. All she needed was time alone to let it happen and put herself back together, and she hated to have to explain it to anyone.

She darted into the elevator and pressed the button to close its doors, hoping no one would get on with her. When the elevator doors opened on her floor, thankfully Maudy wasn't seated at the hallway table. "She must be in Brian's room or the bathroom," Cate thought as she sagged with relief then scurried down the hallway, dashing to her room as quickly and quietly as possible. She prayed she would get herself inside without encountering Maudy or waking Brian, then she could run a hot shower and cry as long and hard as she needed to. She waved her keycard in front of the sensor, then slowly and smoothly pressed down the door handle until she met resistance. She carefully pushed the door open just far enough to step inside, then she slowly eased it shut, keeping the handle depressed to eliminate thumps and clicks.

She'd made it! She started to take off her jacket, but she was humid all over from a hot flash's sweat inside her clothes and chilly rain dampness on the outside. Everything was sticking together, and she wrestled with the layers that rolled and stuck to each other, locking her up. She felt as uncoordinated, rageful, and powerless as a toddler and was on the verge of screaming and cussing when she heard a woman's voice next door in Brian's room. It brought her to a complete stop. She thought, "Maudy?" But she knew immediately that it wasn't.

A new burst of adrenaline boosted Cate's heart rate, but it brought her to a standstill of motion that made her hands and feet burn with pinprick sensations. She moved closer to the door that separated their rooms which was just barely open, with only a hairline gap of light coming through. She was still stuck in her jacket, trying to listen and maybe see what was going on without attracting any attention. A woman was talking sternly, and it definitely was not Maudy. Was it Clodagh? Or Mags? No. Who was it then? And where was Maudy?

"I'm not supposed to have visitors," Brian said, coughing.

"I won't stay long," the woman replied.

"What do you want?"

"What do I want? I want my life back!" she snarled.

"Who are you?"

"I'm Anna Dooley, the widow of the one you murdered."

"But I never did!" Brian protested, wheezing.

"I know that, ye gobshite! But ye caused it, and ye get the credit!" In a mocking falsetto voice she continued, "'Claire is in a bad way and I want you to do right by her. She doesn't know what to do. I only want to help her.' All Tim did was shout back and the starch went right out of ye. Ye took off running, coward! But Tim didn't see me comin', no. Ye left me to do the business and I been takin' care of it all ever since. But ye couldn't stay gone, could ye? Ye had to come back and stir things up again and forced me to put down my Billy this time. Ye're a curse, Brian Atley."

"I never even saw Billy!"

"Ye as good as kilt him, same as Tim!"

"I had nothing to do with it!" Brian's wheezing was increasing.

"Ye had everything to do with it! Waltzing back into town, acting the innocent. Tim was no loss, but ye took Billy too. Ye'll take nothing more from me, Brian Atley, for ye're only going to take yer own last breath now."

It was Anna Dooley in Brian's room! Cate slowly eased out of her jacket as she listened to Anna's rant, admitting to killing both Tim and Billy, and now she was going to kill Brian too. Where the hell was Maudy and why hadn't she seen this on the monitor? Cate thought frantically, "What should I do? I can try to get in there and help Brian or I can go for help. But I can't see into the room and have no idea if Anna has a weapon. And she sounds full-on crazy. Even if she's unarmed, she's probably going to be scary strong."

"Give me that!" Brian croaked.

"Stay down!" Anna roared as a thud sounded.

Brian cried out and Cate could hear him gasping. If he was having trouble breathing, there was very little time to help. She moved quickly to the door of her room and eased it open as quietly as she had come in. It was a good thing she'd just had practice, because her hands were shaking and slick with sweat.

Across the hall, the table and chair were still in place for the garda. Behind it a mop handle was jammed horizontally through the door handle and across the doorframe, preventing the door from being opened from inside. Cate hadn't noticed it earlier in her mad dash to her room. Now the hotel room door was rattling and bumping as Maudy tried to get out. Cate lunged to pull the mop handle out. Then she pushed the door as Maudy pulled it and they tumbled into each other.

"Anna Dooley's attacking Brian in his room!" Cate hissed.

"I know! She locked me in. I've already called for help, but we have to get in there now." She showed Cate the image on the tablet. Brian was sprawled halfway out of the chair. His walker was tipped over as if it had been thrown across the room, and Anna stood in eerie profile with his oxygen concentrator and tubing dangling just out of his reach. His hands were waving weakly, begging for the oxygen.

Maudy directed Cate, "Give me your key. I'm going into your room. After I get in there, you go to Brian's door. Go in loud and stay out of her reach. I'll grab her and you help him."

"Alright."

Cate took her position by Brian's hallway door as Maudy slipped into Cate's room. Cate counted to five to give the guard time to get ready, then she banged on the door and pushed it open calling "Brian!" Anna jumped and turned toward Cate, her face distorted with rage. Her silvery charcoal hair was wild and her right eye was bruised and nearly swollen shut. She screamed like an animal, rearing back with the oxygen concentrator in one hand, and raising a crowbar in her other hand.

As Anna swung the crowbar at Cate, Maudy tackled her and drove her to the ground. The crowbar mostly missed its mark, tangling in Cate's sleeve and flying from Anna's grasp. Anna was disproportionately strong, but Maudy was well trained and had surprise on her side. Their few seconds of wrestling stretched out in Cate's mind as she scrambled to get the crowbar out of Anna's reach.

Anna continued to scream and writhe even when she was laid out on the floor, handcuffed. Cate wrenched the oxygen supply from under Anna where she had fallen on it, and the woman howled and snapped her teeth trying to bite. Praying it still worked, Cate turned it to its maximum delivery and stuck the cannula in Brian's gaping mouth. She was relieved to see he was breathing on his own, though he was barely conscious. "Brian!" she called, rubbing his sternum with her knuckles to wake him up with pain. "Take deep breaths! Brian! Wake up!"

"Whaaaa," his eyes fluttered open, and he cringed away from her.

"Breathe, Brian, you have to breathe deep! Wake up!"

He was looking around, groaning and becoming more alert.

Cate spared a glance at Maudy. She had stepped back from Anna who was still kicking and flailing with her hands pinned behind her. Spittle flew from her mouth as she cursed and ranted, and her charcoal hair fell forward over her eyes. "Don't let her get over this way!"

"Yeh, yeh, got it. You're bleeding." Maudy pointed to where the crowbar had torn through Cate's sleeve, then reached for her radio to report in.

Cate nodded back, "So are you."

Rooney and two other guards burst into the room before she could make the call. "Jaysus!" He shook his head, surveying the situation, "Alright, Maudy?"

"Yeh," she swiped with the back of her hand at a trickle of blood on her forehead.

"Alright, Ms. Jenks?"

"Yes, I'm okay. She just grazed me," Cate confirmed as Garda Ryan knelt beside her with Brian. "Can you hand me the pulse oximeter?" she asked him.

The next few minutes were full of activity all around her while Cate remained focused on monitoring Brian. The gardaí attempted to get Anna up to a chair, but she fought tirelessly, and it was safest for all to keep her on the floor. The suite became very crowded with her still flailing while paramedics entered the room with a stretcher, and Moira and Hughey peered in from the hallway. Brian was alert but shaken. Cate gave the medics a brief report of history and current problems, and they helped Brian onto the stretcher to be taken to the hospital to get checked out. He protested, coughing, "I don't need a doctor!" Rowan Ryan went with them as they wheeled out the door.

Another set of paramedics arrived and bandaged Cate's arm before attempting to pick up Anna. No one was able to reason with her or bring calm, and her screaming and thrashing only diminished after an injection. When she finally settled down, they placed her on the stretcher and the other garda left with them. Rooney, Maudy, and Cate remained in Brian's room.

"Now," Rooney said, "What's the story?"

Chapter 15

Brian's condition had not required admission to the hospital, and he had been discharged directly from A&E after just a few hours' treatment and observation. Cate got him settled in his room late in the night and they both slept until mid-morning when an unusually sunny day set their rooms aglow. There was no guard outside the door, and the murder charges had been dropped. Cate made them tea and Brian sat in the blue wingback chair with his walker stationed within reach. "They'll give me back my cane today."

"I know you'll be happy to have it again, but it might be a good idea to keep the walker too. It gives you more stability."

"Absolutely not!" he growled.

A knock sounded and Cate spied Mags through the peephole. Opening the door, she cried, "I thought you were going to call when you were on the way! We would have met you downstairs."

The two women hugged and then Mags marched purposefully past Cate with a basket on her arm. The smell of brown bread wafted in with her. "There's no rush. I want to talk to me brother."

"Okay, I'll go get changed. Just let me know when..."

Mags cut her off, "No, you need to hear this too, pet. Please stay." She set the basket on the table and hugged Brian where he sat.

"Mornin', Maggie," he patted her back until she pulled away.

As she released him, she took his hands in hers briefly, sighing, "My dear!" Emotion overwhelmed her for a moment, but then she settled herself to speak as she found a chair, "When the two of you first came to me door, I was unwelcoming."

Cate protested, "But, Mags..."

The older woman raised a hand in a quieting gesture, "Please, let me speak."

Cate froze, then exhaled without another word, sinking back into her chair.

"I was just... distraught... that you had returned to Bunclody," Mags said to Brian. "Of course, I knew what you were accused of. I knew what was in store for you – arrest. Prison. What I didn't know was that you knew nothing of it. And when you said you came back to 'make amends'... How do you make amends for murder and abandoning a child? I was so upset that you came back to throw away what was left of your life. That's why I turned you away that day. I wanted you to disappear. To go back where you'd come from."

"But, Mags..." Brian protested, and she cut him off too.

"There's more. Please, let me finish my piece. When all the terrible things happened long ago, I could understand that you and Claire got together. She was beautiful and sweet. What I couldn't accept was that you had run away from her and from your child. And I couldn't accept that you had run away from me!" Tears filled her eyes and her voice faltered, then she continued, "I always believed you innocent of Tim's murder. I knew there must have been more to it, that it was self-defense or something else you could have explained. But I did believe you fathered Mary Margaret and abandoned Claire and I couldn't get past that. I couldn't. I have been so angry with you for leaving all of us. That is why I treated you as I did, and I'm sorry for it, even though I couldn't have known different."

Brian's breath caught with a stifled sob and Mags took his hand again. Cate's nurse face nearly broke, and she had to pace her breathing to keep from weeping along with them.

When Mags regained her voice, she continued, "So almost all of the mysteries have been cleared. We now know it was Anna who killed Tim and Billy. And it was Tim who fathered Mary Margaret. You weren't responsible for any of that, and yet I still don't understand why you left us."

Brian looked down at his hands, avoiding her eyes, and cleared his throat before finally saying, "It'll have to keep a little longer, Maggie, just a little longer. I've someone else to consider yet, so I have to ask you to trust me even though I don't deserve it."

With a sigh, Mags squared her shoulders, "Alright then. The bread will keep for later. Come down to the car, and I'll take you back to me house for a proper welcoming. We'll be just in time for elevenses."

"Elevenses?" Cate asked.

"Ah," Brian smiled, "That's the tea time between breakfast and lunch. You're the best, Maggie."

A short time later, they were once again stationed around Mags's table. The kitchen was warm and felt like home to Cate. Comfort was the word. Mags's kitchen felt like comfort. Cate looked at the people sitting with her: Brian, Mags, John – all strangers really, and yet, the feeling of deep kinship filled her. Her eyes met Brian's. He lifted his cup of tea at her, "Here's to you, Cate Jenks, the woman of the hour, and for sure the hero of this little band of Irishmen."

Cate smiled and blushed a little, "Well, it sure has been an adventure. Not at all the trip I was led to believe I would have."

Mags asked, "And what did Brian tell you the trip was going to be?"

Mimicking Brian, Cate grumbled, "Just make the travel arrangements. Just monitor my health. Just help me get there, that's all. A little getaway from home. You'll be back in a few days, he said."

Mags and John guffawed at her impersonation of Brian, who laughed himself into a coughing fit. Cate began to help him but he put his hand out to stop her. "I'm fine," he wheezed, still laughing.

Mags said, "Well, I am so grateful he suckered you in. But to think of you and Maudy wrestling that crazed woman! How's your arm?"

"It's just a cut and a bruise that will heal fast. It didn't even need stitches," Cate replied. "Maudy is the real hero though. She pinned Anna down and kept her there. That wasn't easy. Anna's strong and determined. It was all very surreal."

"We'll be ever grateful to the both of you," Mags said with her eyes shining. She took Brian's hand and patted it. Quiet filled the kitchen as they each reflected on their private thoughts of what might have happened. A knock sounded at the door and a man's voice called, "Hullo, hullo!"

"That'll be Mick," Mags went to the door, greeting him loud enough for all to hear, "Come in, come into the kitchen with us." She set him a place with tea and scones.

Rooney nodded to everyone, looking quite worn out, seated himself, then drew a deep breath, "Thank ye, Mags."

Mags nodded back, "Of course. Tell us what ye know when you're ready, Mick."

He pointed to the mask covering his face, "The gardaí are all wearing these to protect from the virus, so I'm sorry to miss your scones. It's for your protection as well as mine." He placed his palms flat on the tabletop. "I want to give ye the news of what I've been putting together. Cleaning up, I would say, getting all the pieces of the puzzle to fit."

They waited patiently as he readied himself. "Alright, here it is. A terrible story, actually. Of course, Anna is mentally unstable at best. Hearing that Brian had come back and then seeing him unexpectedly in the hotel broke whatever had held her together for fifty years. She concluded that the truth would not come out if Brian died, so she took advantage of her access at the hotel and stole a key card. Apparently, she knew of Cate's every four hours checks on Brian. She managed to let herself into a vacant room looking like a hotel guest, then watched the hallway through the peephole. She spent hours with her eye pressed to it. That's why her face was already bruised when you saw her, Ms. Jenks. She waited for her chance, with you gone from the hotel and Maudy gone to the toilet. Brian's door lock was disabled, of course, and she was able to go right in. As you all know, Ms. Jenks returned unexpectedly and overheard Anna attacking Brian. Maudy saw her enter Brian's room on the tablet's video feed, but she was trapped in the guard's room and could only call for help. Fortunately, Ms. Jenks was able to let her out and they put a stop to Anna's attack.

He continued, "I was already close by because Brian had asked to see me, to tell me everything he knew. We had set a time. I have to say, I was gob struck walking in on that melee. I first assumed Anna was after Brian for vengeance of Tim, but as she fought her mouth was running and it became clear she wasn't just a weeping widow. I heard plenty that answered some questions, and also spawned new ones. But she had to be sedated for a safe transport and I was only able to question her further this morning. She killed her own husband and let Brian take the blame. In the end, she confessed to killing both Tim and Billy."

Mags gasped, "Why did she kill Billy, for the love of God? He was her helpmate and made that farm profitable."

Mick nodded, "Indeed he was. He stayed on after Tim was killed. He knew she needed lots of help and she relied on him. He was always there for her, still driving the truck until his dying day. Maybe he even loved her. We'll never know now. At some point through the years, he took care of Anna when she ran a high fever and in her delirium she spoke about the night of Tim's murder. Billy questioned her about it after, so she said. That's how she knew that he knew, but he promised to keep her secret.

"I'm guessing when Billy learned what Anna did to Tim and why she did it, he believed it brought less harm letting Brian keep the blame. But when Brian returned to Bunclody, Billy changed his thinking and called to meet.

Anna said she didn't want to kill Billy but had to. He was going to choose Brian over her and tell the true story."

"And what was the story?" Mags asked.

"You'll remember, Anna was pregnant with Scott when Tim was killed. Claire Fitzpatrick had fallen pregnant with Mary Margaret Atley at the same time. Anna came in through the back of the barn and overheard Brian pleading with Tim to help Claire, because he was the father. She heard Tim's response, his ridiculing and threats to expose Brian and his friend. Anna stated she went into a rage as Brian left, but Tim was unaware of her there. She came up behind him without a word and smashed his skull with a crowbar then she ran out the back and hid it. She had no plan at the time. It was pure luck that Billy saw Brian leave the farm that night, and he ended up wrongfully assigning the blame.

"Anna used the crowbar again when she killed Billy, and she brought it with her to kill Brian, too. She says it's the only thing she can depend on." Rooney shook his head slowly and continued, "She said after killing Tim it was years before her dreams of that night finally stopped, but then they started again when Brian returned. After killing Billy, she was having the dreams in the daytime too. She said she knew that killing Brian was the only way to make them stop, and that she was only doing what she had to do.

"So there it is. But there is a question that remains," Rooney concluded. He looked to each person at the table and then all eyes turned to Brian.

"Well," Brian cleared his throat, "As I was going to tell you before I was so rudely attacked by Anna, I did go see Tim Dooley that night, to try to convince him to take care of my dear friend Claire. I guess I thought I could force him, but instead he mocked me and threatened to expose me to the town. I left because I didn't want to bring shame on my family. I later felt it was cowardly, but at the time it seemed the only solution."

"And that shame is...?" Rooney prompted.

"That I am gay. I didn't know that Tim Dooley had seen me with someone and when I pushed him about Claire, he pushed back. He was going to out me. Us. I didn't want to hurt my family, and I couldn't have my friend outed because of me."

"Oh, Brian!" Mags cried, "Mam and Da would have understood. I would have understood."

"No, Mags. It was a different time for people like me. You all would have suffered the stigma of my 'unnatural state.' You know it. The church openly decried homosexuality, and it was still illegal. Mam would have been devastated. Da would have been humiliated. You would have had to defend me. *You* defend *me*, your older brother. And it wasn't just our family. My friend's life would have been ruined too, and he was younger. I had to go. It was the only way to protect everyone."

John said softly, "You don't have to protect me anymore."

Brian nodded gratefully, "I had no way of knowing that until we spoke yesterday. It was such a disaster I'd returned to."

"I see," said Mick. "So, you and Anna concur that Tim Dooley is Aiden's grandfather."

Cate added, "The DNA test will confirm it. As soon as the swabs arrive, we'll get it done."

"Mmhmmm," Rooney continued, "So, Brian, Tim Dooley was going to make your life hell, and that of your family, and John's too. You had no way of knowing he would have kept your secret if he'd lived."

"That's correct," Brian agreed.

"Telling your version of the complete story wouldn't have cleared your name, would it? In fact, it would have given you motive."

Brian hung his head and hoarsely replied, "Yes."

"I suppose you were lucky Anna attacked you, then."

"Mick Rooney, you arse!" Mags roared.

Rooney sighed, "Ah, no. I was having doubts about your guilt anyway, as surprised as you were by the date of Tim's murder. No one is that fine an actor. And as for Billy's murder, I don't mean any offense, but you hardly seem strong enough to lift your cane from step to step, let alone bash someone with it. I continued investigating you, and the evidence wasn't holding up."

"Then why did you keep me under arrest!?" Brian sputtered.

"If it wasn't you, I also had some thought for your safety with a murderer about. You could consider it a protective custody."

"Well you nearly blew that assignment, didn't you?" Brian growled.

"And yet, here you are," Mick stood and clapped Brian on the shoulder gently, "Maybe not so sound, but safe at least. Now I must be getting back to the station. All this has created a great deal of paperwork."

"What of Anna, Mick?" Mags stood to walk him out, "Will she be kept in the station?"

"No. I've sent for a crew that will take her to a psychiatric facility. She's in that bad a state. From some of her rantings, it sounds as though Tim may have done much worse to her and my cousins than stray outside the marriage."

"Have ye talked to her family?"

"I've interviewed each of the Dooley boys and feel confident they were not aware of Anna's crimes, nor were they involved in any of her plotting." He looked directly at Cate, "Scott did admit to hiding the microfiche you had used, but only to inconvenience you because he believed you were an associate of his father's murderer. He did pick up the to-do list you dropped, and we can assume Anna gained information about your medical checks from it, but Scott did nothing further with it. Of course, just like Aiden, the Dooley boys are adapting to these revisions to what they had always taken as truth. It's a terrible thing to think of Anna deliberately sending young James out to find his murdered father that morning. The four brothers will have each other to lean on as they deal with it all."

"Of course, of course. Thank you, Mick," Mags said.

Brian raised himself from his seat to a standing position, offering his hand to the detective sergeant. Their handshake was warm as Rooney said, "Welcome home, Brian." Then he looked to each of them, "Good day, Mags, John, Ms. Jenks."

"Call me Cate," she replied.

"Good day, Cate."

Mags saw him out and when she returned to the table, she topped off their teacups and settled back into her seat, "So now what happens?"

"Well," Brian said, "I'll need to start looking for a place to live."

The End.

About the Authors

Daughter-mother duo A. Elwood and C. Chapman found solace in writing when their planned trip to Ireland was canceled because of the COVID-19 pandemic. Drawing inspiration from their disappointment, they created Cate Jenks who was able to embark on a cozy mystery adventure in the beautiful Irish countryside while they were confined at home in Florida, U.S. They hope that readers will enjoy traveling vicariously through Cate as much as they have.

The second Cate Jenks, RN, Irish Cozy Mystery *The One Who Found Him* will be available in all the usual places. Learn more at ElwoodAndChapmanBooks.com.

Made in United States
Orlando, FL
14 June 2024

47866224R00167